MASTER OF HOUNDS

C.Steven Manley

This is a work of fiction. Names, characters, businesses, places, events and incidents are either the products of the author's imagination or used in a fictitious manner. Any resemblance to actual persons, living or dead, or actual events is purely coincidental.

For more information and to keep up with new releases, please visit www.cstevenmanley.net

Cover by Kid Mindfreak

ISBN 10: 1718754914

ISBN-13: 978-1718754911

Dedication

For Don Heinisch who told me about the downtown cave and distracted me from my other work.

For Ralph Kern, Scott Moon, and Josh Hayes; podcasters extraordinaire and damn fine storytellers in their own right. Thanks for putting up with all my law enforcement questions, guys!

CHAPTER ONE

Outside the Warner Residence
203 Lowe Avenue
Hunstville, Alabama
28 October, 1:37 a.m. CST

Arlo knew something was wrong the moment he laid eyes on the place.

It wasn't that there was anything wrong with the house itself. It sat in the shadows of the tall oak trees that filled the city's historical district. There were so many of the things that most of the light from the street lamps was all but completely blocked, hiding the details of the restored Queen Anne style structure in a layer of chilly, autumn darkness. No, the house itself was fine. The source of his apprehension was something less tangible.

"What is it?" Deana said, looking up from her phone screen. The glow cast a faintly blue shadow over her light mocha skin. The Tahoe's engine hummed and warm air blew from the vents between the two front seats just hard enough to tickle the back of Arlo's thin hand. The two agents in the front were quiet, their eyes sweeping over the vehicle's surroundings.

Arlo didn't bother looking over at Deana. He didn't have to. After seven years of working together he could have described the look on her face just from her tone of voice.

"I'm not quite sure," he said, letting his eyes and his deeper senses sweep over the place. "I feel something but it's obscured somehow. Muffled. Are we certain it's here?"

"As much as we can be. We know that one of them contacted the seller on the dark web and payment was made. It's had time to make it across the ocean."

"But no visual confirmation?"

"Of course not. We just got here."

"I'm feeling… something. It's just off normal enough to notice."

Deana considered it. "The relic? Could you be sensing that? It would confirm things. I mean, if the intel on it is right then the damn thing's probably got its own aura."

Arlo nodded. "If it's actually one of the seven crypticals then, yes, without a doubt. That could be it, I suppose. It's odd, though. Where are the perimeter teams?"

"Half a klick out in four directions," she said. "I give the word and they can be here in well under a minute. Why? You checking my work?"

Arlo suppressed a momentary impulse to smile. "I wouldn't dream of presuming so much. I just wanted to know how many celebratory drinks I'd be buying if this goes to plan."

Deana gave a small laugh and said, "All of them, money bags. Getting this thing out of circulation would be a big win for everybody."

Arlo nodded and then looked over at her. "Shall we?"

"Copy that," Deana said. "Miles, Frank," she said to the two agents in the front seats, "you guys hold here and keep your eyes on the place. The two of us are going to be weird enough knocking on their door in the middle of the night. No need to give these old folks a coronary."

The two men acknowledged the order and turned their eyes towards the Warner House as Arlo and Deana got out of the SUV. The cold night air was like a slap on Arlo's skin as he stood and waited for his partner to join him. He shoved his hands into his coat pockets and pulled the dark wool closed tighter against the soft breeze. The assortment of rings that he wore were like small bands of warmth on his fingers.

Deana came around the back of the Tahoe and said, "Crap it's cold. Couldn't we have done this at noon?"

"Not for this," Arlo said. "High priority acquisition. No delay. So, who are we tonight?"

"Standard DHS cover," Deana said, handing him a folded leather ID case. "Terrorist connected intel, blah-blah-blah, secure the relic and disappear."

"Terrorists," Arlo said. "It's always terrorists."

Deana shrugged. "It's in vogue. Scary enough to get attention but not as scary as the truth. Now let's get this done so we can hit a Waffle House or something for all the hot chocolate they can pour."

This was usually the point in their pre-mission banter that Arlo would make some comment about her drinking coffee like all the other grown-ups but he let the reference go without responding. His mismatched eyes were fixed on the house. Something was tickling his awareness, buzzing around his senses like an insect he couldn't quite catch sight of.

He started a little when Deana poked him in the arm and said, "Hey, Gandalf, you good? Didn't forget your meds, did you?"

Arlo looked at her and nodded, "Yes, I'm fine, and you know I never forget. Let's go."

They crossed the street and approached the wrought iron fence that surrounded the property. It was one of the four foot high models and as near as Arlo could tell encompassed the double sized lot that the house was centered in. He dropped his hand on the gate and said, "There might be a dog."

Deana said, "Maybe, but I haven't heard or seen any sign of one. Cold night like this, they probably brought him inside."

Arlo nodded and lifted the latch. The gate swung open with a soft, creaking sound. The heavy iron ring on his index finger scraped against the gate as he pushed it aside. The house stood before them dark, silent, and draped in tree cast shadow. Dried, brown leaves rustled and fell as the breeze moved through the trees, filling the night with a faint, whispered rattle.

"Come on," Deana said, "move it or lose it. You're blocking progress."

Arlo headed up the walk. The wide front steps gave a wooden groan under their weight as they climbed them and moved onto the long, angled porch. Arlo raised his hand to knock on the stained glass front door but stopped when he saw a thick line of deeper blackness between the door and the frame. He looked at Deana and said, "It's open."

Deana took one look and drew her Glock-22 in a single, fluid motion. It rested in her hand like it had evolved there while she keyed her collar mic and said, "All units, the structure has been breached, move silent to tight perimeter positions and stand by. Escort team, cover the back."

She returned her free hand to her shooter's grip and said, "Think maybe they forgot to lock up?"

Arlo responded by raising his hands and whispering something in a language that sounded a lot like he was gargling marbles. Faint lights of varying colors came to life in each of the ten rings he wore and glowed just bright enough to see in the dark. He stepped to one side and let Deana take the lead.

She carefully nudged the door open with her boot until it was open wide. Arlo glanced inside quickly and then shook his head at her. "Light?" he whispered.

"Let's try the normal way first," she whispered back.

Arlo nodded. They'd done this so many times that no more words were needed. Deana swept in with her Glock up and dropped into a kneeling stance. Arlo came in behind her and felt around for a light source. His hand brushed over a panel of four plastic switches. He tried them all but nothing happened.

"Okay," she said. "Light it up, Gandalf."

Arlo reached into his pocket and pulled out a small glass orb about the size of a golf ball. He held it up to his mouth and fogged the clear sphere with his breath before whispering something into the glass. He extended his hand as a white glow bloomed in the orb and lit the area with a stark light.

They were in a foyer with switchback stairs leading up to the second story. A hallway extended out before them but the light only illuminated a portion of the space. An open portal to the left led into some sort of great room. There was a closed door a little further up the hall on their right. Rich, ornately carved wood filled decorated the banister and rows of family pictures lined the walls.

Arlo inhaled through his nose. The air was tainted with a thick, metallic scent that was all too familiar. He glanced at Deana and she nodded. She smelled it, too. "Bowl a frame," she whispered.

Arlo took the glass sphere and sent it rolling down the corridor. He put enough strength behind it that the orb bounced onto a thin carpet runner that was in the center of the hallway and kept going. Shadows danced as the light moved. The glass made a slight sound as it left the runner and struck the hardwood floor in the room beyond. It suddenly slowed when it hit a thick puddle. The light's hue shifted to something darker with a subtle hint of red.

Deana cursed and rose to her feet. Arlo stayed to her right and had his hands up, spots of multicolored lights glinting from his rings. He drew in a breath as they moved down the hall, floorboards creaking under their weight.

Just as they'd suspected, the glass orb had come to rest in a puddle of slowly coagulating blood. The muddied light revealed a room filled with book shelves filled to capacity, comfortable furniture, a stone faced fireplace alight with the embers of a dying fire, and the bodies of Walter and Alice Warner.

The elderly couple had died badly. Walter's corpse was tied to a chair with duct tape. He was a bloody mess from head to toe which was no surprise since there was an empty cavity where his abdomen should have been. Alice was on the floor in front of him and was so savaged that Arlo had to close his eyes against the sight. Parts of her were lying about her body like pieces of a broken figurine.

"God almighty," Deana said, her voice a whisper that threatened to end in a gag.

"Oh, that old Judeo-Christian chestnut," a cold voice said from behind them.

Arlo and Deana spun back and faced the way they had come in. A man stood between them and the front door, just far enough into the light to make out his features. He was tall and handsome in a lean, cigarette-cowboy kind of way. Pale hair that was slicked back from his scalp glistened with something dark in the light. Equally dark stains covered the shirt, sport coat, and slacks that he wore.

Arlo's rings flared brighter.

Deana lined up her pistol with the center of the man's chest and snapped, "Federal agent! Get your hands up or I'll shoot!"

The man laughed. It was an icy sound, devoid of any feeling, humorous or otherwise. "Spare me the floor show, brownie. You're as much a federal agent as I am. Well, that is, unless the Pickmen have gone through some really radical changes since I've been away. I somehow doubt that, though"

"Who are you?" Arlo said.

The man studied Arlo for moment. There was a smile on his lips that reminded Arlo of a shark. "Oh, little magus, I'm just a man looking for a good book. Much like the two of you, I imagine."

"Get your damn hands up or I swear to God I'll put every round I have straight into your creepy-ass heart," Deana said.

The man's smile vanished and he gave Deana the kind of look that promised murder. "You know," he said, "I remember a time when someone like you would never have spoken to a white man like that. Why, back then, we'd have set the dogs on you for that kind of disrespect."

Deana replied but Arlo didn't hear what she said. Dark, violet-blue light had flared in the man's eyes, though Arlo knew that his partner couldn't see it. He opened his mouth to speak but a movement behind the man caught his attention. There were shapes there, large shaggy patches of black that shed wisps of arcane power like steam from their midnight black hides.

"Deana," Arlo whispered. "We-"

The sound of a single gunshot from the backyard echoed through the night followed fast by an unearthly howl. Arlo heard a man scream. He thought it was Frank.

The shadows came for them as Deana opened fire.

CHAPTER TWO

Huntsville Hospital Emergency Room
101 Sivley Road
Hunstville, Alabama
28 October, 1:59 a.m. CST

Clint Mercer signed out of the patient record he'd been updating and pushed the keyboard back into its slot beneath the monitor. He swiveled in his chair to face the doctor sitting next to him at the nurse's station and said, "No."

"Why not? You'd make a great doctor," Sarah Powell said, leaning back into the seat and adjusting her lab coat so the stitched letters showed clearly. "Just picture it; Clint Mercer, M.D. I'm telling you you'd be great."

"Better than you?" Clint said with no attempt to hide his smirk.

"That's just crazy talk," Sarah said. "Still, you'd be damned good."

It wasn't the first time they'd had this conversation. Sarah had already been on staff for nearly a year when Clint had come to work after graduating from nursing school. It hadn't taken long before they'd become friends and she'd taken an aggressive but well intentioned interest in his career path. At first, he'd thought it was some kind of romantic overture but soon discovered that he was the wrong gender for that kind of attention. It was always on the slow ER nights that she seemed determined to make him climb the educational ladder.

"I'm good with the R and the N after my name," he said. "Thanks, though."

"That's even better," she said. "Between nursing and your military time you'll have more experience than anybody else in your class. You'd be top of the applicant pile, no problem."

"Yeah, thanks. Still not interested." He stood up and grabbed a tablet next to the computer. "I've got to inventory exam three. Walk with me if you want to keep talking."

Sarah rose and joined him as he walked out from behind the desk and headed for the nearest examination room. She stood a few inches shorter than his six feet and change but carried herself as though she could look him squarely in the eye.

"See? Right there. We've worked in the same unit for what? Two years and some? I've never had to inventory an exam room. Not once."

"True," Clint said, "but I don't have to carry malpractice insurance, deal with partners or office management, and have guaranteed days off. I show up, I work a shift, I go home, and I only take about half the call you do. So, you know, I'm good."

"It's not that bad," Sarah said.

Clint locked his wide brown eyes on hers and said, "Being a doctor isn't a job, it's a lifestyle. It's not that bad for you because you chose it. I like keeping my job and my lifestyle in separate boxes."

Sarah met his dark eyes with her slate blue ones and rolled them dramatically. "Oh, for God's sake, Clint. You make it sound like I'm in a nunnery or something. Look, just let me sign you up for the MCAT. We'll see how you do and then you can make a better informed decision."

Clint pulled a light pen from the side of his tablet as he entered the room. They'd had a car accident victim with some minor injuries in earlier so it wasn't a complete mess. He ran the pen over one of the supply drawers and then opened it to check the supplies against his list.

"Tell you what," he said, "I'm signed up for a Tough Mudder in Tennessee this coming April. You do that with me and I'll take the MCAT."

"Oh," Sarah said, absently pushing a strand of dirty blonde hair out of her eyes. "Oh, hell no. Are you kidding me?"

"Why not? You could get ready in seven months."

"Uh, no, I couldn't, and I'm not into all that. I was in med school while you were off being a paratrooper."

"I wasn't a paratrooper," Clint said. "I was a pararescueman. There's a difference."

"Whatever. I wasn't in the Army."

"Air Force."

"See? I didn't even know that. I was in med school while you were learning to jump out of airplanes looking all badass. Become an MD and you'll have that on me even if I am still the better doctor."

"You know," Clint said, "you have some unhealthy control issues."

"Only in the face of under-utilized talent. Come on, Clint, you know I'm right."

Clint closed the drawer and opened the next. "I like my life the way it is. I'm not interested in going back to school. I-"

"We need a doctor over here! I've got a wounded federal agent!" someone shouted.

Clint and Sarah both spun at the sound and saw five people coming in through the ambulance bay doors. One of the men was carrying a smaller man with a bloody shirt and limply lolling head. He was obviously unconscious and blood dripped from one dangling hand. The rest were coming in through the bay backwards with weapons trained on the street outside. Each of them looked as though they'd been in a scuffle.

"What the hell is this?" Sarah shouted. "How did you get those doors open?"

The woman turned, held up a badge and ID so fast that Clint barely had time to register it, and then said, "We're with Homeland Security and that man needs immediate help! Green, contact hospital security and get this area cleared of civilians and non-essentials! Jeffers, get the local leos on the phone and get ahead of the reports! Carlson, stay on the door."

The man carrying the injured agent rushed towards Clint. "Where?" he said.

Clint pointed to another treatment room and said, "There. Room five. What happened?" They moved together towards the room.

"We were attacked," the man said as he placed the injured man on the bed, smearing blood across clean sheets and guard rails as he did it. "An operation went sideways. He's breathing but he's been out for about five minutes now."

"Was he shot?" Sarah said.

"No, it was-"

"Agent Scott," the female agent snapped as she came into the room, "join Carlson on the door. If you even think you see something, sound off."

Agent Scott gave her a quick, "Yes, ma'am," and headed for the ambulance entrance, drawing a heavy pistol from under his coat as he moved. The female agent pulled the exam curtain closed around them, cutting off their view of the main ER floor.

Sarah shouted into the bay for more assistance and then turned to the female agent. "I'm Doctor Powell," she said, grabbing a trauma pack from a nearby bin and tearing into it. "I need to know what I'm dealing with here, agent…" Sarah left the sentence hanging.

"My name isn't important. Just help him."

"Then tell me.."

Their voices faded into background noise as Clint focused on cutting up the length of the patient's coat sleeve so he could get a blood pressure cuff on him. The wool was sturdy but his heavy duty emergency shears made short work of it and the shirt beneath. The man's arms were thin and lean with a lot of intricate tattoos. As Clint wrapped the cuff around his bicep, he let his eyes roam over the patient's body, assessing his condition as he went.

The patient was well under six feet and thinly built. He was pale from blood loss but Clint got the impression that even under the best of circumstances the guy wouldn't look like he'd been in the sun much. The front of his clothing was soaked in blood but Clint could make out three long rips in the fabric and the lean torso beneath. If he'd lost as much blood as it looked like he had, then they needed to get a large bore IV into him as fast as they could so they could replace his lost blood volume.

Clint hit the button to cycle the blood pressure cuff and grabbed the small fingertip clip that would give them a reading of the patient's blood oxygen saturation. He lifted one of the man's clammy hands to apply the device and realized that there was an assortment of odd rings on his hand. One for every one of the man's digits.

He grabbed one and started to pull it off when the female agent said, "Hey! What are you doing?"

"I need to take these off," Clint said without looking up. The ring didn't want to budge.

"No," she said. "The rings stay. He needs them."

"No," Sarah said, he doesn't." She had pulled a large pad of absorbent material from the trauma pack and was pushing hard on the worst of the patient's wounds. Blood was starting to show at the edges.

"Do not remove those rings," the agent said.

Clint kept pulling. The damned thing was stuck but he couldn't understand why. The guy's fingers were slender and the ring looked as though it should slide right off. "Ma'am, if his extremities swell with this jewelry on then-"

Something cold pressed into the side of Clint's head. The old but familiar scent of gun oil and spent cordite tainted the air. Clint stopped pulling at the ring and lifted his hands away.

"What the hell are you doing, lady?" Sarah shouted.

"Listen to me, both of you. I'm sorry. We wouldn't be here unless we had to be. I know this is weird and confusing but you've got to listen to me.

He's not a normal patient but I don't have time to explain the details. I just need you to do what I tell you and I promise the explanations will come. Consider it a national security matter. Do you understand me?"

Clint looked back down the pistol at the dark-skinned woman. Her eyes were hard, cold, and had a look he'd not seen in a long time. It was the look of someone that was on a mission and not to be trifled with. Clint nodded.

"I swear to God-" Sarah said.

"Hey, doc," Clint said, "we should do what she says, okay? She's serious." Clint met Sarah's eyes. Apparently his expression said everything she needed to hear.

"Fine," Sarah said, "but I need another set of hands in here if you want me to properly treat this patient."

"No," the agent said. "My men are already clearing your staff out for their own safety."

"What?" Sarah snapped. "You can't-"

"I can and I did." The agent holstered her weapon and faced Sarah. "Look, I'm not interested in hurting you and I'm sorry about the gun but I needed your full attention. This is a high risk situation and we need everyone as far from this area as they can be in case something else goes wrong. You're going to have to make do with the three of us."

Sarah glared at the woman so hard Clint was surprised that the agent didn't flinch. "Fine," Sarah said. "Since you're so free with your six-shooter why don't you tell us what's so special about this patient. What does he need?"

"First, the rings stay. Second, he needs blood and lots of it. Get him that and he can do the rest."

"What's that mean? He's not even conscious!" Sarah said.

"We don't have time to argue," the agent snapped. "Just do what I say. All of this falls under confidentiality so you won't be liable for anything. Just do it."

Sarah looked at Clint and nodded. "Get a 16 gauge into him and start a line."

Clint started grabbing what he needed from the supply bins by the bed. "Do you know his blood type?" he said over his shoulder.

"It doesn't matter for him. Any blood will do."

Clint looked back at her. "Ma'am, it does matter. Unless he's a universal recipient, the wrong blood type-"

The lights went out. Emergency lighting kicked in almost immediately, bathing the room in a cold, blue tinged LED glow.

The agent's gun was back in her hand. "Dammit," she said, training her weapon on the open door. "He caught up to us."

Before Clint could ask who, a chorus of baying howls rose from the street outside the ambulance bay.

CHAPTER THREE

"What the actual hell was that?" Sarah said.

"Another problem. A big one," the agent said. She looked at Clint and said, "Get him what he needs. Trust me. He's not like any other patient you've ever had."

She turned to Sarah. "I've got to get out there and help my people secure the area. Is there a back way out of here?"

"Back way out? Why would-"

"There's an elevator," Clint said. "Goes up a floor to the surgery department."

"What about from there? Can you get out of the building?"

Clint thought about it for second and said, "Yeah. There's a door to the employee parking structure at one of the back stairwells. Maybe a minute from the elevator."

"We can't move this patient," Sarah said.

The agent looked at her and then back to Clint. Her eyes paused on him for a moment, as though she'd spotted something she was trying to work out. She dropped a hand from her weapon and grabbed his arm. "Get him the blood and then you two get him out the back way," she said. "He'll know what to do when he wakes up. Take care of him. That's the mission."

She lifted his scrub shirt's short sleeve and fully revealed the tattoo that was inked on his upper arm. It showed a robed angel of death holding a globe in its bony hands and a parachute rising above its hooded head. A curling banner beneath the globe read *That Others May Live*. Clint looked at it and then back at her.

"This tells me that you know what that means. His name is Arlo and he's important. Promise me you've got this." Her eyes held the same intensity they'd had when she'd held the gun on him but there was something else now. It wasn't fear, exactly, but desperation. It was the look of someone who was afraid to fail.

"Yeah," he said. "We've got this. Go do what you have to do."

She gave him a quick nod and headed out of the room, barking orders to her men as she went.

"Excuse me, nurse," Sarah said, "would you mind telling the *doctor* what the hell is happening here?"

Clint slid the rest of the IV supplies into one of the lower pockets on his scrub shirt and said, "Honestly? I have no idea. Between you and me, I think that bitch is crazy. This guy needs blood regardless, though, so I say we get this line started and then get the hell out of here just like she said. There are other ER's in this town that I'll bet haven't gone insane."

Sarah looked over the patient and then nodded. "Yeah, I like it. Crazy woman with gun, evacuated unit, patient safety concerns; yeah, we can move him."

There was another chorus of howls. Clint thought they were getting louder.

"Then there's that," Sarah said.

"Yeah," Clint said. "That. What the hell *is* that?"

He quickly snapped a pair of gloves onto his hands and pulled the IV supplies from his pocket. Sarah let up the pressure on the man's chest and gestured to the supplies. "Gimme," she said. "I'll do that while you get the blood. Grab O-neg if we have it."

"If we don't?"

Sarah shrugged. "Then we do what the crazy lady with the gun and the badge says. Maybe he actually is a universal recipient. It doesn't sound like we have time for a type and cross so just go."

Clint ducked out the exam room curtain. He fast stepped out of the room but stopped suddenly at the scene before him. The agents had collected everything that wasn't nailed down and formed a barricade at the ambulance bay doors. The emergency lighting was casting thick shadows from the mish-mash of furniture, carts, and everything else that they had piled up to block the entrance.

Clint could still see over the barricade, though. The ambulance bay doors were thick glass but the exterior lights had gone out with the power. Mostly, he could see the reflections from the ER floor but he swore there were shapes out there, moving fast at the glass and veering away suddenly.

A howl went up from outside, quickly answered by a choir of others. It was so close now that Clint could feel it in his head. He turned and sprinted for the ER's blood cooler, trying hard not to think about what was happening.

He reached the cooler and punched in his code. With the main power down, it seemed that the processor was running more slowly than usual or something- he really wasn't much of a tech guy -so it took a few seconds longer than it normally did. Clint gritted his teeth impatiently while he waited and snatched the glass and stainless steel door open as soon as he heard the lock disengage.

He scanned the dimly lit labels until he spotted what he needed; a plastic tray with four bags of O-negative blood. Usually, there was a process of bar code scans that he'd go through for inventory purposes. He ignored that and grabbed the entire tray. He made a point of not looking outside as he sprinted back to room five. He came in just as Sarah was taping down the IV.

"I swear to my time that howling is going to give me nightmares," she said. Clint could hear the tension in her voice as plainly as he could see her rapid, nervous breathing.

"Focus on the job," he said. "That out there is their problem. This guy is ours."

Sarah nodded. "Yeah, okay. Let's get that line hooked up and start pushing those units in."

"Yes, ma'am, doctor, ma'am," Clint said. He hoped the teasing would help to break down some of Sarah's tension. She didn't even seem to notice.

Clint hung all four units of blood onto the bed's IV pole and opened a tubing pack with a plastic spike and dip chamber on one end. He handed the other end to Sarah, made sure the line was clamped and inserted the spike into the port on the bottom of the blood bag. Once it was secure, he opened the clamp enough to bleed the air out of the line so that Sarah could hook up the IV with a fluid to fluid connection. As soon as it was taped down, she nodded to Clint and he grabbed the bag with both hands and squeezed, forcing the blood into the patient's body faster than gravity could.

"Too slow," Sarah said. "He needs a central line. Honestly, I don't see how he's even still with us. It looks like something mauled this guy."

As though on cue another chorus of howls filled the air. Sarah's eyes got wide. "What the hell, Clint? Is somebody turning attack dogs loose on us? Where are the cops?"

"I don't know," he said, squeezing harder on the bag. "This one's almost in. Want to get another started and push it on the move?"

Sarah was staring at the privacy curtain. There was a tremble in her hands.

"Hey, doctor," Clint said. "The patient needs you, okay? That's our job. Trust those guys to do theirs."

She nodded. "Right. Sorry. Get another unit going wide open. I'll get him on the portable O2. Grab some epi and an ET kit for the road just in case."

"Will do," Clint said.

"I guess we're taking the bed," Sarah said.

"Guess so," Clint said. "Most of the wheel chairs are blocking the doors right now."

"What?"

"Never mind. Are his wounds packed?"

"Yeah, for all it's worth," Sarah said. "Let's get the hell out of here."

Clint grabbed the supplies and tossed them onto the bed. He started unlocking the wheels while Sarah placed a nasal cannula under the patient's nose and hooked the line behind his ears. Pure oxygen hissed into the tubing as she opened the tank valve.

"Straight to the elevator," Clint said. "Don't look at anything but the patient and the hallway."

"Getting kinda bossy there, buddy" Sarah said.

"Yeah, well, they covered situations like this in badass parachuting school. Not sure you got that at UAB Medical."

"That's fair," Sarah said as she grabbed the blood bag and squeezed. "Let's go."

Clint swept the privacy curtain aside pushed open the wide door that led to the emergency suite. He pulled the bed out into the corridor just as something heavy slammed against the Ambulance bay doors. There was a shout of alarm that was answered by the female agent shouting, "Hold your fire!"

Clint pulled the bed faster and nearly whipped Sarah into a wall as he hauled the bed around a corner that led to a set of double doors. Normally, she wouldn't have missed the chance to give him a hard time about it. Instead, she just set her feet and pushed the bed forward without comment. Her eyes were fixed on the patient.

Clint let her focus and kept pulling. He came to the doors and hit the release. The hospital's back up power kept the magnetically locked doors locked but the motors that were supposed to automatically open them weren't functional. Clint turned his shoulder into them and used his and the bed's weight to force them open. The hallway beyond was dark with small islands of LED emergency lighting leading to the elevator.

More shouts came from behind them followed by crashing sounds.

"Almost there," Clint said.

"Keep moving," Sarah said, "I'm spiking the third bag. I think some-"

A kaleidoscope of lights suddenly flared from the patient's hands and torso. The thin man's back arched and he gasped in a deep, ragged breath. Clint felt his own breath catch in his throat as he watched a silver glow radiate and then fade from the patient's eyes and open mouth. As quickly as it had come, the lights faded and the man collapsed back onto the bed.

Without even realizing it, they had stopped in the hallway. Both Sarah and Clint had taken a few steps back from the bed. The LEDs cast stark shadows over everything.

They looked at each other, eyes wide, and Clint said, "What the hell was-"

Behind the ER doors, a man screamed and the sound of gunshots erupted through the shadows.

CHAPTER FOUR

"Go, go, go!" Clint shouted, grabbing the bed and hauling it forward.

There was a roar from beyond the closed doors followed by another burst of gunfire. Sarah grabbed the bed and pushed. They ran down the hallway so fast that they couldn't slow the bed fast enough to keep it from pushing Clint into the closed elevator doors.

His thigh hurt from the impact but he shoved the bed back enough to swipe his ID badge through a reader next to the elevator's call button. He pressed the single button that was there. Since this was the elevator they used to get trauma patients to surgery as quickly as possible, backup generators were supposed to keep it working even in a blackout. Clint had never had to test that, though, so he was relieved when the button lit up.

There were more screams from the ER. Clint looked at Sarah. Her eyes were wide and looked a little wild in the emergency lights. He imagined he looked much the same. He was about to say something when the elevator doors opened. He let the words die on his tongue and jerked the bed forward.

The elevator was built for patient transport so there was plenty of room for the bed and both of them. Unfortunately, a design oversight had left a gap between the elevator and the floor that was just wide enough for the wheels on the hospital bed to slip down into if they struck it as just the right angle. This fact was brought home to Clint and Sarah as the bed suddenly stopped moving when one of the wheels on her end got stuck.

"Oh, are you frigging kidding me?" she snapped, jerking at the bed as she tried to dislodge the wheel.

Something heavy hit the ER doors hard enough that the sound echoed down the hall. There was a frustrated roar from the other side and another loud impact. Clint thought he heard something crack.

"Squeeze in here," Clint said. "Let me get it."

"No, I can-"

Another impact. The door bounced partly open as something gave way.

Sarah jumped at the sound and said, "Okay, tough mudder, you're up!"

She squeezed around one side of the bed while Clint came around the other and took her place, He grabbed the bed frame and jerked it upwards while leaning into the bed. The wheel popped free and rolled into the elevator, hitting the back wall hard.

There was a sudden pop and crash as the heavy screws that secured the magnetic locks to the ER doors gave way and the doors flew open. Clint looked back and saw what had been forcing its way through.

The thing was huge. At first, he thought it was the biggest dog he'd ever seen with its front shoulder easily four feet high. That was wrong, though. The thing's head was stooped too low and didn't have a proper snout. A think mane of something that wasn't really fur but moved like loose spines ran from the stooped head all the way down the length of its six foot body and gathered into a heavy tail that swept the floor. It was nearly ink black in color with small, crimson eyes that studied him from the other end of the hall and sat above two rows of long, gray teeth that dripped something dark from its lipless mouth. Claws as long as Clint's fingers scratched at the tiled floor as he and the monster stared each other down.

The thing roared and charged down the hall.

Sarah and Clint both shouted in panic as Sarah stabbed at the elevator's control panel with her fingers.

Clint watched the thing charging at him on clawed feet that left gouges in the floor with every loping step. The thing's eyes seemed to burn in the shadows, leaving tracers of red fire in their wake.

The doors slid closed just as the thing closed in and collided with the carriage hard enough that Clint felt the shudder through his feet.

"What was that what was that what *was* that?" Sarah shouted.

"How the hell should I know?" Clint snapped back.

"What kind of crazy shit is this?" Sarah said.

Clint shook his head. "I don't know. Let's just get to a car and get out of here. We can figure the rest out later."

Sarah nodded. "Yeah, okay, we can take this guy to Crestwood. Call the cops on the way. My car's in… shit."

"What?" Clint said as the elevator chimed and the doors slid open to reveal an empty alcove with a single hallway leading away from a set of locked double doors that led to the surgery suites.

"My keys are in my bag and my bag is in my locker."

Clint hauled the bed into the alcove and turned into the hall. Between the time of night and the blackout, there was no one else in sight. "We'll take mine. I'm on the fourth floor. We're going to have to carry him, though. The bed won't work for the stairs."

"After that little light show I'm not sure I want to touch this guy. I know I keep saying it but what *was* that?" Sarah said, pushing the bed while letting Clint lead the way.

"Yeah, again, no idea. He's still our patient, though."

"Is he? Look at him, the bleeding's pretty much stopped. We didn't do that."

Clint glanced at the man's wounds. Sarah was right. No more rivulets of fresh blood ran from the bandages and sponges that had been packed into the wound. In fact, some of the packing had fallen away from the worst of the injuries and the flesh beneath looked far less worse that it had in the exam room. It looked like it had partially healed.

Clint alternated between hauling the bed around a corner and looking back at the wound. "That isn't possible."

Sarah shook her head. She was breathing hard from the exertion and her hair was falling in loose blonde strands in her face. "I'm starting to wonder if that word means what we think it means," she said. "Look, if this guy suddenly wakes up and tells us he's good then I say we take him at his word and get as far away from him as possible. Whatever's going on, he seems to be at the middle of it."

Clint nodded. "If he wakes up, I'm good with that."

They skidded to a stop in front of a door with an exit sign hanging above it. The word 'Stairs' was stenciled in black on the cream colored door.

"All right, lose the O2 but let's keep pushing the blood. If that's really what's making him heal then maybe more will bring him around. You grab him and I'll carry the blood."

Clint didn't bother to respond. He pulled the nasal cannula off the man, spent a second making sure he wouldn't tangle the IV lines and then lifted him from the bed into a cradle carry.

Somewhere, something howled.

Sarah and Clint looked at each other. "That wasn't downstairs," Sarah said.

Clint shook his head. "It's tracking us or there's more than one. Leave the bed in front of the door. It might slow it down."

Sarah pulled the bed into position and let the stairwell door bang shut behind them. Clint started up the stairs. The patient was light enough that he managed to take them two at a time. Sarah was breathing hard but she kept up and didn't complain.

When they reached the door for the third floor garage access, she said, "Hang on. I need to spike the last bag."

Clint nodded and stopped. His legs were starting to burn a little. He ignored it and looked down at the patient. A faint glow was coming off the space on his abdomen where he'd been injured. His hands were folded over his chest. Tiny symbols on some of the rings were glowing like multi-colored Christmas lights that he could see from a distance.

His first instinct was to drop the man. Every sense he had was telling him that what he was seeing wasn't normal and that he shouldn't be anywhere near it. Clint fought back that fear, though, and readjusted his grip on his patient.

"Done," Sarah said. "I don't hear anything coming after us."

"Don't jinx it, doc. Let's keep moving."

She nodded and they headed up the last flight of stairs.

CHAPTER FIVE

Clint and Sarah came through the doors to the parking garage at nearly a full run. Clint nodded toward the ramp that lead up to rooftop parking and said, "That way, about halfway up. It's a Jeep Rubicon, black four-door. My keys are in my right hand pocket. Grab them and go lay the back seats down so we can spread this guy out."

Sarah balanced the last of the blood bags onto Clint's right shoulder to keep it above the patient so gravity would keep the blood moving, though slowly. "Try not to jostle it," she said and reached into the scrub shirt pocket Clint had indicated. A moment later she held up a heavy key chain engraved with a Fleur De Les and the words *"New Orleans - Let The Good Times Roll"* in a circle around it. Two keys dangled from the chain. Sarah had no problem finding the one with the Jeep logo. She ran ahead, clicking the unlock button on the key fob as she went.

Clint slowed to a careful walk so that the blood bag remained balanced on his shoulder. Now that he was outside, he could hear police sirens coming from the street below. The gunfire had stopped but an occasional howl filtered out from the building. Clint knew that there were still a lot of people in the hospital even in the middle of the third shift. With all the shooting and the power outage, most of them would be secured in rooms of some kind and not in the public spaces. Still, if those dog-wolf things had given up on them and were wandering the halls then a lot of people were in danger.

He looked down at his patient. What had the other agent called him? Artie? No, Arlo. That was it. His color was better and the rings were still glowing steadily on his hands. Clint chose to assume that was a good thing since he couldn't really assess the injuries on the man's torso.

It didn't take long for him to make a decision. He would get the patient into the vehicle and tell Sarah to take his Jeep and get out of there. He'd left his hiking pack in the back of his Jeep the day before. He kept a well sharpened K-bar knife there. While he would have preferred a fully loaded Remington 870 and a squad of equally armed shooters to back him up, the knife was what he had so that's what he'd go back in with. There were too many people inside the building for him to just drive away.

He looked up to tell Sarah his plan just as a man dropped down from the rooftop parking overhang.

He landed as though he'd just stepped off the back of a truck instead of the nearly twenty foot fall he'd just taken.

He was lean and dressed in a stylish black sports coat and matching slacks. A tight, gray shirt showed beneath the jacket with dark stains marring his otherwise neat look. The same kinds of stains were smeared across the man's hands, neck, and lean, chiseled face. Clint was sure he saw some in his light colored, slicked back hair, as well.

Sarah looked up just as the man landed a few feet from her. Before she could even say anything, he had crossed the distance between them and grabbed her by the throat.

"Hey!" Clint screamed taking a sudden, instinctive step forward. The blood bag slid off his shoulder and onto the ground.

The newcomer didn't even seem to notice him as he lifted Sarah off her feet and delivered two vicious punches to her gut so fast that Clint barely had time to realize what had happened. His hand darted in a third time and grabbed a handful of her clothing near her waist. Without so much as a grunt of effort, the man pivoted and threw Sarah through the air like she was nothing.

Clint watched in disbelief and horror as his friend went flying across the parking garage and collided with the back of a parked Lexus so hard that the back window burst into a spider web of cracks. Time seemed to slow for Clint as he watched her limbs bend in ways they weren't meant to. She skipped off the Lexus's trunk, collided with the side of an SUV and fell to the concrete between the two cars. There was a smear of dark red down the side of the SUV. Clint could see one of her feet sticking out past the Lexus's rear tire. It didn't even twitch.

"There," the man said, straightening his dark jacket. "Now the menfolk can have a private conversation, as is proper."

Clint stared at Sarah's still foot. He shifted the patient's weight in his arms slightly to get a better grip. He slowly took a step backwards as he shifted his eyes to the man who had attacked his friend. The blood bag hissed against the concrete as he dragged it.

"Of all the things that have changed over the centuries," the man said, adjusting his cuffs, "this whole equality of the sexes thing has been the most annoying, I think. Well, that, and freeing the slaves. Honestly, though, I think the whole idea of equality is to blame. Owning people was just too much fun."

He met Clint's eyes for the first time and for an instant they flared with a dark, violet light, like something you'd see lighting up fluorescent paints in a nightclub.

Clint gasped suddenly despite himself and took another few steps back. He turned to run, blood bag scraping along behind him, when a chorus of howls from the floors below brought him up short. He stopped and looked around fighting hard to keep his fear under control.

"Be glad you parked near the top," the man said. "I told my hounds to start at the bottom and work their way up while I came in from above. If you'd encountered them instead of me, you'd be in pieces by now."

Clint was sure he could make it to either the stairwell that would lead him back inside or the elevator that would take him down to the garage's ground level. He'd have to stop at either, though, whether to try and pull a door open or wait for the elevator car. He glanced to the side as flashes of police strobes started lighting up the night beyond the parking deck and sirens grew louder. He heard the distant chop-chop of a helicopter's rotors.

"Don't get your hopes up," the man said. "All the Pickmen are dead and my hounds will make short work of the police. You're trapped, son. Face it like a man."

Clint thought it over for a second before he realized that the man was right. No matter which way he went, he would get run down before he had a chance to get clear. There was no way out and that meant there was only one thing left to do. He drew in a deep breath, knelt, and placed the patient on the floor as gently as he could. Fear driven breath hissed around his teeth as he turned and faced the man in the stained suit.

"I'm not your son," he said, meeting the other's eyes and planting his feet.

The man's eyebrows rose in surprise. "Excuse me?"

Clint swallowed hard. "You heard me, slim. I'm not your son. And if you're looking to hurt this guy… well, we have a problem if that's the case."

The man's eyes had grown wide with disbelief as Clint had been talking. After a moment, a wide smile crossed his face. "Let me make sure I understand," he said, holding up a hand for Clint to wait. "You've met my hounds, you just saw me throw that female around like she was a lawn dart, and now you're standing between me and my prey even though it's obvious from your face that you have no earthly idea what I am or what you're actually facing. Have I got that all right?"

Clint swallowed again. His mouth was as dry as a desert wind. "I think that about sums it up."

The dark light flared through the man's eyes again and tiny arcs of the same colored electricity danced over his hands. "Give me the Pickman," the man said, his voice suddenly more animal than man.

Clint's stomach tightened as his guts went cold. For just an instant, he almost ran but the moment passed and he shifted his hands and feet into a defensive stance. He forced himself to hold the other man's blacklight stare as he shook his head.

Suddenly, the lights were gone from the man's eyes as though they'd never been there. "Really?" he said. "Usually that little display sends you humans running like rabbits. It's been decades since anyone's stood up to me like this. Why would you? You must recognize that I can kill you easy as sliding off a horse. Why would you risk that for someone you've just met? He can't possibly be anything to you."

"He's my patient," Clint said, forcing the words past the lump in his throat. "He's mine to look after until he's well. That and I made a promise. Besides, you said it yourself, I'm boxed in here. If this is where I go out then I'm sure as hell not going to do it running."

The man studied Clint through narrowed eyes, his smile dropping into a thoughtful line. "You would die for a promise? Son, that makes you a rarity in today's world." He raised a finger to his lips absently, as though considering his options, and then said, "I'll tell you what; since you've shown some obvious courage I'll make you a deal. You walk away unmolested by either myself or my hounds. Gone, free and clear, to live out as long a life as you can manage. Only you, though. The Pickman stays with me."

Even Clint was surprised by how fast he replied. "No deal, freak-show. This man's under my protection."

The man with the blacklight eyes shook his head thoughtfully. "A rarity, indeed," he said. "It's very nearly a shame to kill you." The man studied him a moment longer then shrugged and said, "Oh, well. Omelets and eggs." Energy flared around his hands and he thrust them towards Clint.

Clint saw the hands coming up, the dark energy crackling between them. At the same time, though, he felt someone grab his ankle from behind. Warmth like walking from a cold room into a hot summer day flooded through him at the same moment searing pain seemed to light up his chest and head.

For an instant, everything went dark. He felt as though he were being shredded apart from the inside out and pulled into a trillion molecule sized lines that stretched out into a black forever. He had no throat to scream with or eyes to weep with or limbs to defend himself with. For that instant, he was little more than a stain of pain and terror stretched across the world. Then, the instant was over.

Clint didn't feel himself fall, didn't feel the concrete bite into his face, didn't hear the sobbing scream that rushed from his throat. In those last instants before the darkness came for him again and his vision was clear, all he saw was his patient rising to his feet and stepping past him.

CHAPTER SIX

Southline Consolidated Headquarters
Bank of America Financial Center
600 Peachtree Street NW
Atlanta, Georgia
28 October, 7:22 a.m. EST

Jeffrey Lemaster stepped off the elevator on the fifty-fifth floor and jostled his cell phone as he switched hands with his laptop case. "Yes, I promise," he said into the phone, nodding to the attractive young woman who rose from the desk that was just outside the elevator. "I'll be there. No late night tonight. I'll be fully present and attentive."

The woman mimed drinking coffee and Jeffrey nodded.

"I know, honey," he said, rolling his eyes as he made his way past his assistant's desk. "Last time couldn't be helped. Come on, I explained that." He listened for a moment as he used the hand with the computer bag in it to open the door to his spacious office. "Oh, come on," he said. "She's twelve. I'm pretty sure me missing one middle school band concert isn't going to scar her for life."

He listened some more as he crossed the office and put his bag on the mahogany desk that dominated the space in front of the glass wall that overlooked the city below. "I understand," he said, watching the clouds that were hanging low in the October morning. "Look, unless the world economy crashes sometime today and we lose all our business, I'll be at the concert. I promise"

There was a knock at the open door. He looked back as Melissa, his assistant, entered with a dark wooden tray that held a black carafe of coffee and a dark stoneware mug. Jeffrey nodded towards the desk. She smiled and put the tray next to his bag and poured him a cup.

"Okay, honey, I'll be there. Gotta go now, I'm at the office." He ended the call and looked at his assistant.

"Good morning," she said, a broad smile crossing her face. "Sounds like you were getting scolded."

"Not really. It's Kiera's first concert since I missed the last one and Vanessa's stressing herself out over this one. I love that woman but I swear she thrives on anxiety."

"Most of the good mama bears act that way," Melissa said as she handed him his mug.

"I suppose," he said. Jeffrey took a sip and let himself smile. It was hot, bold, and just a little bitter, exactly how he liked it. "Was your mom like that?"

Melissa laughed. "Oh, lord yes. Dad used to say she could worry the rust off a bumper. It all came from a good heart, though."

Jeffrey nodded. "Well, you and that boyfriend of yours make it official and maybe you'll get a chance to find out if you follow in her footsteps."

"I don't know. We're kind of exploring more nontraditional relationship models at the moment."

Jeffrey stopped with his mug halfway to his lips and locked eyes with her.

"And before you use the word 'millennials' in some kind of derogatory way, you might want to remember who makes your coffee," Melissa said, the smile turning into a playful smirk.

Jeffrey finished taking the drink and said, "Fine, oh future of the human race, what's on this silver-haired old man's schedule for today?"

"I just updated your calendar. Conference calls with Texas, Brazil, and Long Beach this morning, then a lunch meeting with the rep from the mayor's office and the city tax people, capped off with a quarterly check in with the U.S. district managers. Pretty routine stuff."

Jeffrey nodded. "Good. I should be able to keep my promise about the concert and not have to watch my wife go through a psychotic break."

"Oh, stop it. She's a sweetheart."

"That, she is," Jeffrey said.

"Anything else, boss?"

"Not at the moment. Make sure I'm the last one to join the conference calls."

"You'll be business fashion late, as always."

"Thanks, Mel. Close the door on your way out, please."

Melissa smiled and left the office, closing the door behind her as she went. Jeffrey watched her go and then turned back to the windows once he'd heard the doors click shut. He took another pull from his mug and snorted, "Non-traditional relationship models, my ass. Frikkin' millennials."

He spent a few minutes going over the day's schedule in his head. He'd want to call up the Long Beach account reports before that first call. He recalled seeing a downturn in their last-

He started at the cold squirm in the back of his neck. It was like a frozen worm wriggling lazily just under his skin. It always startled him a little whether he was expecting the sensation or not. He paused just long enough to finish his coffee and then placed the mug back onto the tray with the carafe. He drew a deep breath to steady his nerves and then sat down at his desk.

When they'd done the remodel for the top floor of the building, Jeffrey had made sure to install a remote lock for the office doors. He pressed the concealed button underneath the desk and saw a tiny red light appear in the wood paneling just above the office doors, indicating that the doors had been silently sealed. This done, he removed a small, silver bladed pen knife from a drawer and pressed it into his left thumb until a fat drop of blood swelled next to the blade.

His desk was inlaid with pieces of brass that gave it a kind of art deco appearance but that was all for show. He'd had some very particular craftsmen build the desk from scratch for him with the sole purpose of making sure that the hidden compartments he needed were easily accessible and secured by- and he chuckled at this - 'non-traditional' means. He pressed his bloodied thumb against one of the small, brass diamond shaped inlays. It gave a satisfying hiss and a flat section of the desk popped out a couple of inches.

He pulled it open the rest of way to reveal a thin, silver disc resting in a padded drawer. The disc's finish was dull and non-reflective. Not exactly tarnished, just not polished. He carefully removed the disc and placed it on the desk in front of him.

Jeffrey squeezed the cut in his thumb until more blood flowed and he used it to draw a series of swirling and jagged lines onto the metal. Satisfied, he sucked the remainder of the blood from his thumb and placed his left hand over the symbols, palm down.

"Mgah'ehye ya ph'nglui ymg' 'ai throdog fhalma," he whispered, his voice growing deeper with every syllable. Twice more he spoke the incantation. With

every utterance, the disc beneath his palm cleared into an unmarred surface of silver purity that shimmered like a puddle of mercury. The cold bloom at the base of his skull grew into a rushing wave of icy discomfort. He closed his eyes as the world fell away from his senses and was replaced by a sense of dark, cold, and the presence of something that could swallow him whole.

"Summoned, I come to you, Mother." He didn't speak the words, exactly, but rather forced them into the frozen black with a well-practiced force of will.

There was the sense of movement around him, of something long and huge sliding to encircle him. Jeffrey resolutely kept his focus pulled in, not allowing it to stray too long on The Mother's form.

"One of my Favored has come once again to your lands. You will grant what aid he requires of you." The words came to him much as he had sent his. It was like they were being shoved into his mind.

"Your will is my hand, Mother. The many gifts you have bestowed to me are the tools of my service. How will I know this Favored?"

"He is the one called Jubal Mott. Obey him as you would me. His task is one of great import."

"It will be as you command, Mother."

As suddenly as blinking, Jeffrey was back in his office. He opened his eyes and took a steadying breath. His hand still rested on the metal disc but it was back to its original tarnished state. There was no trace of blood on it.

With careful reverence, Jeffrey replaced the disc into its hidden compartment and closed it. He rose and poured himself another cup of coffee. Communing with The Mother was always a mentally taxing experience and the older he got, the harder it seemed to be. Still, though, it was worth the pain. He owed his success to The Mother. Every financial gain, every eliminated rival, every secret carnal impulse he'd satisfied; they were all the result of boons granted him by The Mother. He owed everything to her, really, even his family and they had no idea she existed.

Jeffrey stood again and returned to studying the cityscape stretched out before him. He'd only ever dealt with one of The Mother's Favored once, many years back, and that was just a momentary exchange to arrange some off the books travel. If there was one in town now, then somebody down in that mass of humanity below him was in for a very, very bad time.

A slow, smirk of a smile crept over Jeffrey's lips as he took another sip from his mug and whispered, "Sucks to be that guy."

CHAPTER SEVEN

Private Care Facility
799 Arrington Blvd South
Birmingham, Alabama
October 28, 3:20 P.M. CST

It had been years since Clint had dreamed the dream.

He was back in South America, back in the helicopter that was filled to capacity with half drowned flood victims. Children were crying. Women were weeping for what they'd lost. Men sat in sullen silence or prayed in a language that Clint didn't understand. He didn't see them praying, though. He only barely heard the lamentations or the steady thump of the rotor blades. He was in the chopper's open door, staring down at the disaster below.

The village of sturdy shacks that made up the community these refugees had come from was being swallowed by flood waters and mudslides. Buildings were breaking apart, homes washed away by rain that just didn't want to stop falling. He watched as a tree washed from its roots and tore through a home smashing what were once someone's walls into nothing more than random flotsam. That was when he would always seem them.

The family of four was huddled together on a tin roof that was already showing signs of degrading. They were screaming, pleading, begging for the chopper to descend and pull them from their certain death.

Instead, the helicopter flew on. They were too full, too heavy to take on any more passengers. Physics cared nothing for human need so the decision was simple math in command's eye; lose four or lose them all.

Clint watched as the waters and the mud swept over parents that held their children tight. He watched as children who were probably too young to have ever gotten their first kiss were swallowed by dark water and torn from their parent's desperate grasps by currents that could uproot trees.

He would always lose sight of them then. The helicopter would get too far and the rain would cloud his goggles. He told himself it was the rain.

That was when he would tear the goggles from his face and wipe the moisture from his eyes. He would look to the ones they had saved hoping for some sense of solace. What always looked back, though, weren't the kinds of things that knew what solace was.

Milky, dead eyes stared out from slick, death gray faces. Hair, lank and saturated with dark rivulets of brackish water, hung in cloying stands and sheets from heads that were lolling loosely forward and rolling with the bob and shifts of the chopper. The eyes were fixed on him, though, and held an intensity that felt like needles on his skin. Then, as one, the compliment of dream dead lifted their hands to point at him, to accuse and condemn him. Gone was the weeping, gone were the prayers. In their place was only a damning silence and the weight of those dead, drowned eyes on his own.

Then, in the dream, they would come for him.

Clint snapped awake from the nightmare with a sharp breath. The room was a wash of bright blurs with shapes moving through them like out of focus ghosts. He started to sit up but the dull, throbbing ache that filled his head encouraged him to lie back down. He went along with the notion, blinking as he tried to clear his vision.

One of the shapes leaned over him and said, "Mr. Mercer? Clint? Please lie back. You're safe here. Give yourself a moment."

It was a woman's voice, strong yet soothing, punctuated by a heavy British accent. It reminded Clint of something you'd hear in one of those old, hardboiled detective movies.

"It's all right, Clint. Take as long as you need. You've been through quite the ordeal," the voice went on. "I'm Doctor Smythe. Everything is fine, now."

"Not sure I'd go that far, Rani," another voice said. It was a male this time with a sharp, impatient tone and just enough of a southern drawl for Clint to notice. It seemed to come from the brightest blur. Clint tried to squint and bring the speaker into focus but all he managed was to make his eyes water.

"Hush, Arlo. That's not helping," the doctor said.

Arlo; Clint felt like he should know the name but the bright lights and the pounding in his head was making it hard to collect his thoughts. "Too bright," he said, though his voice was like a croak coming from his dry throat. He tried to raise his hand to shield his eyes but something held it fast. He thought maybe it was tangled in the heavy blankets that covered him.

"Lie still, Clint," Doctor Smythe said. "I'll get you some water. Arlo, close those blinds."

There was some rustling and the brightest of the blurs faded into something more tolerable. Clint saw a small framed man moving in front of what he realized was a large window. The sun must have sitting low in the sky because even with the blinds closed he could see lines of brightness between the slats. The man was still indistinct, though.

"Here you go, dear," Doctor Smythe said.

Clint looked towards her voice and blinked some more, finally managing to clear his vision enough to make out her features.

Doctor Rani Smythe had tawny brown skin and large eyes that were the color of roasted cinnamon. Her black hair was long enough to reach past her lean shoulders and framed a face with prominent features that were just the right balance of handsome and beautiful. Her mouth was full lipped and serious but carried a curve that suggested a soothing smile. She was in her late forties, Clint guessed, with all the lines that came with four decades of life. Clint thought they looked good on her, though, and accented the deep intelligence that lingered behind her eyes.

"Drink," she said as she held out a small plastic cup with a straw sticking up over the rim. "You've been out for quite a few hours."

He raised his head enough to take a sip. Ice cold water washed down his throat and, in that moment, was the most glorious thing he'd ever felt. He tried to reach for the cup but felt his hand come up short again. Clint tried to free it from what he thought was a tangle of blankets but couldn't. It only took a moment for him to realize his hands and feet were all bound by heavy leather restraints.

Clint jerked against them and said, "What the hell? Why am I in restraints?"

"Just a precaution, Clint. We wanted-"

"We had to make sure you didn't wake up bad," the man called Arlo said, cutting the doctor off.

Clint looked at him and immediately recognized the man he had carried from the emergency room. Cleaned up and with a change of clothes, Clint realized that his earlier assessment had been pretty accurate. He wasn't tall, well under Clint's own six-two, and was built like someone who'd never lifted anything heavier than a large book for most of his life. His skin was pale and his hair was only a few shades darker than that. His face was a mask of severity around a nose that was long and hawkish. The most striking thing, though, were his eyes. Even in the dimmer light, Clint could see that one was a dark blue and the other a shade of green that reminded him of fresh limes.

"You're the guy from the ER," Clint said. "The DHS agent."

"Obviously," Arlo said. "How are you? Any strange cravings? Feeling irrational or violent? Think about dead puppies and tell me what you feel."

Clint stared at him for a moment before he said, "Think of what? What the hell are you talking about?" His voice was better. Some more water would be nice but then he remembered the restraints. He looked back to Smythe and said, "Doctor, what's happening here?"

"Don't answer that," Arlo said. "We need to make sure he's clear."

"Arlo, I think-"

"I'm fine," Clint said, looking at Arlo and then back to Smythe. His head felt like it was turning a second or two later than his brain. He did his best to ignore the pain and said, "Why am I restrained? Did I do something while I was unconscious?"

"No," Doctor Smythe said. "Clint, what you've been through is-"

"Do not give him any information, Rani," Arlo said, "not until we're sure he's clean."

Clint felt his temper flare along with the throb in his head. "Hey, skinny, how about you shut up a minute and let me talk to the doctor. I carried your narrow butt out of the hospital so I think you at least owe me that."

"For what? Doing your job? They pay you for that, right?"

"Look, you ungrateful-"

"Gentlemen!" Doctor Smythe said in a voice that was accustomed to being heeded. "Enough of this nonsense. Arlo, contain yourself. I'm as good at my job as you are at yours. Clint-"

"Oh, for God's sake," Arlo snapped. He crossed the room fast eying Clint the whole way. "Sorry," he said, "you're not going to like this."

Before Clint could say anything, Arlo had slapped one ring laden hand over his forehead, fingers stretching back through his hair.

Everything was pearl white and silent. Clint couldn't feel anything. No body, no breath, no anything.

Suddenly he was overwhelmed by a rush of memories that flashed by like a video in fast reverse. He saw the parking garage, the man with the blacklight eyes, the hounds, the stairwell, Sarah, all of it streamed across his mind in a matter of moments and then reversed again to flash forward to the moment the man named Arlo had grabbed him. Reverse, forward, reverse, forward, Sarah alive, Sarah dying; back and forth it went like some kind of perverse punishment.

Clint tried to cry out, tried to shout for it to stop, but he had no voice with which to protest. Finally, it stopped. The pearl white nothing shimmered in again and Clint was grateful for it.

"There's something," Arlo's voice said. It seemed to echo in from every direction. "Something," he repeated, "but not an entity. You've changed but you're not infested."

Clint tried to speak again but nothing happened.

"I was wrong, Mercer. It happens but not often. I should have been less aggressive. Rest now."

Clint felt the pressure leave his head and, just like that, darkness overwhelmed the sea of white.

CHAPTER EIGHT

Clint woke from a dreamless sleep to a room that was dark save for the glow coming from a television that was mounted in one of the room's corners. The sound was turned down but irregular, black closed-caption boxes flashed words on the screen. There were faint sounds coming from the street outside the window that had been blinding him earlier. Air hissed from an overhead vent and seemed to fill the room with the kind of clean, antiseptic aroma that was a staple of every hospital he'd ever been in.

He took a deep breath and propped himself onto his elbows, looking around the room but seeing nothing outside the television's flat-screen glow. His head still hurt but what had been a throbbing ache had dulled to a more manageable pain that sat behind his eyes like a sore muscle that only hurt when you used it. He glanced down at his wrists and realized the restraints had been removed.

He kept still for a moment, taking stock of how he felt, trying to piece together everything he remembered. Every joint is his body ached as though he been stretched out on one of those old medieval torture devices. He slowly rolled his shoulders to work out the soreness while he thought things over. His eyes strayed to the television and the words *Huntsville Domestic Terror Attack* grabbed his attention. He spent a few minutes reading the commentator's account of an anti-government militia group's attempt to kill federal agents by setting attack dogs loose on them. They were blaming the attack on a group called The Sons of Confederate Liberty. The moment Clint read that he muttered, "Bullshit."

"It is, isn't it?" a familiar voice said from the dark corner beneath the television. "The people that come up with these cover stories are a little too habitual sometimes. It's always terrorist this, terrorist that."

The man named Arlo stepped out from the shadows and looked down at Clint. The glow from the television cast his severe features into hard lines. The one green eye seemed to glitter in the dark.

Clint sat up straighter and tightened his jaw. "I not tied down anymore, slim. Try to touch me again and I promise I'll break the arm you do it with."

A smirking, half smile touched Arlo's lips. He held up a tablet computer he'd been holding and said, "I have no doubt about that, Mr. Mercer."

Clint glanced at the tablet and said, "What do you have there?"

Arlo's expression turned confused. "My iPad, obviously. Haven't you-" he shook his head and said, "No, silly of me, of course you've seen an iPad, you're a professional. You want to know what I'm reading."

Clint furrowed his brow and studied the man, his patient assessment skills slipping into play automatically. "Yeah, that's what I meant."

Arlo nodded, "Of course. I'm reading your records."

"What records?"

Arlo shrugged. "All them. Grade school report cards, high school yearbooks, military after action reports, college transcripts, employee evaluations; pretty much everything that's ever been put into a computer with your name on it."

"Hold on. Everything? Military records? Look, man, who the hell are you? Where am I and what's happening here?" Clint's head was beginning to clear, his memories coming back into clearer focus; the ER, the big dog-things, the man in the parking deck, Sarah.

Oh, God. Sarah.

"My condolences on your friend, Mr. Mercer." Arlo said it as though he'd read the memory on Clint's face. "I'm told that her death was near to instantaneous, if that's any consolation."

"It's not," Clint said, his voice a cold, angry whisper. For an instant, he was back in the dream watching as dark waters swept over desperate faces while he sat useless and safe hundreds of feet above the danger.

"I'm sincere in my condolences," Arlo said. "I'd likely not be here right now were it not for the two of you."

"Which is where, exactly? What is this place?"

"Oh, of course, you must be confused. We don't usually bring civilians here. We're in Birmingham. It's a private care facility that the organization I'm part of maintains. We've got at least one in every state. You're just a couple of hours from home."

Every answer seemed to take a little more steam out of Clint's growing grief. He pushed aside that last memory of Sarah colliding with the parked cars and tried to focus on the moment. Grieving could wait. "Okay," he said. "Why am I here? Why not just keep me in Huntsville? I did get hurt in a hospital, after all. What's going on here?"

Arlo nodded and stepped over to the foot of the bed so he could face Clint squarely. "You want answers, I understand that. What you need to understand, though, is that the answers aren't simple ones. It could take some time to explain it all. Why don't we start with this; tell me your story. If you'll recall, I was incoherent when I came into your emergency room. Tell me what you remember starting just before that."

So, Clint did. When he was finished Arlo said, "Right, then. That fits with all the other information that we've managed to gather."

"The other agents," Clint said. "What happened to them?"

The other man's features grew stiff. Clint saw a tiny shadow swell and contract in his jaw line. "There were no survivors," he said after a moment.

Clint shook his head. "Damn, man. I'm sorry."

Arlo's eyes seemed to blaze through the shadows for an instant. "Your sorrow is in no way relevant to the problem at hand. They knew the risks and did their jobs." The words came out tight and fast. Clint knew the tone, he heard it from a lot of survivors, and let the comment go.

"Fine," he said. "I assume the problem is the man that attacked us?"

"He wasn't a man. He was a warlock."

Clint blinked at that a couple of times. Arlo watched him.

"Is that a call sign or a codename or something?" Clint asked.

"No," Arlo said. "A warlock is a mortal human who has bargained with an extraplanar entity to house some portion of said entity into their flesh on this plane in exchange for access to a portion of that entities eldritch knowledge and power. Usually, it's proportional to the amount of free will the host is willing to sacrifice but it varies, really. It rarely turns out well for the mortal."

Clint blinked some more. "Huh," he said after a minute. "Warlock. Guess you learn something every day."

"If you are wise, yes," Arlo said.

"Eldritch power. You mean like... you know, magic?"

"Exactly that."

Clint nodded for a moment and pursed his lips as he thought it over. "Yeah, I'm going to have to stop you there, slim. There's no-"

"Don't say it," Arlo snapped. "You're smarter than that. I know you are because I just memorized your life story." He waggled the iPad at Clint.

"Don't say what?"

"That there's no such thing as Magic."

"Well, there isn-"

"Don't."

Clint glared at Arlo. "You know, this is going to be a pretty one sided conversation if you keep cutting me off."

Arlo nodded. "Very well. How do you explain the hound that pursued you? The things the warlock did? What you saw me do?"

Clint thought it over carefully. "Some kind of weird mutation for the dogs, gene manipulation, maybe. As for you and the guy in the garage..." Clint's voice trailed off. He had nothing. He looked up and met Arlo's mismatched eyes. They stared each other down for a few seconds while Clint searched the other man's face for some sign of deception or some hint that he was being punked. There wasn't any he could see.

"This can't be real, man. It just can't."

"Can and is," Arlo said. "There is far more wonder to the world than you know, Clinton Matthew Mercer. Wonders and horrors alike."

Clint kept watching the man's expression for a crack in his sincerity. There was none. He shook his head and said, "Okay, fine. There's a lot I don't know. Can't say that surprises me. What now?"

Arlo nodded. "Good. He has a nimble intellect and an open sense of the real. I can work with that." Arlo was staring hard at Clint while he spoke.

"Excuse me?" Clint said.

"What?" Arlo said, his expression momentarily confused. "Oh, damn, I said that out loud. Never mind. It was complimentary."

Clint looked around and said, "Where's Doctor Smythe?"

"Yes, about her. Here's the thing; strictly speaking, I'm not supposed to be here right now."

"Why's that?"

"Well, the organization I mentioned, the one that operates this facility, they've made some decisions I'm not willing to go along with but I haven't really told them that yet. They think I'm sticking to protocol which would dictate that I have no further contact with anyone involved in last night's incident. As such, anything I do here won't have their stamp of approval or their authority to back me up."

"Okay," Clint said. "And you're here to… what, exactly?"

"Offer you a job."

"Excuse me?"

"Look, here's the situation; I can sneak us out of this facility without any problem and already have a vehicle waiting. It's roughly a two hour drive back to Huntsville which is where I need to be and where you live. So, you come with me now and listen to what I have to say in the car. If you want the job, we get back to Huntsville and get to work. If you don't, I drop you off at your apartment and you never see me again. Either way it's a free ride home and a handful of those answers you were looking for. I'm certain you can see the logic in that."

"I'm pretty sure I've still got a job."

"Not like this, you don't. Also, your emergency room is currently a crime scene. It will be shut down for a while."

"And I assume we're sneaking because you're not supposed to be here."

"Correct."

Clint thought it over. "I haven't even heard from any doctors yet. Am I good for travel?"

"I wouldn't be here if you weren't, would I? You're not much good to me if you're stuck in a bed."

"Okay, fair enough. Why me, though? Surely there are other people you could reach out to. People who you wouldn't have to explain things to."

"Numerous reasons, not the least of which is the fact that you stood your ground. I was coming around last night for that bit. The warlock was right. The vast majority of people would have left me, fled to save their own lives, but not you. You are man who finds identity in service to others and to things larger than yourself. You take these things very seriously."

"You sound pretty sure about that."

Arlo waved the iPad again. "Memorized it, remember? I believe that if you accept my offer and promise to see it through then I can count on you to do so, no matter what. Plus, you know your city better than I do."

"And if I decide to stay put?"

"Then I'll go anyway and you can sit here and wait for the team of lawyers that will most certainly be visiting you at the crack of dawn. They'll have a whole stack of confidentiality forms and non-disclosure agreements for you to sign under threat of… well, let's just say 'reprisal'."

Clint thought it over. His head hurt and his joints were sore but more than any of that he wanted to know what he had gotten pulled into. Sarah had died for it and that couldn't go unanswered. It didn't take him long to decide.

"All right," he said. "Let's take a road trip."

CHAPTER NINE

Lemaster Residence
3560 Castlegate Drive
Atlanta, Georgia
29 October, 01:20 a.m. EST

Jeffrey's eyes opened and banished the dream of cold, soothing water and fleshy things he couldn't see propping him up above the churning water and the other bodies that thrashed and drowned there. He knew that other people might call his dreams nightmares. He had to laugh at that. Other people had never known The Mother's touch.

He looked over and saw his wife, Vanessa, sleeping soundly. Her silhouette was still but he could hear her even breathing. Jeffrey didn't need any light to see her pale skin, gentle eyes, and easy smile. He knew every curve, crease, and beautiful wrinkle in that face better than he knew anything else.

He gently pulled back his blankets and rolled out of bed. Methodically placed house shoes were waiting for his feet as they made contact with the floor. He slipped them on and grabbed the flannel robe he favored from the chair beside his bed. All of this happened in the dark since he made it a habit to keep things in the same places at all times.

Staying as quiet as he could manage, Jeffrey crossed the room and let himself out of the bedroom. The door closed with a barely audible click. His bedroom was on the second floor and opened onto a hallway that overlooked the main foyer. An enormous crystal chandelier hung from the ceiling there. Vanessa loved the way it glittered when the lights were up but in the dead of night, the crystals seemed more like pockets of captured shadow hanging motionless in the air and refracting what minuscule light there was from the huge windows that adorned the front of the house. Jeffrey liked it better like this, he thought, but he had a hard time refusing his wife anything.

He made his way downstairs, through the keeping room and den, and into the kitchen. There was even less light in the back part of the house but he could see well enough to make his way to the fridge. He saw the silhouette of Kiera's school backpack on the massive, marble island that dominated the center of the space and frowned a bit. If he could sit through an hour of listening to a bunch of pre-teens butchering classical music, then the least she could do was put her blasted backpack away like he'd asked. He'd have to remember-

"Good evening, Mr. Lemaster."

Jeffrey nearly screamed when he heard the voice. He turned his back to the refrigerator and scanned the dark for the speaker. He needn't have bothered. There was a soft click and the three pendant lights hanging above the island came to life. A man was sitting across the island, casually sipping on one of the beers from Jeffrey's fridge.

Despite the fact that he was seated, Jeffrey could tell the man was tall. His skin was pale but flawless in way that made his age hard to judge though he obviously wasn't young. His straw blond hair was brushed straight back over his head and hung in straight lines to the nape of his neck. His features were strong, like a leading man in an old movie, but lean. Jeffrey was willing to bet there wasn't an ounce of fat under the man's clean, dark blue slacks and sport coat. Ice blue eyes glittered at him from across the island.

"I hope you don't mind," the man said, holding up the beer. "It's been a long and somewhat disappointing trip to get here. Get yourself one and we'll talk."

Jeffrey's mind raced but finally stopped on the only thing that made sense. "Are you Jubal?" he asked.

The man smiled. "Oh, that's a name I've not used in many, many a year. Yes, though. I'm Jubal Mott."

Jeffrey immediately averted his eyes. "Favored," he said. "Please, forgive me. I didn't realize it was you. I was expecting a call not a personal visit."

"Oh, I hate phones. All technology, really. Everything after gunpowder was a damned mistake, if you ask me. I can tolerate automobiles and the like but that's about it."

"As you say, Favored."

Jubal made a clicking noise with his tongue. "Enough of that. I'm not about to make a loyal adherent grovel in his own kitchen in the middle of the night. Get yourself that beer and sit down, Jeff. Then we can talk about what brings me back to Atlanta."

Jeffrey replied with a single nod and removed a beer from the refrigerator. He opened it with hands that trembled just a little and then sat down across from Jubal. He tried to remember everything he knew about The Favored. They were touched somehow by The Mother, granted power and authority beyond any of her other worshipers. They were rumored to live impossibly long and have magic that could kill with a gesture. Jeffrey made a point of not meeting his eyes or doing anything that might be misconstrued as defiance.

"Jeff, relax. I come in fellowship, brother. The Mother will embrace the world and all that. It's all right."

Jeffrey nodded nervously and took a pull from his beer. "Of course," he said. "Again, please forgive me. I've never-"

"Ohhh," Jubal said. "I see now. I'm your first warlock."

Jeffrey looked up though he still kept his eyes slightly below the other's. "Warlock?"

Jubal shrugged as he took a drink. "That's what the Pickmen call the Favored. Truth be told, I kind of like the word. Sounds a little more aggressive than 'Favored', I think. It is it what it is, though. My point is; relax. So long as you do what I say and give me what I need, I'll conclude my business and be on my way."

"As The Mother wishes," Jeffrey said. "How can I serve?"

"I need a team of congregants," Jubal said. "The toughest, most loyal you've got. Initiated, of course, and loaded for trouble. We've got some business in Alabama and the Pickmen are already involved."

Jeffrey remembered a news story he's seen on his computer feed. "Alabama? Do you mean that thing in Huntsville?"

"Yes, exactly that. It got very loud. A lot of that was my fault. I'd forgotten how quickly things can get publicized in first world countries. See what I mean about the technology? I hate it."

"I understand. How many congregants do you need?"

"With the Pickmen involved? Let's say a baker's dozen just to be safe. And make sure at least one of them is good with technology. I've let my education on that sort of thing stagnate. I'll need someone who can handle it. No women and no coloreds. I don't trust either of them in a fight."

Jeffrey nodded. He hesitated to ask the question but decided to risk it. "If I may, Favored, what is the mission? So that I can let the congregants know what's expected of them."

There was a long moment of silence as Jubal locked his eyes on Jeffrey. The Favored took a slow drink from his beer but his eyes never left Jeffrey's face. Just about the time Jeffrey thought he'd made a mistake, Jubal said, "The *Nnnkadishtuor ot Cthon* has been revealed."

Jeffrey felt his eyes widen. "That's..." he rolled the idea around in his head, his memory collecting what he'd heard or read about the book over the years. "That's one of the seven texts," he said. His breath was a little clipped. "You mean a copy has been discovered, right?"

Jubal shook his head. "Nope. This is the original as scribed by Hsun the Greater."

Jeffrey's mind reeled somewhat at the possibilities. "But that's... The Mother could do great things with that text."

"Yes, she could," Jubal said. "Which is why I was willing to make so much noise to get it."

"Did the Pickmen beat you to it?"

"No," Jubal said. "They did not. I didn't get it either, though, but I'm certain it was supposed to be in the house where I ran into the Pickmen. The occupants were entertaining but not at all helpful. I didn't get to finish my search before a magus and his pet mortal interrupted me."

Jeffrey's head snapped up at that. For an instant, his eyes met Jubal's but he quickly averted them. He'd been an adherent in the Church of the Black Cosmonogy for more than two decades. He'd started as a congregant and risen through the ranks to become High Adherent for all of the southeastern United States. In all that time, he'd always managed to keep himself and his congregants off the radar and in the shadows. He'd brushed up against the Pickmen a few times but never in a way that had amounted to anything. He had never drawn the attention of any of the magi in their employ. Now, in the space of a single day he was entangling himself with a Favored that was very much on their radar. Jeffrey didn't like that. He didn't like that at all.

"Jeff? Is there a problem?" Jubal's tone made it very clear that he wasn't interested in problems.

"Not at all, Favored," he said, swallowing. "I was just thinking of a list of congregants that would best serve you."

"Good man, then," Jubal said. "You get them together and tell them to meet me in the parking lot at that big space center in Huntsville. You know it?"

Jeffrey nodded and said, "I do."

"Very good. I do appreciate efficient minions. Now, you tell those boys to be there before the sun is full up. If they're not, I'll be disappointed. Nobody wants that, right?"

"No, of course n-"

"Dad?"

Jeffrey's head snapped around and he saw his daughter come into the room yawning and rubbing her eyes. She was dressed in a baggy tee shirt and a pair of loose pajama bottoms. "Who're you talking to?"

Jeffrey looked back at Jubal. He wasn't surprised to see that the Favored was gone.

CHAPTER TEN

Northbound Interstate 65
Birmingham, Alabama
29 October, 12:33 a.m. CST

"Vampires?" Clint said, guiding the car into the lane that would take them home.

"Yes, but not exactly as you think of them," Arlo answered.

"Werewolves?"

"Yes, along with a number of other therianthropic subspecies. Again, though, not exactly as you've heard of them."

"Okay, okay, "Clint said. "Bigfoot?"

Arlo closed his eyes and drew in a patience building breath. "Yes, they're actually a very peaceful and notably intelligent species, in their way. Look, Mercer, essentially every supernatural entity or myth that you've ever heard of is in some way real, just not the way that's been presented to you in popular culture. Vampires don't sparkle, not all shape-shifters are teenage underwear model lycans, and the creatures that you refer to as 'bigfoot' do not pose for photographs or leave any evidence for humans to show off on YouTube. That's one of the things that proves them to be intelligent."

Clint nodded in understanding. "Freddy Krueger?"

Arlo ignored him. "You need to understand that what you've been shown and have absorbed through social osmosis is a combination of carefully constructed misdirection and good old fashioned fiction. Movie mythology, religious dogmatism, comic book mysticism; you have to discard all of that if you want to learn the truth of the world. You'll need to come at this with a mind like a clean canvas. Ask questions even if you think you already know the answer because, likely, what you think you know is flawed."

"Okay," Clint said. "So, zombies; slow or fast?"

"I'm getting the impression you're not taking me seriously, Mercer. If we encounter that warlock again, you'll likely wish you had in the moments before he murders you."

Clint considered that and wriggled a little in his seat to ease some of the ache in his hips. The car that Arlo had provided was a brand new Lexus SUV that still smelled and looked as though it had just rolled off the lot. When Clint had seen the car, he'd asked Arlo where he'd gotten it. Arlo had on shrugged and said, "I bought it earlier today. That's how people get things, right? They purchase them?" He then went on to explain that he hoped Clint felt like getting behind the wheel because Arlo "didn't drive." Clint had tried to question that but had only been told how it was irrelevant to the problem at hand, that they were on a time table, and needed to get going. So it was that Clint was driving a brand new car that he wasn't sure even had license plates. He didn't have his wallet, his phone, his clothes, or his shoes because sneaking out of the private hospital hadn't allowed them the time to get them from the nurse's station before ducking out of a back exit. Clint was dressed in a pair of dark green scrubs and was pretty sure he looked like an escaped mental patient. To top it off, the ache behind his eyes was showing no signs of letting up.

He'd hoped that he could lighten the mood a little by peppering Arlo with questions- the guy seemed to be wound pretty tight -but the mention of the warlock brought Sarah and the parking garage back to him. That was something that sent a little shudder of fear through his guts and killed any notions of teasing.

"Fine," he said. "I was just yanking your chain a little. This is all pretty hard to take in."

"I don't see how. I'm providing you with a rational explanation based on the evidence that you witnessed firsthand. I've never understood why people have such a hard time with facts presented that way."

"Rational? *Magic,* Arlo. You're telling me that *magic* is real. Kinda goes against everything I and everyone I know believes about the world."

"Ah, 'believes', yes. Emotional reasoning."

"What?"

Arlo studied Clint for moment. Clint glanced at the other man and could see that he was finding the best way to frame his response. "Have you ever heard of Chris Evans?"

"The actor? Sure. He's the guy that plays Captain America."

"Correct. Is he real?"

Clint took his eyes off the road long enough to give Arlo a questioning look. "Yeah," he said. "I think it's safe to say he's real. Millions and millions of people see him in those movies."

"Are you sure? All kinds of things can be altered and faked these days. For all you know, everything you've seen in the movies are just enhanced special effects or computer generated imagery. Every public appearance made by a carefully prepared body double. Have you ever met him? Have you ever met anyone who has met him? Actually spoke to him or shook his hand?"

"Well, no. I did date a stunt woman once, though."

"Lucky you. So, really, all the information you have about Chris Evans is what you've heard and seen. Information that's been filtered and altered and sanitized by layers of public relations and media spin. You don't really *know* who the man is, you just know what other people have told you. So, really, you're trusting a virtual mob of strangers to tell you the truth. You are, in short, choosing to have faith in that truth and make your decision about the reality of Chris Evans based on that *belief* as opposed to actual first hand evidence gathered with your own observations and intelligence. Belief is an emotional construct so, therefore, you have indulged in emotional reasoning."

Clint considered it and then said, "Okay, I see where you're going with that. Chris Evans is real, though, right?"

"So far as I know."

"Good. I really liked Winter Soldier."

"Do you see the point I'm making, Mercer?"

Clint shrugged. "People think with their feelings a lot. Welcome to the human race."

"True but that's not the thrust of it. Celebrity is a lot like the supernatural. Most people live the whole of their lives hearing about it but never actually encountering it. They hear stories, enjoy fictional accounts, maybe even try to do some legitimate research into it but never really brush up against it in their lifetimes unless they take major steps to seek it out. Sticking with our Chris Evans example, if someone were to quit their job, move to Hollywood, and then get into the movie business then their chances of actually meeting the actor increase exponentially. It that were to happen, then they would *know* that Chris Evans is real and if they spent enough time with him, they would likely learn the truth of the man and not the characters he plays or the pre-packaged version of him that is pushed by studios and publicists. Not filtered information or people telling others what they want them to think but first hand, tangible evidence of this thing that they had previously only *felt* that they knew."

Clint nodded impatiently. "Yeah, okay, celebrity media doesn't always tell the truth. Big shocker, Arlo. Thanks for the revelation. What the hell does any of that have to do with me?"

"I'm just trying to frame in a way that the common person would understand."

Clint snorted a laugh. "I'm going to give you the benefit of the doubt that by 'common' you didn't mean 'stupid'."

"Good, because I didn't, and all of this applies to you because what happened to you the other night was the supernatural equivalent of walking into the middle of an a-list Hollywood Academy Awards party that you didn't know you were attending and finding out all of your favorite celebrities were cardboard cutouts. Your introduction to the supernatural was the most dramatic I've ever heard of and that's saying something since I'm one of the leading authorities on the topic of preternatural and paranormal phenomena."

"Humble much?"

"That's not vanity, Mercer, it's an established fact. Just like it's a fact that if you hold to your common preconceptions about the supernatural, you're likely to get one or both of us killed."

"What preconceptions?" Clint said, a snap to his voice that he hadn't intended to put there. "How the hell am I supposed to have preconceptions when I don't have a damned clue what I saw? I've never even heard of anything like what I saw last night and, now, I've got you sitting here telling me it was magic. *Magic*, Arlo! You talk about magic like it's science but that doesn't actually explain anything. You keep talking about the guy in the garage but you know what? He wasn't the only person making the crazy. What are you? How are you walking around? Because about twenty four hours ago you had a laceration in your gut I could have fit my hand into. What was with those rings? Are you like that other guy? Are you something else? Nothing you've told me amounts to an answer I can latch onto, Arlo, and until I get an answer like that then this is just going down as the weirdest ride home I've ever gotten."

Silence descended inside the car after that, broken only by the occasional muffled thump of tire over a rough piece of highway. Arlo was staring out the passenger window at the mass of shadows and lights that made up the passing cityscape. Clint kept his eyes on the road and took deep, quiet breaths to get his frustration under control. He knew that all of this was going to catch up with him, that he would have to deal with the fear, anger, and grief that came from what had happened, but now wasn't the time. Now, he just needed to get home and get his head together.

"I'm not like him," Arlo said.

"What?"

"The warlock," Arlo said, looking over at him. "We aren't the same. We both practice the Arts but how we do it is what makes the difference. That difference is a radical one."

"Well," Clint said, "I think I can buy that. You haven't tried to kill me with… what the hell were those things, anyway?"

"They've collected a lot of names in the course of human history; Black Dogs, Hellhounds, Hairy Jacks, Churchyard Grims. Just depends on the region they were seen, really. These days the arcane academic community refers to them as Barghest, though the popular mythology around that name doesn't completely match the reality of the beasts."

"Where do they come from?"

Arlo held up a hand to stop him. "Let's table that for the moment. I think that I made a mistake in trying to give you too much of the big picture about the situation we're in. You're correct, none of that answers the questions that are in front of you in any usable way. It's an interactional flaw of mine that I don't always see things from other's perspectives. I propose we start again and I try to explain just the essentials of what happened."

Clint nodded. "Okay. Yes. Start small and expand out. I like that. Let's hear the summarized version."

"Very well. I am a member of an organization that investigates and polices supernatural threats. One of the duties entailed by that charge is the acquisition and impounding of objects that may be a danger to the public. That's what my team and I were doing in Huntsville last night. During the course of the assignment, we were ambushed by the warlock you encountered. I was injured in the ensuing fight and cut off from the supply of blood that I would have normally used to heal myself. With my death seemingly imminent, the decision was made to obtain the blood I needed from the closest emergency center. That turned out to be yours."

"Why the blood?" Clint's eyes grew a little wide and he cast a quick look at Arlo. "Wait, are you a…" he let the question hang between them.

Arlo rolled his eyes. "No, Mercer, I am not a vampire or any other category of undead. I'm very much alive. Blood just happens to be a powerful component for certain types of healing magic."

Clint nodded. "All right. So, this warlock, he just followed you and was trying to finish what he started?"

"Correct."

"All right, then. That's something I can get my head around. I'm guessing you didn't manage to get the warlock after I got stunned or whatever."

Arlo's expression shifted a little at that. His mismatched eyes swept over Clint's face like he was looking for something. It only took a moment and then he said, "That's correct. Local police and reinforcements from my own organization arrived and he fled the scene."

"Okay, so why are you and your organization disagreeing? If you've got backup, why aren't you using them instead of recruiting me?"

That searching look returned to Arlo's face. Clint flicked his eyes back and forth between the road and his passenger. "What?" he said.

"I'm recruiting you, Mercer, because according to everything I know about magic, you should be dead right now."

CHAPTER ELEVEN

Seven Pines Apartments
1580 Sparkman Drive
Huntsville, Alabama
October 29, 12:35 A.M. CST

Andy Wright's eyes snapped open. While his vision showed him nothing but the shadows of a dark bedroom, his ears and his head were still filled with the steady whispers that had pulled him from sleep. He put a hand to his head and drew in a breath. His forehead was slick with sweat that had beaded there while he'd been dreaming. The specifics of the dream eluded him, coming only as a vague impressions of dry, dark places and shapes that were never really where he thought they should be. The whispers, though, sharp and unintelligible, those remained like a distant ringing in his ears.

Beside him, Jasmine was breathing in a deep, steady rhythm that told him he hadn't disturbed her. As his eyes adjusted to the faint light coming through his bedroom window, he could see that she was lying on one side with her back to him. She had pushed down some of the blankets and her smooth, chocolate dark skin shined ever so faintly in the glow. Justin couldn't help but smile at the curve of her shoulders and back. She was still naked, they both were, having fallen asleep almost immediately after they'd made love. He could just make out the faintest curve of her breast under her arm. Between that and the memory of earlier that night, he felt his lust stirring once more. Rather than risk waking her, he silently swung his feet off the bed and stood up.

The whispers were still there, hanging in his mind like a barely audible static. Andy took another deep breath and blew it out slowly, trying to clear his head. He couldn't remember the last time he'd had anything resembling a nightmare, his mind was far too logical and orderly for that, but this certainly felt like one. They had always faded as soon as he woke which was fine with him since he never put much value on the rambling of the unconscious mind. Psychology and all those other soft sciences never held much interest for him which had made his engineering major a logical choice. If that other-

His foot hit something and broke him from his train of thought. Looking down, he saw a pair of jeans on the floor, discarded during the earlier foreplay. They had landed in the doorway between the small bedroom and the combined living room and kitchen that was the apartment's only other living space.

Andy glanced back and the bed and furrowed his brow in confusion. He didn't remember taking the steps to the living room. In fact, he was certain he intended to go to the bathroom, not the living room, and had no recollection of moving from the spot where he had stood up.

The whispers came again, louder this time, insistent and seeming to crawl over his pale skin in a slow shiver. They were… calling him? He shook his head against the notion. No, that wasn't right, wasn't possible. Memories of a dream didn't call to people. That was just nonsense.

Still, it persisted. He felt his eyes being pulled towards the package that he had picked up from the FedEx store earlier that day. Professor Warner had said he'd call when he had the address that he wanted Andy to deliver it to but he hadn't heard from the old guy. Which was weird, because the professor was usually-

With a start, Andy realized he was standing over the box, his hands on its sides, brown paper creasing but not quite tearing under his fingertips. Again, he couldn't remember crossing the room. The whispering was like a breeze blowing through his head.

He pulled his hands away quickly, as though the package were hot to the touch. He looked around at his apartment as if something might jump out at him but there was nothing there. Just him and the shadows and that damn whispering.

"Andy? You okay? What're you doing, bae?"

Andy's head snapped around in surprise. It was Jasmine. She'd pulled on a loose t-shirt that was too short to cover much below her hips. Even freaked out as he was, he couldn't help but note the silhouette of her legs below the shirt's hem.

"I'm sorry," he said. "I didn't mean to wake you."

"It's okay," she said, coming forward and wrapping her arms around him. "Were you talking to somebody? I heard you out here."

He returned the embrace. "Talking?" he said. "No, there's no one here. My phone's in the bedroom."

She pulled away a little and looked up at him. She was nearly a foot shorter than he was so he got a good view of her wide eyes and full features. "Really? I swear I heard you talking. Maybe we're both sleepwalking."

Andy forced a laugh he hoped didn't sound too nervous. "Maybe. I told you how mind-blowing you were tonight."

Jasmine laughed a little. "Well, mister, I don't have a class until noon and it feels like you might need a little help getting back to sleep. Come back to bed and let's see what we can do about that."

She rose up on her tip toes and kissed him then. Soft lips meeting his own and reigniting his passion. She broke the kiss and walked back towards the bedroom, pointedly pulling the t-shirt over her head and dropping it on the floor as she went.

The whispering faded under the weight of his need. Andy followed her into the bedroom, leaving the package on the kitchen counter as though it were waiting for him.

CHAPTER TWELVE

Northbound Interstate 65
Birmingham, Alabama
29 October, 12:39 a.m. CST

"I'm supposed to be what now?" Clint said.

"Dead," Arlo said. "Deceased, crossed-out, expired; call it what you want but your time on this Earth should have ended in that parking garage. Yet, here you are. Not only alive but, essentially, unharmed. I don't understand how that's possible, Mercer. I don't often encounter things that I don't understand. That makes you interesting to me but an unknown to my organization. In short, they don't trust the fact that you survived but since you don't seem to pose any threat they made the decision to release and surveil you. I disagreed."

"Why?"

Arlo shrugged. "As I said, your survival is a matter of some interest to me. A puzzle to solve, if you will. I think I'm best suited to solving that puzzle while in your company. You, in return, seem capable of helping me in turn."

"I'm so happy that I get to make your life interesting. Why are you so sure that I should be dead?"

"Because I saw what happened to you. Tell me, what's the last thing you remember from the garage?"

Clint considered it. "I remember thinking there was no way out. That no matter what I did one of those bar-ghost things-"

"Barghest," Arlo said.

"Yeah, that. I decided that even if I tried to run for it, we wouldn't get away. So, I put you down and got ready to get bloody. Then, he hit me with some kind of weird Taser or something."

Arlo rolled his eyes. "Taser?" he said. "Really? After everything we've talked about, everything you witnessed, you still can't accept that it was a spell? A *magic* spell?"

Clint's only reply was to shrug and keep his eyes on the road.

"Well, that's what it was, regardless of what you might believe. I woke up when you put me down. I was lucid enough to catch the last part of your conversation so I knew what was coming. Just as he attacked you, I tried to defend you, cast a working around you that would absorb the brunt of the attack. That's why I grabbed your leg. I was too slow, though, Mercer. My spell wasn't complete when the blast hit you. You were defenseless in the face of something that should have quite literally immolated your entire nervous system. All you did was fall down, though. Why do you think that is?"

"How the hell am I supposed to know? I can tell you that it *felt* like that's what was happening. You're the magical guru or whatever. You tell me."

Arlo nodded. "I hope to be able to. That's one of the reasons we're here."

"One of the reasons? What are the others? We still haven't gotten around to the job offer you mentioned."

"No, we haven't," Arlo said. He grew quiet after that. Clint assumed he was gathering his words but couldn't really see his face. They had passed out of the city and were entering the long stretch of interstate that cut through more rural and less well-lit areas. Now, the only light was from the instrument panel and the distant tail lights of the only other vehicle on the road. It wasn't enough for Clint to make out any details on Arlo's face. He'd have preferred to be able to see the man's face as he spoke but he found the dark helped to ease the ache in his head.

"The job I have for you is two-fold," Arlo said. "The first part is best described as bodyguard. Just someone to watch my back while I work."

Clint gave a little grunt of understanding. "Security work's not really my thing."

"Don't forget I read your military records. Top marks throughout all of your pararescue training including a marksman rating with both rifle and sidearms. Over a dozen combat and humanitarian rescue missions to your credit in Afghanistan and South America. To top that off, I know that you did some extra hand to hand training on your own. Krav Maga with a little Jiu-Jitsu, I believe it was."

"Doesn't make me a superhero," Clint said, staring at the asphalt stretching out before them.

"Of course not but it does make you a little more qualified than the average Registered Nurse."

"Okay, fine, I can watch your back. What's the second part of the fold?"

Arlo drew in a breath. "That's the odder part. I'm not good with… humans. People, however you choose to refer to the more mundane citizens of the world. I need you to be my face to them. My spokesman or go between, as it were."

"You need me to do what? You're a grown man. You can't speak for yourself?"

"Of course I can. I just don't always do it well when I'm working. I get… impatient. I forget about the banal insincerity of societal norms when I'm focused on my work. I usually end up, quite unintentionally, insulting people in my fervor. I've found that having someone to run interference and conduct interviews for me yields better results than if I work alone even if it does slow things down."

"Is this about your eyes?"

"Excuse me?"

"That's a pretty pronounced case of Heterochromia Iridus you've got there, Arlo. I'm assuming it's congenital. Do you get tired of people asking about it?"

"You're correct about it being congenital and no, this isn't about my eyes. My concern with people's opinions of my physical appearance is somewhere just below my concern over whether or not fish can ride bicycles. This is about the fact that I have trouble with social interactions on a normal basis and it's amplified when I'm working."

"You seem to be doing fine right now."

"Right now, I'm not trying to find a dangerous warlock and I'm freshly medicated. I'm focused on this conversation and this moment. I get… more detached when I'm working. People become these shapes moving through negative space to me and they're either useless, potentially useful, or distracting. That's a non-productive way to see the world but that's where my mind goes. I need a translator, if you will, someone to help me interact."

"And you think I'm that person?"

Clint heard Arlo draw in a deep breath, as though he were collecting his patience. "You're a professional caregiver in a level one trauma center, Mercer. Dealing with people in stressful situations is literally in your job description."

Clint shrugged. "Fair enough. What do you mean 'freshly medicated'?"

Arlo took another breath. "Power, magical or otherwise, always exacts a price. In my case, I struggle with some behavioral issues that I control with medication that Rani, that's Doctor Smythe from earlier, monitors. I took a dose shortly before coming to see you."

Clint took a moment with that. "What kind of meds exactly? Anti-psychotics?"

"Only when absolutely necessary and that isn't often. As I said, Rani monitors my needs quite closely and the dosage and types vary according to… changing circumstances. As with everything else about this situation things are not what you are accustomed to. I'm not a psychiatric patient in the traditional sense. I can assure you, I will have my wits about me at all times should we end up working together."

"I'll hold you to that. What kind of payday is attached to this?"

"Meet the terms of our agreement and I'll match one year's salary at your current position."

Clint managed to keep his jaw from dropping. "That's quite a payday, Arlo. Are you sure whoever you're working for is willing to come through with that much?"

"They won't. I'll provide the funds. Money isn't really an issue for me. So far as the amount goes, you've seen what we face. The rewards should match the potential risk, don't you think?"

Clint kept his eyes on the road for a few more silent seconds. "What if we show up and they shut the show down? Tell you to walk away and take me with you?"

Arlo half snorted a short laugh. "I'll just have to ask you to trust me when I say that won't happen. I have a unique skill set that gives me a certain amount of leverage."

It was Clint's turn to laugh. "I'll bet. So, if I'm going to watch your back I'll need to be armed. What happens if things go sideways and I have to defend myself. Am I covered legally? I need to know if I end up shooting somebody I won't find myself cuffed and stuffed for my trouble."

"I assure you, so long as you are acting in good faith to defend yourself or others, you will not be held as criminally liable. Think about it; we showed up in your ER with DHS badges that would pass as the real thing. We have ways of covering ourselves."

"So you aren't actually with some black branch of the DHS?"

"Oh, no. the government uses us in much the same way they use private military contractors though we have a very specific focus. They give us a certain latitude when it comes to presenting ourselves as law enforcement. It's all a bit convoluted, really, but it allows us to get the job done."

"Yeah, about that. Tell me about this organization you keep talking about. What's it called?"

"That, I'm afraid, I will have to keep to myself for the moment. You have to understand that we work under a condition of secrecy that is very strict, hence our need to impersonate law enforcement. If you choose to decline my offer, I'd prefer that you know as little about the details of our group as possible."

"The Pickmen, right?" Clint said, smiling a little at what he imagined Arlo's reaction to be. The other man's voice didn't reflect the mental image.

"Obviously the warlock mentioned us. Consider that all the information you need on the subject."

Clint nodded. He'd done enough classified work when he was in uniform that he could understand the need for secrecy. "Fair enough," he said. "Let me think on this a while. I'll give you an answer by the time we cross Huntsville city limits."

"As you wish," Arlo said. The rustle of cloth and leather upholstery told Clint that he was settling into his seat as though getting comfortable enough to rest.

They stayed silent while Clint drove. He considered turning on the radio but thought better of it since it seemed that Arlo was trying to get a nap in. He considered the odd little man with the unbelievable story but then shook his head at that word 'unbelievable'. Arlo had a point and Clint knew it. The hounds, the glowing rings, Arlo's miraculous recovery, the man in the parking garage; these were all things that Clint would have sworn was impossible mere days ago. Now, though…

now, he'd seen them with his own two eyes, felt the pain from whatever it was he'd been hit with. All of that was very real and Arlo's explanation was the only one that fit.

Magic.

Magic was real. Magic was real and, by all accounts, as dangerous as any weapon Clint had ever encountered if not more so. It could heal, too, though. Arlo was proof of that. He'd gone from someone who Clint wouldn't have given good odds for survival to walking and talking like nothing had happened in less than twenty four hours. Did that say something about magic itself or just the way Arlo used it? Were there different kinds? He'd said that the warlock was different from him but how?

There were too many questions about that. If he stuck with Arlo, he'd get at least some answers if not all but did he even want them? Clint had always thought that knowledge was the remedy to fear but recent events had made him question that. This knowledge, these answers he thought he could get, were the kind that could fundamentally change his perception of the world. He wasn't sure that understanding these things would make them any less bizarre. Were these things he necessarily wanted to know? It took another mile before he admitted to himself that the answer was an unqualified 'yes'.

Of course he wanted to know. More than that, though, he felt he had some unfinished business with the warlock. Clint didn't know whether or not Arlo's people had some kind of legal system for dealing with warlocks but he didn't much care. That man had taken a friend from him and Clint had every intention of making him pay for that. It had been going on five years since he'd so much as touched a weapon much less fired one. He'd told himself that the days of wielding the tools of death dealing were behind him, that he'd spend the rest of his life helping people to heal. He'd meant it when he'd told himself those things.

That was before the warlock and his hounds, though. That was before he'd watched Sarah die. To balance that scale, Clint knew he'd gladly take up arms once more.

The next hour passed quickly for him as he guided the Lexus through the early morning dark. There was no moon or stars, just a dark sky with gray clouds that floated like massive ghosts on the horizon. Interstate 65 crossed the Tennessee river before Clint had to exit onto Interstate 565 to reach Huntsville proper. Lights started appearing along the interstate again and brought some illumination back into the car as he approached his home town. In the distance, he could see the blinking red light that topped the Saturn 5 rocket display that stood outside the U.S. Space and Rocket Center. No matter where he'd gone in the world, that sight had always told him he was back home.

By the time he was driving past it, he'd made his decision.

CHAPTER THIRTEEN

Clint had to say it twice before Arlo responded. Clint didn't think that he woke Arlo up, exactly, because he didn't think that the man had been sleeping. It was more like he had interrupted some sort of deep meditation exercise or something.

"Yes, what?" Arlo said. Clint could see his eyes blinking in the light from the lamps that lined I-565.

"I said I'll do it," Clint said. "You've got a deal but with one additional condition; if we run into that dog whisperer from hell again, he doesn't walk away from it. We deal with him in an extreme and permanent way. You get what I'm saying, Arlo?"

"If you're saying that you want to kill him then, yes, I fully support that action. It's really operating procedure whenever we come across a warlock, anyway."

Clint frowned. "How many warlocks are there?"

Arlo shrugged. "I haven't the foggiest. It's as though someone keeps making them. Regardless, I accept your terms." Arlo extended his hand to shake on the deal.

Clint stared at the offered hand. "The last time you touched me some weird shit went down. Is that going to happen again?"

"Only if I will it. I have no intention of doing so."

Clint looked between the hand and Arlo's eyes. His expression was filled with thoughtful doubt.

"We can't very well work together if you don't even trust me enough to shake my hand, Mercer."

Clint sighed and said, "Point taken." He shook Arlo's hand. The smaller man's grip was surprisingly firm but that was the only remarkable thing that came from the gesture.

"All right then," Arlo said, "first thing's first. We need to go back to the house where-"

"Uhm, no," Clint said.

"Excuse me?"

"The first thing is for me to swing by my place for a shower and a change of clothes. In case you haven't noticed I'm running around barefoot in a set of stolen scrubs. I don't even have any ID on me. I'm not going anywhere until I get changed."

Arlo appeared confused, blinked a few times, and then looked down at Clint's outfit. "Oh," he said, "right. Of course. To your apartment and then to the work at hand."

Twenty minutes later, they were parking on the street outside Clint's apartment. It was actually a townhouse that was built on land that was adjacent to the small state park that capped Monte Sano Mountain. The curving road that led up the small mountain was freshly paved and had houses and apartment buildings of varying sizes scattered among tall trees and grass shrouded boulders. Clint's townhouse was at the end of a line of half a dozen similar structures that all shared at least one wall with their neighbors.

Most of Clint's neighbors were older than him and too settled in their ways to be up at such an early hour so he wasn't surprised to find the street and all the windows dark. All the windows, that was, except his. A light burned clearly through the living room window.

"And what the actual hell is this?" he said, pointing to the window.

Arlo looked up and drew in a breath. "I thought she'd take longer," he said. "Either she's getting better or I'm getting too predictable."

" 'She', who?"

"Rani. I told you that I'm not supposed to be associating with you. I'm sure she's here to remind me of that."

"And they just broke into my place?"

"Don't worry. James is very skilled at getting into places. I'm sure he managed to pick the locks without doing any actual damage." He studied the townhouse for a few more seconds before continuing with a deep sigh. "Nothing for it, then. Let's go get this over with."

"Get what over with?" Clint said but Arlo was already out of the car.

Clint shoved the door open with a whispered curse and followed Arlo up the short, flagstone path that led to his front door. There was a small, concrete porch with three steps leading up to it. Arlo virtually marched up them, opened the door, and went in without waiting for Clint.

By the time Clint got inside, the confrontation had already started. Arlo was standing in front of Doctor Smythe with his posture stiff and his hands clasped firmly behind his back. His face was set in an expression of adamant defiance that made the nostrils on his long, pointed nose flare.

Doctor Smythe was in front of him. She was tall enough that she had to tilt her head down a little to meet his eyes. She was speaking to him in hushed, controlled tones. Even though he couldn't understand what they were saying, Clint could tell from the cinnamon flush on her dark face that she was not happy with Arlo in the least. Her black hair fell across her face as she accentuated one of her words with a slight jut of her face.

Clint's attention was drawn towards the entrance to the kitchen as another person entered the scene. He was a large man, six and a half feet at least, with skin tone and features that were plainly some variety of native American. He was dressed in a dark suit with white shirt that was open at the collar. His neck was thick and the suit bulged in all the places that would suggest the man could juggle engine blocks. Hair as black as night was pulled back from his face and tied into a neat bundle at the top of his spine. Steam floated over his lips as he took a sip of coffee from Clint's favorite mug. He looked at Clint with dark eyes and gestured for him to come into the kitchen.

"Sure," Clint muttered, glancing back to Arlo and Smythe, "what the hell? I only live here." He shook his head as he walked into the kitchen and pinched the bridge of his nose for second. The headache was getting worse.

The kitchen was a small, galley style space that was well suited for one or two people. There was a bar that overlooked a small, sunken seating area with a fireplace and numerous windows that looked out on the trees in the small yard though all there was to see at the moment was dark. The big man was leaning on the bar sipping at his coffee.

"I'm going to guess that your name is James and you know how to pick locks," Clint said, eying him up and down once more.

The big man laughed. "Yeah. The boss tell you that?"

Clint nodded.

"Try not to take it personal. Just the job," he said. He sipped at the coffee again, noticed Clint staring and then said, "Hope you don't mind. It's been a long day and we weren't sure when you guys were going to get here."

"Yeah, I'm picking up on that. I guess breaking and entering's a big part of what you guys do?"

"When we have to. I don't need to tell you how far outside the lines we work. I read the report about what happened to you. You were in it deep, brother."

Clint nodded. "So I'm told." He made sure not to smile when he said it.

The big man stood up straight and said, "You know what? Let's try this again." He stuck out his hand to shake. "I'm Jim Lonebear. I'm sort of a field security specialist for the doc out there," he nodded towards the living room. "Her and the boss keep me around for when they need to open pickle jars or pick up heavy stuff."

Clint tried not to crack a smile but wasn't completely successful. He accepted the man's hand and said, "Clint Mercer."

"Oh, I know. I had time to read your file."

"Did they post that damn thing online or something?"

Jim shook his head. "Nah, it's just for us grunts on the line. You're a PJ, right?"

Now Clint did laugh. It had been a long time since anyone had called him by the Pararescueman nickname. "Yeah. You serve?"

Jim nodded. "Marines. Force Recon then some embassy work before I went to work for the boss."

"Semper fi," Clint said, grinning.

"Semper fi," Jim said, returning the smile. "So, PJ, I'll bet you've got questions. What all did the boss tell you?"

Clint wasn't sure where to start. "He told me magic's a real thing," he said.

"Yeahhh," Jim said, drawing the word out. "That."

"You're backing it up?"

"Oh, yeah."

"Really?"

"Hey, I get it. It was a tough one for me to swallow at first, too. Couple years back me and my unit came across something in the desert outside Trek Nawa. It got in our heads. The boss and his people had to come in to deal with it. That's what landed me with an embassy security assignment. It was months before I really accepted that I'd gotten spell smacked. I reached out to the doc to talk it out and ended up with the boss offering me this gig. Been riding shotgun for them ever since."

"Spell smacked?"

Jim shrugged. "That's what I call it. The boss can give you the fancier words. What else did he say?"

Clint told him everything that Arlo had shared up to and including the part about putting down the warlock. When he was finished, Jim was rinsing out his coffee cup and putting it away.

"Sounds about right," he said. "He told you more than he should have and less than he could have. Either way, I can see why the doc is pissed."

"Look," Clint said, "don't take this the wrong way but who the hell are you people? If I'm going to be working-"

Jim held up a hand to stop him. "That is not a done deal. Let's see what the boss and the doc say about it when they're done arguing. In the meantime, all I can say is that we're the people that deal with the things that most everybody doesn't believe in. We fight the fights that no one knows need fighting."

Clint gritted his teeth. The pain in his head continued to grow. "Are you government?"

Jim shrugged. "Yes and no. That's all I can say, PJ. You know how this classified stuff works."

"Yeah, I'm just finding it hard to care at the moment," Clint said.

Jim nodded. "I hear that. Look, the doc and the boss tend to go on for a while when they get like this. Why don't you grab a shower. We'll probably have something for you by the time you're out."

Clint studied the big man for moment and then nodded. "Yeah, that's a plan. Just don't drink all my coffee. I think I'm going to want some once I'm out."

Jim responded with a smile and a wink. "You got it."

Clint shook his head a little and headed up the narrow stairs. The carpet was worn and a little slick under his bare feet. He ascended from the living floor into a small hallway that connected the upstairs bath, master bedroom, and second bedroom though he had chosen to fill that room with a treadmill and dumbbell set instead of furniture. He passed through the unlit hall and into the bathroom between the two bedrooms.

Soon, he was in the shower letting hot water wash over his head and neck. He wished that there was some way to apply the same kind of cleanse to him memory, just turn on some mental faucet and wash away the images of Sarah's body lying broken between those cars. Maybe he could wash away more than that, older memories that-

Pain spiked between his eyes and blossomed like rolling wildfire behind his eyes. The dim light in the bathroom was suddenly too bright, the steady rain patter the shower too loud, the water's heat on his skin to intense. Every sensation down to the air on his flesh was suddenly a grating, piercing point of pain that overwhelmed him as though he had suddenly burst into flame.

Clint screamed but even the explosion of sound from his throat and the rush of air from his lungs was agony. He thought he cut off the scream but the pain was all there was, rising and rising like a whirlwind of fire straight up through the center of his body, spiking higher and hotter than anything he had ever imagined a human being could feel. Clint was sure he was dying, sure that the pain would end him and render what was left to a pile of ash and charred teeth.

When the darkness swept over him, he embraced it.

CHAPTER FOURTEEN

Clint dreamed the dream.

He was back in the chopper, looking down at the flood choked jungle and watching as lives were snuffed out by the black water like so much candle flame. He tore the goggles from his face, as he always did, and wiped at his eyes. Dream-Clint looked back at his passengers. Some distant, waking part of him knew what he was going to see but knew equally that he would look, regardless of what horrors awaited his sight.

So he turned his head and found the dead staring at him with their gray eyes. They were like they always were, drowned and accusing and terrifying, but there was a new face in the group. She stood in the center of the mass of dead like she was bolted to the center of the chopper's deck. It was as though she were somehow immune to the rocking and sudden shifts that the chopper was experiencing in the storm. She stood stock still while the dead all sat and crouched around her staring at Clint and moving with the storm tossed helicopter.

Sarah looked much like she had the last time Clint had seen her. Her dark blue scrubs and starched lab coat stood out like a beacon of color against the grays and blacks of the dead things that surrounded her. Her wavy blonde hair fell well past her collar but was as immune to the wind in the cabin as she was to the shuddering deck. Blue eyes set into a stern but impassive face looked around the cabin. She looked over the dead at her feet and then at Clint. Her expression shifted into a confused frown.

"Sarah?" Clint stammered. It was the first time he could remember talking in the dream. "Oh," he said. "Oh God, I'm so sorry."

She kept staring, the confusion on her face getting deeper.

"I'm sorry," he said again. "I should've helped you. I should have-"

"I am not your friend," she said. "Why are you dreaming deceit like this?"

"I know," he said. "I know. A friend would have fought for you. Kept that monster from hurting you."

"That is not what I am saying, Clinton Mercer. What I mean is that I am not Sarah. Your friend is gone, never to return, but when I felt the call this memory of her was near to the fore of your mind. It seemed fortuitous so I assumed its likeness."

"What?" Clint said. "I don't understand."

She gestured around her. "What is this? This memory-dream you have created is cloaked in a fiction. I see the shape of truth in its curves and edges but not in its surface. Why would you try to deceive yourself? That does not seem reasonable, even for a mortal."

"A what?"

"A mortal, Clinton Mercer. That is what you are. I am different from that. It has been quite some time since I have interacted with one of your kind. I don't recall them being quite this dense of mind."

"I don't understand anything you're talking about," Clint said, shaking his head.

"See? Dense."

Clint rubbed his eyes with the palms of his hands. He was suddenly more aware of the dream than he ever had been before. It was as though Sarah's presence was bringing things into focus, almost solidifying them into something he could carry into the waking world. "Hang on a second," he said. "What is this? Is Arlo doing this?"

"What is an 'Arlo'? No, wait a moment," she said, looking around the cabin again. "Ah, the magus, of course. No, he has no presence here. Forgive my ignorance, Clinton Mercer. Whenever I touch a new mortal mind there is a period of adjustment. It will pass soon enough."

"What are you talking about?" Clint snapped. "If you aren't Sarah then who- no, scratch that- what are you?"

"My kind holds many titles none of which are completely accurate or completely incorrect. Know that we are drawn to those who should not be or have stepped into places best left untrodden. Those like yourself."

"I didn't do anything."

"No, you didn't. Not with intent, in any case. I see it in your mind, though, the memory of the moment that should have been your last and wasn't. The instant when you were torn apart and existed in multiple realities in the same instant. Mortals aren't supposed to be able to do that, Clinton Mercer. It is one of the Immutable Laws of corporeal life. Yet you, through whatever means, broke that Law. That kind of thing thrums the web strings of the interconnected multiverse and draws the attention of my kind. So, I am here."

Clint sighed and said, "I'm getting really sick of saying that I don't understand."

Sarah just stared at him.

"What do you want from me?" Clint said.

"Do you know what has happened to you?" She asked, ignoring his question. "Not just the event but the result of the event, the truth of it. Do you know?"

Clint opened his mouth to speak but then just shook his head.

Sarah stared at his face as though searching for something. They stayed that way for what seemed like hours of dream time before she said, "This is not what I was expecting. You are not what I was expecting."

"Is that a good thing or a bad thing?"

"For whom?"

"Just for fun let's start with me. What's happened to me?"

She studied him for a moment before she said, "You have broken that which was is meant to be unbreakable,

Clinton Mercer. A mortal does not do such and walk away from it unaltered or unnoticed."

Clint nodded and said, "Okay, thanks, that was vague but unhelpful. I appreciate it."

"I am limited in what I can reveal both by Law and my own lacking knowledge."

"What Law? What are you talking about?"

Sarah but not-Sarah shook her head. "I had forgotten how fragile your kind are."

Clint looked up at her. Sarah's features were there just as he remembered them but with none of the warm expressions. Gone were the small smiles and energetic shine of life in her eyes and its place nothing but flat impartiality. He saw it then, the stranger beneath the features, unknown and alien. He'd never dreamed anything that had felt so real before. It really was like he was back in chopper over South America and he knew it felt this way because of the presence standing in front of him.

"What are you?" he said. "How are you in my head?"

"The Dreaming is one of the few places our kind may interact, Clinton Mercer. Such things require very specific circumstances. This is merely one of the more convenient. That and your altered nature make it a simpler matter for you."

"My 'altered nature'? Altered how?"

Not-Sarah stared at him. "That is more complicated than I have the time to explain. Even now, I feel you withdrawing from The Dreaming."

"What? You mean I'm waking up?"

"Yes, that is the correct phrase."

"Good. I am more than ready for this weird ass dream to be over."

Her expression shifted a little then into a familiar look of empathy that he had seen on Sarah's face hundreds of times when she was dealing with patients. "This is not anywhere close to 'over', Clinton Mercer," she said. "It has barely begun to begin. Stay with the magus, if you are able, for you will see but he will know. Tell him about me or not, the choice is yours, but you will need each other. There is far more here than I expected. Far more."

Clint opened his mouth to ask her what she meant but she was suddenly gone. The dream lost its clarity and hard edges.

As though released from cages, the drowned things in the chopper surged towards him.

He opened his eyes to early morning sunlight.

CHAPTER FIFTEEN

Seven Pines Apartments
1580 Sparkman Drive
Huntsville, Alabama
October 29, 06:58 A.M. CST

It was all Andy could do to ignore the whispers. They had distracted him while he had made love to Jasmine and then woke him from a troubled sleep afterward. He stood naked in the living room of his small apartment staring at the package on his kitchen counter and fighting the urge to cross the room to tear it open.

Why? He couldn't say. He didn't even know what was in the damned thing. It was Professor Warner's, after all, but the old bastard hadn't called him yet and the thing was whispering and it was driving him nuts but that's impossible because boxes can't speak so-

"nog forth ng raise f' yogor, nog forth ng raise f' yogor, nog forth ng raise f' yogor," he said, his voice a kind of bubbling hiss of a whisper.

Wait; *his* voice? How could that be his voice? He hadn't tried to say anything. What language was that, anyway? It wasn't like anything he'd ever heard before and didn't sound right coming out of his throat because it was like something was shooting it out past his lips with a flamethrower-

Andy groaned and shoved the heels of his hands against his temples. His thoughts were coming too fast. The whispering was getting too loud. The language was wrong, something was wrong, all of this was wrong but the whispers, the whispers, the whispers-

"Andy?"

He jumped and twisted towards the voice as if something had shocked him. Jasmine stood there in the big tee shirt from the night before. She was staring at him with a blend of fear and confusion simmering in her eyes.

"What are you doing, bae?" she said. "What was that you were saying?"

He felt his lips moving but there was no sound from his mouth. The whispering was still in his mind, though, and he blinked hard trying to focus enough to answer Jasmine even though the question was already sliding behind the whispers.

"Andy," she said, her voice more forceful and concerned. "Hey, are you okay? What's going on with you?"

"I… I can't," Andy said. He knew his voice was breaking and hesitant but it was all he could do to speak without the words morphing into the wrong language between his brain and his lips. Anger spiked in him and he growled in frustration.

"That!" he snapped, stabbing one finger towards the package. "Professor Warner. It's his. We need to get it to him."

"Okay," Jasmine said with more than a little caution in her voice. "Do you know where he lives?"

Andy shook his head.

"That's fine. Look, why don't you get ready for class and I'll-"

"No," Andy said through gritted teeth. "Just… we need to get rid of it. It needs to be gone, Jas. Now." He could feel his jaw quivering with the words.

Jasmine looked from him to the package and back again. Andy could see she was getting scared and he felt another surge of the frustration and anger. "Look," he said, trying hard not to stammer, "I know I'm acting weird but there is something about that thing that is freaking me out. We need to get it to Warner and then I'll be fine, okay?"

She stared at him for a moment and then gave a hesitant nod. "Okay, bae. You're sure about missing class, though? I could-"

Andy gritted his teeth against the sudden urge to cross the room and knock the stupid right out of that bitch. Knock her on her fat ass and beat-

Wait.

What… what had that been? Where had… he would never do something like that, never hurt anyone like that and especially not Jas. He loved her but the whispers were driving him mad, driving him-

"Andy, please stop staring at me like that," Jas said. Her voice was small and more than a little afraid.

He blinked again and said, "I'm sorry. I'm so sorry. I'm going to get dressed. Could you try to find Warner's address and we'll just take it to him? Everything will be okay after that. Yeah, that'll make it stop. Please, Jas, just find his address for me, okay?"

She nodded. "Okay, let me get my phone and I'll track it down." She went back into the bedroom.

Andy turned and faced the package again. He fought to keep the whispers at the back of his mind, clenched his teeth to keep from whispering along with the maddening chorus of sounds that thrummed against his thoughts. Just give the package to Warner and it would stop, right? Of course it would because then it would be gone and he'd be away from it and he could go back to loving Jasmine without the constant whispers, whispers, whispers.

As he stared at the box on his counter, his lips started forming silent words once more.

CHAPTER SIXTEEN

Mercer residence
2237 Tollgate Road
Huntsville, Alabama
October 29, 07:01 A.M. CST

He opened his eyes to early morning sunlight.

Clint was lying in his bed watching the light stream past the open blinds and curtains. He didn't move. Instead he studied the light. It looked different, he thought; more detailed. It was like could see the shift in its quality as it filtered through the heavy clouds that were floating in the mostly blue sky.

Cold air touched his face but he was warm beneath the blankets. He yawned and let the lazy warmth suffuse him all the way through. His eyes started drifting closed again.

"No time for that, Mercer. Your nap is over," Arlo said.

Clint's eyes snapped open and he sat up quickly. The magus was sitting in the chair Clint kept next to the small fireplace that comprised one corner of his bedroom. He was dressed in slacks, a dark business shirt, and a long black leather coat that would probably hang to his knees had he been standing. He held his hands with steepled fingertips and was looking at Clint through the space between them. The rings glittered with tiny points of multicolored lights and Clint swore that, for a moment, his pupils mirrored their colors.

"Is this going to be a regular thing?" Clint asked. "You watching me sleep, I mean. Because it's creepy."

"I wanted to make sure there was no psychic damage. That required that I commune with you."

"That you what with me?"

"You can relax, Mercer, it's not a sex act. Remember what I did the first time you woke up in Birmingham? Like that but less abrupt."

"Yeah, I remember. I remember not liking it."

"Trust me, it's better than having a Baku take up residence in your psyche."

"A what?"

"Baku. One of a dozen or so entities that can hide away in a person's spirit and prey on them while they sleep."

Not-Sarah flashed through his memory and Clint said, "And?"

"And you are free of any psychic parasites that I can detect. Still, something feels slightly off with your mind but it's not like anything I've experienced before. It's a small thing. I don't think it will affect your ability to work. We can it explore it at a later date."

"So I guess you and the doc decided to keep me around."

"We did. Consider it a kind of paid internship."

"Okay. How'd I end up in bed?"

Arlo dropped his hands and stood up quickly. "You collapsed in the shower," he said. "There is no history of any narcoleptic disorder in your medical records so I am assuming it was just a reaction to the current situation's stressful nature. Rani examined you and declared that you needed rest. You've had it. Now, it's time to work. Please dress and join us downstairs." With that, he turned for the door with a fast twist and left the room.

Clint watched the door close behind him and muttered, "What the hell have you gotten yourself into, Clint?" When no one answered, he shook his head and threw back the blankets. He was still naked from the shower and grimaced when he realized that at least one of the people hanging out in his condo had seen him naked. He really hoped it hadn't been Arlo. That guy was… different.

He found a pair of pajama bottoms and slipped them on long enough to go to the bathroom and spend a couple of minutes brushing the bed-head out of his dark, wavy hair. He'd let it grow since he'd separated from the military but kept it trimmed and neat. A few minutes later he was dressed in a sturdy pair of hiking boots, cargo pants, and a dark work shirt with the sleeves rolled up to just below his elbows. He grabbed his favorite leather jacket from his closet and slid it on with a small smile. The worn brown leather always made him think of Indiana Jones. He spent another minute digging through a bedside table until he found his spare Jeep key and then headed downstairs.

He found his guests, he'd decided that was the best way to think of them, gathered in the kitchen. Rani and Jim both looked just rumpled enough that he guessed they had napped on the downstairs furniture while he'd slept. They were sipping from steaming mugs and the aroma of coffee scented the air. Arlo was standing near the door leading to the living room looking impatient.

"Hey, there he is," Jim said, pushing a third mug down the small bar in Clint's direction and flashing him a big grin. "Get this in your system. It'll wake you right up."

Clint thanked him and picked up the mug. As soon as the coffee passed his lips, his stomach gave him a small reminder that he hadn't eaten in quite a while.

"How are you feeling?" Rani asked.

Clint shrugged. "Good. Great, actually. My headache's gone and most the pain in my joints is down to something a couple of Aleve will handle."

Rani nodded and then glanced at Arlo. Clint didn't miss the look on her face.

He took another slow drink from his mug and then said, "Any idea why I passed out?"

"Not really. I checked your vitals and everything else I could without a lab at my disposal. You seem fine but I think you've been through more physical stress than a lot of people ever get exposed to. I think you just got back home and relaxed enough that it all caught up with you at once. In short, I think you fainted."

Clint nodded and said, "Passed out. I don't faint. I pass out."

Rani's smile lit up her face. "Of course," she said. "My mistake."

"No problem," Clint said. "So how come I'm not dead? Arlo says I should be."

Rani shot a sharp look at the smaller man. "He's exaggerating," she said.

"No, I'm not," Arlo said, meeting her eyes with equal intensity.

"Uh-huh," Clint said. He looked at Jim and said, "Do mom and dad always argue like this?"

Jim held up a hand and wagged it back and forth a little. "Fifty-fifty," he said.

"This is all very entertaining," Arlo said, "but could we continue this discussion in the car? There is still a dangerous relic out there that we need to recover." Clint noticed that the man was practically twitching with anxiety.

"I don't see what the rush is, Arlo," Rani said. "The investigative teams have scoured the house and grounds. Their reports should be uploaded in the next few hours. Jim has security in place in the meantime. We can finish our coffee."

"You know very well that I can discover things that they cannot," Arlo said.

"Yeah, well, slow your roll, Arlo. The new guy needs an orientation," Clint said.

"Meaning what? I told you about the job in car on the way here."

"You were a little light on the details. First thing's first, though; I need to get my stuff from wherever it was I was in Birmingham. Can you guys arrange that?"

"Consider it done," Jim said.

"Great. Second thing; I need to swing by the hospital and get my Jeep."

"That might be tougher," Jim said. "It's still behind crime scene tape. I'll make some calls. Until then, you can ride with us."

"Okay. Third thing; the person or thing or whatever that killed Sarah. Who and where is he?"

No one responded except to exchange knowing looks with one another. Clint watched in silence and, after waiting what he felt like was an appropriate five seconds or so, said, "Well?"

"I'm sorry about your friend, PJ" Jim said. "You know I know what losing one feels like. Believe me when I tell you, though, that you need to stay frosty about this. Be professional. This isn't the kind of threat you can just track down and put a bullet to. Looking for revenge will only land you in a body bag." The big man held Clint's eyes with his own while he spoke and Clint could see that every trace of good humor was gone from them. The part of Clint that remembered wearing a uniform recognized the deadly seriousness of that look.

"Fine," he said. "Fill in the blanks for me."

"His name is Jubal Mott," Arlo said. "He was born the son of a wealthy southern landowner in 1835. He grew up with a love for hunting both wildlife and runaway slaves. During the Civil War, he fought on the side of the confederacy and was, by all accounts, a nearly zealous devotee to the cause. From what we can tell, in early 1865 when it was becoming obvious that the Confederacy was going to lose the war, Mott found a way to strike a bargain with an outside entity for the eldritch power to continue the fight. Whether this was a selfish thing or if he thought he could somehow rally the war effort is unknown. All we know for certain is that that was when he became a warlock. He roamed the countryside slaughtering Union forces right up until the end of the war and beyond. Eventually, the victims of his ire expanded until it was just a matter of whim for him, it seems."

"Did you say 1835?" Clint said

"I did," Arlo said. "It's common for warlocks to be very long lived and difficult to kill. Sort of boilerplate language in the contracts they strike with the outsiders. It makes a kind of sense when you consider that the entities that they deal with want agents who can enact their will in this world for as long as possible."

" 'Outside entities', 'this world'; what's all of that mean?"

Arlo drew in one of those deep, patience inducing breaths that Clint recognized from the car. "There are other places, Mercer. Call them worlds or dimensions or planes or whatever other term suits your sensibilities but they are places that are not *here*. Just like *here,* though, they have inhabitants all their own. Collectively, we refer to those inhabitants as 'outsiders' and they come in many shapes and sizes. Some of them, many of them actually, are intelligent. Among those entities are beings that are older than any of us can imagine and are as close to the embodiment of pure evil as the human mind is capable of framing the concept. These beings want dominion over all other places and the life those places hold. There are barriers, though, things that keep them from crossing over and just wiping us out. So, when a human discovers a way to contact these beings, they seek to entice them into allowing a small piece of their extraplanar substance- a piece of their flesh, if you will -into their bodies. The presence of this remnant grants the host varying degrees of power depending on the amount and type of outsider influence. We call such hosts 'warlocks'."

"Okay," Clint said. "I remember some of that from what you said in the hospital. This drives the person crazy or something, right?"

"More or less," Rani said. "It's really dependent on the base personality but there is always a suppression or outright elimination of all sense of conscience, shame, or guilt. It's as though it brings out the host's inner sociopath."

"And the barghest? Where did they come from?"

"Very good, Mercer. You were paying attention," Arlo said. "They're Mott's hounds, as it were. He summons and controls them. I'm unsure as to the mechanics of how he works the summoning but I'm hoping I have the chance to find out more."

Clint nodded. "Why is he in town?"

"Guess that's my cue," Jim said. "Before the other night, our most recent intel on dog-boy was nearly a year old. We had some solid information placing him in North Africa up to his neck in a variety of human trafficking networks. Now he's here at the same time a local guy is supposed to be getting his hands on a major relic. The facts point to him wanting that relic, same as us."

"And the relic is what?"

"All we know for sure is that it's a book," Arlo said. "One of a very special set. We just don't know which volume."

"A book? Seriously? There's, like, three Barnes and Nobles in town."

"Remember what I told you, Mercer. Forget what you think you know. This book is like getting your hands on the original typewritten script for…" Arlo seemed to search for a reference but looked at Rani when he came up short.

"Citizen Kane," she said. "Only this book is more rare. And could kill us all in the wrong hands."

Clint thought that over for a second and then said, "Okay, that's dramatic."

"Don't worry about that spooky shit, PJ," Jim said. "Just look at it this way; we've got a target to acquire and secure before a covert and likely overwhelming enemy does. Just treat it like a mission."

Clint studied the man while he considered it. "All right, then. I can work with that." He took on big swig of the coffee to finish it, put the mug on the counter, and headed for the front door. As he stepped past Arlo he said, "Move it, Arlo. You're wasting daylight."

CHAPTER SEVENTEEN

Jim and Rani had parked a few doors down from Clint's place so the four of them walked towards the car with Clint and Jim leading the way. Clint glanced up at the townhouses as they passed and saw one of his neighbors pull back from the window. He imagined that they made up a pretty intriguing group for such a quiet street. The ink black Chevy Tahoe with the tinted windows that they were headed towards just added fuel to what was likely to become a wildfire of gossip for his neighbors.

"Hey, PJ, hold up a sec," Jim said as they approached the vehicle. He stepped to the Tahoe's rear and lifted the cargo door, gesturing for Clint to join him as he did so.

Clint stepped over and saw that the big man was tapping a code into a small keypad that was set into the end of the cargo space. The whole rear floor of the vehicle seemed to sit a little higher than a normal SUV.

"All our rides are custom," Jim said, gesturing to the interior. "We had them pull the third row seat and expand the under floor cargo space so we could have this." He hit the last number on the keypad and there was a soft whirring sound as the floor panel separated up the middle and opened towards either side like a set of folding shutters lying face down. As they opened, Clint saw an assortment of handguns, two M-4 carbines, two Mossberg pump action shotguns, a small stack of armored vests, a backpack sized medical kit, and a small red cooler. There was also a bulky laptop that looked like it could take a blast from one of the shotguns and still function. Boxes of extra ammo lined the sides.

"Damn, man," Clint said. "Are you planning on us storming a bunker or something?"

"What are you talking about?" Jim said with a grin. "This is my weekend kit."

The two men shared a small laugh as the shutters clicked into place. "So," Lonebear said, "when I was securing your apartment the only real weapon I found was a k-bar in your bedside table. Gotta say, I was a little surprised."

"Why's that?" Clint said.

Jim shrugged. "Most former spec-op guys I know like to keep a firearm handy. You don't. You anti-gun or something?"

It was Clint's turn to shrug. "I'm not really pro or anti-gun. They're the best tool for the job they're designed for. They're like a hammer that way. I just don't have that kind of job anymore."

"Still," Jim said, "personal safety and all that."

Clint shrugged again. "I live in a good neighborhood in a relatively low crime small city. Just don't see the need."

"Yeah, well, you roll with us and the chances are good that there will be a need. I think I've got just the thing for you." He pulled a familiar looking handgun from the collection and held it up for Clint to see. "Sig P320, chambered for forty-five ACP complete with accessory rail and lots of hollow points to feed her. I think this is pretty close to what you carried back in the day, right?"

Clint nodded. "Mine was a nine-mil but I think the forty-five will work."

"Damn straight it will. Got you a holster and everything." He leaned into the truck and started pulling the armored vests up, looking around beneath them.

"Will this be enough to put down…" Clint thought for a moment and then said, "Mott, right? Jubal Mott?"

"That's the one," Jim said. "If he shows up, we perform a tactical withdrawal maneuver and grab the heavier stuff. Mostly, though, withdrawal."

"Really? He's that tough?"

"Couldn't tell ya," Jim said with a shrug. "I've never thrown down with a warlock. From the reports I've read, though, I can say I'm good with that. Now check that weapon, PJ. Get your head back in the tactical space."

Clint held up the pistol and ejected the magazine. Once he had confirmed that it was fully loaded, he pulled back the slide just enough to check the chamber. Sure enough, he found a round sitting snugly in the pipe. Clint figured that Jim was the sort to keep his gear ready to fire. He replaced the mag and looked up in time to see Jim hold up a black leather holster.

"This'll do the trick," he said. "Secure that onto your belt and I'll find the spare mag carrier for the other side."

Within a minute or two, Clint was armed and had two spare magazines to boot. He adjusted his belt on his hips as Jim talked.

"Here are the rules," the big man said. "You keep it holstered unless we are under direct hostile action or the boss or myself tells you different. You're with us but you're still not one of us so you need to follow our lead. We've got DHS badges but you don't. Anybody asks, you're a consultant and point them towards us. We probably won't run into anybody that will challenge you but that's the story if we do. Also, when we get to the scene, the doc will stay in the vehicle. She doesn't normally do the field stuff."

"I guess she's here because of the agents you guys lost?"

Jim nodded. "Yeah. One, in particular."

"Let me guess," Clint said, "whoever it was that had this gig before me."

"Deana," Jim said, nodding. "Deana Sanchez. She was with the Miami P.D. before she signed on. Hell, truth be told, she's the one that talked me into this job. She was good people. Her and the boss were a helluva team."

Clint nodded. He remembered the female agent from the ER and realized that he didn't need to ask if that had been her. Her adamant need to protect Arlo told him everything he needed to know.

"Anyway," Jim said, drawing in a breath. "Got any questions?"

"Keep my head down, follow your lead. I think I can handle it."

"All right then, PJ. Let's roll."

Clint walked around to the passenger side while Jim secured the rear compartment. He saw that Arlo and Rani had gotten into the rear seats so he opened the door and slid into the front passenger spot. Jim's phone rang just as he was buckling in and he took the call by answering, "Go for Lonebear." His voice was strong and authoritative, a shift from his friendly banter while they'd been getting Clint kitted out.

Jim listened for a minute without speaking and then said, "Copy that. Light a blowtorch under the evidence guys on this for me. The boss is waiting and he's got an itchy feeling about this one." He ended the call and looked back over his shoulder. "Boss, Our guys-"

"Drive," Arlo said with a glare, "then talk." He said it with the kind of impatient tone that Clint usually heard parents use with misbehaving children.

Clint looked back at him, then at Rani. She gave him a slight shake of her head. Clint glanced at Jim, who seemed wholly unphased by Arlo's abrupt manner, and decided to let it lie. If the big marine wanted to let Arlo's attitude slide then Clint figured that was between them.

Jim pulled the SUV away from the curb and headed towards downtown. Clint kept his eyes on the familiar neighborhood and tried to settle all the recent events in his mind. He felt the pistol digging into his hip a little and made a mental note to try and adjust it better once they were out of the vehicle. What he'd told Jim about his attitude towards guns had been the truth but he had to admit that, all things considered, he felt better having it than not. A little time on the range to fire up all the old muscle memory would have been nice but it was what it was. Now, all Clint had to do was figure what exactly that meant.

He didn't think his current companions meant him any real harm since they'd been the ones to arm him. That didn't mean he necessarily trusted them, though. Whatever their deal was, he figured this was the best way to get to the man- warlock, whatever -that had killed Sarah and deliver a measure of retribution. So long as they kept him going that way, he figured he'd keep his mouth shut and tag along.

That thought brought back the memory of the Sarah/not-Sarah from his dream and he just shook his head. He'd never in his life had so vivid a dream but there was just too much weird there to try and unpack at once.

He was still thinking on it when they pulled into the driveway of a house that was surrounded by crime scene tape.

CHAPTER EIGHTEEN

Warner Residence
203 Lowe Avenue
Hunstville, Alabama
29 October, 7:41 a.m. CST

Clint got out of the car and looked around. The sky was a rich blue and heavy clouds drifted by overhead. The horizon was a haze of gray sky that promised cold wind and rain but he chose to enjoy the sun. A chill breeze swept across the yard but that was okay with Clint. He much preferred a chill breeze to the sweltering heat of a southern summer. He noticed something in the near distance and said, "No wonder you guys ended up in my ER. I can see the hospital parking garage from here."

"Yes, it was fortuitous," Arlo said as he got out of the car and shut the door hard. "Now stop gawking and let's get to work, Mercer." Clint turned his eyes on the man but Arlo was already walking away. He was deciding whether or not to warn him about his tone of voice when Rani came around the vehicle and stood next to Clint.

"Try not to take it personally, Mr. Mercer," she said. "He's a challenging and impatient man."

"Uh-huh," Clint said. "What's his diagnosis, doctor? I think if I'm going to be working with him I should at least get read in on that much."

"I agree but it's not that simple, I'm afraid."

"How so?"

"The kind of man Arlo is, the things he can do, his talent, these all make him a one of a kind patient."

"You're talking about the whole magician thing, right?"

Rani's eyes grew wide. "Oh, do not let him hear you call him that. He's a magus or a wizard, if you must. He'll tell you that he reorders reality and magicians do tricks for tourists and the gullible. He's sensitive that way."

" 'Reorders reality'? What does that even mean?"

"Give it time. You'll see."

"Okay, fine, 'magus' it is," Clint said, "but what's his damage?"

Rani drew in a breath and said, "That's too long a conversation for now but suffice to say that his diagnosis is a fluid one. You have to watch and assess him continually when you're with him. If it seems he's escalating to an unmanageable level you call me and I'll figure out what needs to be done."

Clint looked towards the house. Arlo was watching Jim slice through a line of yellow police tape that was holding the door shut. The smaller man was practically vibrating with impatience. Clint looked back at Rani. "You know," he said, "my psych rotation was my least favorite in nursing school."

"Well," she said with a small smile, "for the time being it might be your most useful. Watch him, intervene with the public on his behalf if needed, and call me if he gets too unruly. I'll be right here." She patted the side of the SUV before walking around the vehicle and climbing into the driver's seat.

Clint watched her go and closed his eyes before muttering, "Sure, I'll babysit the crazy magic guy. Why not?"

"Mercer!" Arlo shouted from the porch, "If you're finished discussing my psychiatric shortcomings with Doctor Smythe perhaps you'd like to join us and start living up to your end of our agreement!" The man's tone was remarkably similar to the one he had used on Jim in the car.

Clint felt his expression grow hard as he looked towards the house. Arlo was already inside while Jim was standing at the door apparently waiting for Clint to join them. He did so with long, controlled steps that gave him time to beat down a little of the irritation that Arlo had sparked in him. As he passed Jim on the porch, Clint held up his index finger and mouthed the words, "That's one."

The big man just smiled and shrugged before gesturing for Clint to go into the house.

He did so and got about two steps before he stopped short. His chosen career had ensured that Clint had seen more blood than the average person but not even the bloodiest of injuries that he'd encountered compared to what he saw in that house. There were dark splashes and smears of dried blood everywhere. Furniture was overturned, bullet holes showed in the walls and windows, long lines of dried blood crisscrossed the ceiling, and there were sets of deep claw marks in the floors and walls. The air stank with a kind of earthy, metallic aroma that Clint knew well. A lot of people had died horribly in that place and Clint glanced back at Jim as though for confirmation.

"First crime scene?" Jim said.

Clint nodded.

"Well, you got a doozy, brother. This is one of the worst I've seen and I've seen my share since signing on with this outfit."

"Mott did this?"

Jim nodded. "Yeah. Him and his hounds. Nine casualties total; the two occupants, five of our people, and two local leos who happened to drive by at the wrong time and tried to intervene. From what I read, the boss might not've made it to you if they hadn't."

Clint frowned and said, "This? All of this-" he gestured at the house, "-over a damned book?"

"It's never just a book, PJ. Or a statue or a person or a… whatever. If there's one thing I've learned in the last five years it's that these things that the Pickmen go after are never, ever, just what they look like. There are things in the dark that no one ever told us about. I can tell that you have yet to really, truly embrace the suck that is that fact. You need to because you got thrown in the deep end first and the things that you can't or won't see out here *will* pull you under."

Clint could hear the sincere concern behind Jim's words but he wasn't entirely sure he understood what it was that he was supposedly not embracing. He was there with them, after all. Instead of asking about that, though, he said, "Pickmen; that was what Mott called Arlo and the rest of the agents at the hospital."

Jim nodded. "That's us. The-"

"If it's not too much to ask," Arlo said from farther back in the house, "I require the two of you to join me."

Jim gave Clint a wink and said, "To be continued. Try not to step in any of the bloody patches. It's mostly dried but you never know."

Clint nodded and the two men made their way down a short corridor towards a large sitting room attached to the kitchen in the rear of the house. Clint frowned when he stepped into the space. This room seemed to have seen the worst of fighting. In addition to the damage he had seen in the foyer, there were a number of large scorch marks the size of dinner plates burnt black into the walls and built in bookshelves.

Jim gave a low whistle and said, "Damn, boss. No wonder-"

"I was here when it happened, Lonebear. Your idle commentary will add nothing to my knowledge of the situation."

"Right. Gotcha, boss."

Clint looked at Jim with an expression that said, *'What the hell?'*.

Jim shook his head as if to say, *'No big deal. Just let it go.'*

Clint shrugged and looked back to find Arlo staring at him. "How are you feeling, Mercer? Be specific."

"Aside from being a little grossed out, I'm good."

"No strange sensations or impulses? Headaches? Do you have an erection, perhaps?"

Clint's face flushed mildly. He could hear Jim stifle a laugh. "A what? No, man, none of that. Something in the air is irritating my eyes a little but that's about it. Nothing bad enough to worry about."

"Really? That's disappointing. There is a remarkable amount of magical residue in this place. I was hoping for a more definitive reaction." He studied Clint for another few moments and then shrugged. "Oh well, further study required and all that. Back to the business at hand."

Arlo stepped to the center of the ruined room and pointed to two separate spots, one with each hand. "We found the Warners here and here," he said. "Each of you pick a spot and stand there facing one another."

Jim stepped forward. Clint hesitated and then followed with his eyes locked on Arlo.

"Very good. They were bound to chairs facing one another. Their chest and bellies were opened but not by the claws of any beast, no. Mott split them to expose their organs so that he could feed them to his pets while the other watched. I suspect he used his magic to keep them alive while he did-"

"He did what?" Clint snapped.

Jim winced and shook his head at Clint.

Arlo closed his eyes for a moment. The internal war between his temper and his patience was plain on his face. When he opened his eyes again, he fixed them on Clint and said, "Mercer, I acknowledge that this is your first experience in the field and while I would have preferred that one of my subordinates-" he shifted his glare to Jim for an instant, "-had explained this to you, I will go ahead and take the time to do so now. I often work things out aloud when I am at this phase of an operation or investigation. When I am doing so, it is very important that you don't interrupt me with inane questions or requests. I very clearly stated what Mott did with his victims and, yet, you let your emotional reaction spur you to ask me to repeat myself for which there is no need since you are standing right here and undoubtedly heard me clearly thereby imprinting the information onto your pre-frontal cortex. Going forward, I must insist that you remain rational and control any impulses that might lead you to similar emotionally based outbursts. Understood? Good."

Clint took a long moment and mentally counted to ten. Arlo kept going, barely missing a breath.

"As I said, I suspect that he used some kind of magic to keep the Warner's consciousness adhered to their bodies despite the lethal damage that was being done to them. Why, though? If the cryptical was here, why the binding and the torture? Why not just kill them and disappear with the prize? Mott is a sadist? Yes. He took perverse pleasure in their suffering? Perhaps, but would that be enough to risk an encounter with us? Again, perhaps, but it seems unlikely. He's an old warlock who hasn't gotten that way by taking unnecessary chances. Still, why such heavy magic to-"

Arlo stopped suddenly, his eyes darting back and forth as he internalized his monologue. He rapidly bounced the first two fingers of each hand against their opposing thumbs like a hyperactive crab as he looked about the room.

"That's it," he said, his hands opening suddenly. "Heavy magic. Like attracts like. Heavy magic leaves behind heavy residue that would have been altered by… yes, I need to perform a working. You two stay exactly where you are. This won't take long."

Clint snapped a nervous look at Jim. The big man just patted the air with his hands as if to say, *'It's all good, PJ.'*

Clint relaxed by a fraction and watched Arlo.

The magus seemed to be oblivious to Jim and Clint's exchange. He was rummaging through his coat pockets and whispering to himself. Clint realized that the coat must have a dozen or more pockets sewn into the lining at about the same time that Arlo pulled out a bent and twisted length of silver wire about eight inches long. He kept whispering to himself as he held one end tightly between the thumb and index finger of his left hand while running the same two digits of his right hand quickly down the length of wire, smoothing and straightening it. He kept muttering to himself the whole time. The thumb and index finger rings on his right hand started to glow with a faint, white light.

Clint's eyes burned as though he'd suddenly gotten smoke in them. He tried to blink away the sensation but it didn't stop with his eyes. Like some kind of minuscule wildfire, the feeling spread out over his face, neck, shoulders, and then the rest of his body in sudden rush. He pushed his palms into his eyes, the feeling was harshest there, and staggered back a step. He thought he cried out because he suddenly heard Jim shout his name in alarm followed quickly by Arlo. Clint staggered away a few more steps and turned back to them. He pulled his hands down and looked at them with his burning eyes.

The house looked… wrong.

Everything was cast in shades of silver, gray, and varying degrees of black. All the hard edges and lines were blurred and indistinct but not so much that he couldn't recognize the shapes of things. Jim had been right in front of him when he'd opened his eyes. The big man's form was surrounded by a faint glow of white and gray that stood out from the rest of the world as though it were more in focus than everything else.

As he watched, Jim suddenly jumped back and drew his pistol. He took aim at Clint and said, "Stay back! Just be cool, PJ!"

"Mercer!" Arlo shouted.

Clint turned to Arlo and gasped at what he saw. Colors swirled about the man in waves and lines like bright paints that refused to blend together into a new color. All of this moved over his body which was a solid slate gray with ten points of piercing light spread over his fingers and thumbs. They left tracers of silver white as he raised his hands palms out in a calming gesture.

"Lonebear, stand down," Arlo snapped. "This is fascinating. Mercer, describe what you're seeing. What-"

Clint didn't hear the rest. He staggered towards the door, leaning against the walls to steady himself as he went. He needed air and sunlight, he thought, something to ground him and clear his head and sight.

His eyes, dammit, his eyes! Was he going blind? What was happening to him?

He tripped and fell through the screen door leading to the porch. It slammed open as he fell and bounced against his side as he crawled towards the steps, rising to his knees to look at the world.

It was like an alien landscape. The shapes were there. The school soccer field that was across Lowe Avenue was there, the single story offices beyond that, the hospital in the distance, the sun, the clouds, the trees; everything that should have been there was but it was all different in ways he didn't understand. Colors flowed through the sky in misty lines like free floating spray paint looking for something to attach itself to. Blooms of red dotted the soccer field like burning spikes though some were far brighter than others. The edge of the buildings wavered and he thought he could see faint lines of color leaking out the black and white shapes of the windows and doors. The whole thing was making him nauseous.

He heard a car door slam and looked towards the sound. Rani had gotten out of the Tahoe and was looking at him from the street. A nimbus of silver gray light surrounded her, clean and distinct.

There was something else, though, something that pulled his attention from Rani. Another car had come to a stop on the opposite side of the road a few car lengths behind their Tahoe. It was a small car. An older model Honda two door of some kind but that wasn't what drew Clint's attention.

Tendrils of perfect black rolled and twisted off the car. They fell to the ground all around it and squirmed into the earth leaving black stains where they landed. Clint thought he could see two passengers but the black was so pervasive that it obscured whatever light they produced.

The whole sight made his guts churn with fear and revulsion. On some deep, untouched part of his psyche, Clint knew that whomever was in that car was in great danger and whatever it was in that car that was threatening them had no right or reason to exist in the world, his world, and it needed to be destroyed.

Hands grabbed his shoulders. He heard Arlo and Jim shout his name. Rani was moving towards the porch. The car with the black infection started to pull away from the curb.

Clint pointed a shaking hand towards it and said, "That car! Arlo, there's something in that car that's… it's just *wrong*."

He didn't see what Arlo did but a few seconds later he heard him say, "Lonebear, secure that car. I can feel the cryptical inside it. Go, now!"

Clint felt Jim brush by him, shouting something he couldn't understand. The hazy, undefined world continued to swim and sway around him. Nausea crept through his guts. Arlo's hands clamped onto his shoulders. His rings had faded to a dim glimmer of what Clint had seen in the house.

"Well done, Mercer," he said. "I'm not sure how you knew but well done all the same. You found the cryptical. Now we can focus on what's happening to you. What-"

Then, someone started shooting at them.

CHAPTER NINETEEN

It wasn't the first time Clint had been shot at. It was the first time he'd ever been shot at while half blinded by… whatever it was he was seeing. Despite that, old muscle memory from long hours of training kicked in and he rolled to his right, getting the sparse cover of the porch railing between him and where he thought the shots were coming from. He planned on using that cover to keep him from getting shot long enough to get his feet under him and get back into the house where he could dig in and get a line on their attackers. As it turned out, Arlo had other plans.

Rather than going for cover, Arlo stood up between Clint and the distant gunman. He thrust both hands out in front of him, palm out, and spread his fingers wide. The rings flared with light that expanded out in front of Arlo and glared so brightly in Clint's eyes that he had to close them against the glare.

Words tumbled from Arlo's lips, alien and unintelligible to Clint. Gunshots rang out in a fast burst. Jim yelled for Rani to get back. Tires screeched on asphalt. More shots, but farther away, as though retreating.

"They're falling back," Jim shouted. "Target vehicle is on the move. We gotta go, boss!"

Arlo stopped speaking in the weird language and Clint heard him exhale hard, like he'd been holding his breath. "Help me with Mercer," he said. "Hurry!"

Jim must have already been heading their way because the words were scarcely out of Arlo's mouth when Clint felt the big man haul him to his feet. "Come on," Jim said, his deep voice thick with tension, "ain't no time for beauty sleep, PJ." They started moving with Jim carrying Clint more than guiding him.

Clint opened his eyes. Everything was a sea of silver white. He closed them again, biting back a cry of alarm as he did so. He opened his mouth to tell them he was blind.

Before he could say anything, Jim said, "Boss, what the hell happened?"

"A reaction to my working, obviously," Arlo said from somewhere ahead of them. He seemed to have caught his breath but there was still a kind of weariness to his tone.

"Yeah, but his eyes. They were-"

"I was there, Lonebear, I saw it as clearly as you. First, the cryptical. Then, Mercer."

Clint heard a car door open and Rani's voice. "Clint? What happened? Who was shooting at us?"

Clint was pretty sure he said something about being blind but no one seemed to hear him. He felt Jim hand him off to Arlo while he tried to blink his eyesight back. Arlo roughly guided him into the Tahoe and got in behind him as the SUV's big engine roared to life.

"He's not injured, He reacted in an unknown way to a minor working, and I have no idea," Arlo said. "Lonebear-"

"Don't lose that car. Got it, boss." The SUV lurched away from the curb so fast that tires squealed and Arlo was thrown awkwardly into Clint.

"Mercer," Arlo said. "Can you understand me?"

Clint nodded. "Yeah, but I can't see. My eyes-"

"I know," Arlo said. "You've mentioned it repeatedly. What happened? Describe what-" the car lurched into a hard left turn, sliding Clint and Arlo around again.

Clint ignored it and said, "You started doing your thing and-"

"Summarize, Mercer," Arlo snapped. "What do you see?"

Clint tried to tell him. He tried to describe the blurred edges and the free floating colors and the hazy shapes and the grayness of it all. He was pretty sure he sounded like a crazy person doing it.

"Do you remember when you woke up in the hospital that first time?" Arlo said, "Do you remember what I did?"

"There!" Rani shouted. "They just took a left onto California!"

"Got 'em," Jim replied.

Clint nodded.

"Then brace yourself because here I come again," Arlo said.

"Hold on," Clint said, "I-"

Arlo grabbed Clint's head with both hands.

Silence.

Perfect, white, silence.

There was no sense of motion or sound of movement from the Tahoe. Jim and Rani's voices were gone. No rush of wind or sensation of the seat at his back. It was as though Clint had suddenly lost his body and become pure consciousness in a universe of perfect absence.

"Oh, please, Mercer." Arlo's voice said from everywhere at once. " 'A universe of perfect absence'? What does that even mean? I didn't take you for the poetic type."

"Arlo? What the hell, man? What are you doing? What is this place?"

"We're in your head," Arlo said. "I'm seeing what you're seeing but I've taken the liberty of dialing down the intensity. I can see why you were in distress. There is

a lot of residue here, both arcane and eldritch as well as something…"

The voice drifted off into the silence again. After what seemed like a minute, Clint said- or thought, he wasn't sure - "Arlo?"

"Quiet," Arlo said, "I'm thinking. Mercer, have you had any unusual dreams recently?"

"What the hell do my dreams have to do with anything? Fix my eyes so I can help with all this."

"I suppose you're right. Priorities. We will revisit the question, though."

"Great, can't wait. Eyes, please."

"Your eyes are fine."

"As the person who's actually using them I can confidently tell you that, no, they are not fine."

"Yes, they are. It's your brain that's having the problem."

Clint spent a moment taking that in. "Can't say that makes me feel any better, Arlo."

"Merely a fact, Mercer. Feelings about the matter are not a consideration."

"Again with the Mister Spock 'logic is all' crap. Just get on with it so we can help Rani and Jim."

"What's the rush?"

"What's the… man, we are in the middle of a car chase."

"Oh, that. You can relax. This is all happening far faster than any of that."

"What?"

"We're operating in the realm of pure thought, Mercer. Communication and action at the speed of firing neurons. It may feel like you're speaking at a normal rate but this is all happening nearly instantaneously. From Jim and Rani's perspective, this whole exchange will only take a second or two. They're so preoccupied with the pursuit that I doubt they'll even notice."

"Seriously?"

"Of course. Why would I mislead you?"

Clint started to answer when Arlo cut in again. "Ah, there it is. I knew it felt odd."

"There what is?"

"The thing that's disrupting your eyesight. The human psyche has... well, think of them as circuit breakers. They're filters the average brain uses to protect itself from input that is too far outside the individual's accepted reality. They exist to maintain one's sense of normality. And their sanity. Mostly their sanity, really. A person sees something like, say, the warlock and his barghest. Their mental breakers kick in to either rationalize it into something that fits their desired normal or blocks it out altogether allowing them to ignore it completely. Ever heard of repressed memories? Kind of like that, just deeper."

"So why didn't mine kick in that night?"

"Because you didn't just catch a glimpse of something. You had a traumatic interaction with it. That's a different kind of experience. Still, though, you've handled things far better than most anyone else I've ever dealt with in

similar situations. That says a lot about your strength of character."

"Thanks, I guess. What do we do now?"

"I need to see more. Think about what you saw right before the shooting started. Really concentrate on it and I'll try to guide us into the memory."

"What-"

"Mercer, despite how easy I make this look, it isn't. I can't keep it up forever. Hold your questions and do as I've instructed."

Clint bit back a retort and tried to focus on the first few moments after he'd stumbled onto the Warner's porch. The world of white suddenly started bleeding colors like a photograph burning in reverse. In what seemed like seconds, he was standing on the porch again and could see his hands and body again though he still felt nothing. Arlo was in front of him and they were separated by frozen images of himself, Jim, and Arlo as they had been when Clint had fallen to his knees.

"I've locked us into this moment," Arlo said. "It's easier when things aren't in motion. I-"

Arlo's gaze drifted from Clint and to the wider world. His face went slack with disbelief as he slowly walked down the steps and into the yard. "Living light, Mercer," he whispered, his face filled with awe. "This? This is what you saw?"

"Yeah," Clint said. "Needless to say it freaked me right the hell out, too."

"Do you have any idea what this is? What you… no, of course you don't, you're barely a neophyte."

"Arlo?"

"Look up there," Arlo said, pointing skyward. "That's the Aether. The actual Aether."

"Arlo, I don't know what that means," Clint said.

"That first night," Arlo said, seeming not to hear Clint, "you were caught in the confluence of two magics, arcane and eldritch. Opposing energies colliding within the confines of a living vessel previously untouched by magic. Devastating energies were released? Obviously. So why wasn't the vessel destroyed? Unknown… unless-"

"Arlo!" Clint said, packing as much force into the word as he could.

The magus's eyes snapped to Clint. They were wide and wild and Clint could see a glimmer of mania smoldering in them.

"You said we were on a clock. I'm no good to you if I'm blind. Can you get me my eyes back or not?"

Arlo nodded quickly, "Yes, I can, but, Mercer, this-" he gestured around him "-all that you can see. You can't understand the enormity of it." Arlo started turning in slow circles, staring upward.

"Then you'll explain it to me," Clint said, stepping down off the porch. He crossed the yard and grabbed Arlo by the shoulders, turning him so they were facing one another. "Hey," he said, "you can explain it to me but not until after we deal with that." Clint pointed down the street and gave Arlo a rough turn so that he was looking in the right direction.

The Honda was there, the perfect black of the tendrils frozen in place. Even as a memory the sight of it sent a cold tremor through Clint.

Arlo stared at it for a few seconds and then said, "Yes. Yes, the cryptical. Hold on, Mercer, I'm going to… uhm… I going to reset your breakers. It might sting a little."

Clint nodded and half wondered if this was the moment he'd get karmic payback for all the times he'd said that to a patient knowing damn well it was going to do more than sting.

The world went white again.

CHAPTER TWENTY

"There they are," Rani said, "taking that side street along the cemetery!"

Sharp pain stabbed into Clint's eyes as he opened them. The normal world with all its colors and chaos filled his sight just in time for him to see another driver flip them off as Jim gunned the engine and the Tahoe swerved past a small sedan. He grimaced and said, "That was more than a sting, Arlo."

Arlo rocked in his seat as the truck swerved. He waved a dismissive hand in Clint's direction. He was pale and staring at him through tired but wide eyes.

The Tahoe swerved again. Clint heard the loud screech of tires skidding. He grabbed the two front seats and pulled himself up between them so he could see out of the windshield.

The Honda had come to a stop in the middle of a small road that cut off from California Street and ran maybe the length of a football field before it terminated at an intersection with Wells Avenue. Clint knew the road well. It was on his route to and from work.

"Why'd they stop?" Jim said, gunning the engine again to shoot around another car and close the gap.

"There," Rani said, pointing past the Honda, "Someone cut them off."

As the Tahoe got closer, Clint could see that a big F150 pickup had angled itself to block the road just ahead of the Wells Avenue intersection. Clint figured that to whomever was in the Honda, it looked as though they were coming in behind them to seal the trap. Even as he thought it, both doors on the Honda opened and two young people, one light skinned man and a darker skinned woman, jumped out and ran through the gate into the cemetery. Clint spotted a package under the woman's arm and didn't have to try too hard to guess what it was.

"Targets are on foot," Jim said, we need-"

Something hit the Tahoe hard from behind sending it into a small skid that Jim expertly maneuvered into a sliding stop that left them at a forty five degree angle to the road. Clint managed to hang onto the seats hard enough to stay upright and looked back over his shoulder for whatever had struck them.

Another SUV, he couldn't tell the make on this one, had come to a stop ten or twelve yards back. Even as he watched the doors opened on this one and three people got out, leaving the doors open to use them for cover as they leveled guns at the Tahoe.

"Contact rear!" Clint shouted automatically and ducked down into the rear seat.

Gunfire erupted and bullets rang out against the Tahoe like someone was beating on the vehicle with hammers. Clint expected shattering glass and shouts of pain but none came. Gradually the gunfire died down. He looked up and saw Jim looking back at him with a relaxed grin on his big, tan face.

"I told you this thing was custom," he said as he drew a heavy 1911 pistol from inside his jacket with one hand and patted the steering wheel with the other. "These assholes are going to have to come a lot heavier than that if they want to dent this baby."

Clint sat up and looked back at the shooters. Whatever the Tahoe was made out of, it had stopped their bullets cold. Clint couldn't help but smile.

"The people in the other truck," Rani said. "They're chasing the targets."

Clint looked past Jim and saw two men climbing over the low stone wall that surrounded the cemetery.

"They have the cryptical," Arlo said at almost the same moment Rani said, "They'll kill them."

Clint watched as the two exchanged a glance that only people with secrets in common can share. Arlo drew in a breath and said, "Fine. Lonebear and I will hold off the shooters and provide cover. Rani, stay in the truck and call in to the locals with the DHS cover. Mercer, go get the cryptical."

Clint met Arlo's eyes. "Excuse me?"

"No time," Arlo snapped. "You're trained, you run military grade obstacle courses for fun, and every second you sit here increases the chances of those two college kids getting killed. Stop being stubborn and go save those people, Mercer! It's what you do."

Clint looked at Jim and the big marine shrugged. "I'm built for power, PJ, not speed."

Clint muttered a frustrated curse then nodded and said, "Fine, but this was not in the job description, Arlo."

"Take it up with your union rep," Arlo said. "Lonebear?"

Jim nodded. "Exit on the driver's side, stick to cover. PJ, me and the boss will lay it down and you go on my word. Boss, you set?"

Clint looked back to Arlo just in time to see him slide a magazine into a Glock and rack the slide. "Ready," he said, looking back at Jim and then at Clint. Clint must have been staring because Arlo rolled his eyes and said, "I can't use magic for everything, Mercer. Let's go."

Clint nodded and opened the door a second behind Jim. As soon as the doors opened, the gunfire started up again but the Tahoe absorbed all of it. Clint squatted low and got near the front tire which was closest to the low stone wall. He kept his pistol holstered and got ready to sprint for the cemetery. He realized that there was plenty of distance between the Tahoe and the wall for him to catch a bullet.

Suddenly the pitch of the gunfire changed as the thunderous boom of a shotgun or some other higher powered weapon joined the fray. Clint looked back at Jim.

"Go on three!" Jim said. "We've got this!"

Clint nodded and faced the wall. Jim yelled out the count over the rapid small arms fire and the shotgun booms.

"Three!"

Clint bolted from cover. He heard a break in the gunfire as Jim and Arlo opened up on their attackers. Clint reached the wall and hurdled over it without missing a step. He mapped his position in his mind as he ran. He knew that at least one of the shooters would have an angle on him the further he got into the cemetery so he ran at a slight angle away from the gun fight, weaving through and behind headstones and magnolia trees trying to keep as much cover as he could between them. The boom of a shotgun and a sudden spray of marble chips from a headstone behind him told him he'd made the right call.

The sound of gunfire continued in sporadic bursts from the road as Clint came to a kneeling stop behind a mausoleum. He scanned the area in front of him and spotted the two men that had gone after the kids from the Honda. They were far ahead but it looked as though they were slowing. Their quarry was younger and faster so that made sense.

Then, one of them drew a pistol from a holster at the small of his back and assumed a shooter's stance. Before Clint could move, the man had squeezed off three shots.

From somewhere ahead, he heard a young woman's distant scream.

Clint gritted his teeth and sprinted for the shooter.

CHAPTER TWENTY-ONE

Maple Hill Cemetery was one hundred acres of tombstones, mature trees, and more than a few ornate mausoleums. Clint dodged and wove his way past all of these things as he ran towards the man that had been shooting at the college kids.

In the back of his mind, Clint was aware that something had come over him. It was something he hadn't felt since that last mission in South America. Maybe it was his long hours of training coming back to him or some kind of adrenaline effect, he wasn't sure, but it was almost as though he were moving on a kind of autopilot. He had an objective to complete and obstacles to overcome. Before, he had been hesitant to engage with these men because he was in the middle of one of his hometown's biggest landmarks in the bright light of day, not in some lawless, back end of nowhere danger zone. The moment he'd seen that man shoot and heard that young woman scream, though, something had clicked inside him that had narrowed his focus to a dangerous degree. The man with the gun was a threat and Clint was going to deal with him.

He cleared a smaller tombstone like an Olympic runner clearing a hurdle and dodged to the right to open up a long path between some of the more symmetrically placed headstones. Long hours of training for Tough Mudder obstacle runs had kept him fit and he was closing the distance with the shooter quickly but he knew he could only keep the pace up for another minute or so. He was in great shape but sprinting was sprinting.

The shooter had started forward again at a jog. As Clint drew closer, he could see that the man was thick in the middle and carried himself like he was middle aged. The man stopped, pulled a phone from his jacket pocket, and then looked at it. Suddenly, he spun towards Clint and raised his weapon.

Whether Clint was just fast enough to see what was coming or it was the second it took the shooter to target him that saved his life, Clint would never be able to say, but he dropped into a baseball slide that ended behind a large, six inch thick marble headstone just as three shots rang out. He heard the familiar cracks and a whining buzz that passed so close over his head that he swore it brushed his thick hair.

Two more shots rang out and smacked into the headstone as he scrambled into a crouch and pulled the Sig from its holster. He drew in a deep breath to steady his nerves and did a quick mental count; three shots at the kids then three and two more at him. From what Clint had seen of the man's weapon it was a compact model and not really large enough to have very many rounds in the mag. Odds were good that the shooter was either empty or close to it. If Clint was fast enough-

He popped up over the top of the headstone and found the shooter in a kneeling stance partially behind the cover of another headstone. Clint and the man squeezed their triggers at the same time. The shooter's shots went wide and low, smacking into the headstone and kicking up bursts of pulverized marble. Clint didn't miss.

The man's head snapped back and Clint's second two shots hit him high on the torso on low on the neck. He slumped to one side and didn't move.

Clint blinked at the sight. He'd killed before, in the line of duty, but never this close and never in such an everyday setting. It was different. This wasn't a war zone or some kind of rescue operation. He was only a couple of miles from his home for God's sake and he'd just gunned a man down. Self-defense or not, he didn't like it and it wasn't what he wanted to do. He knew that didn't matter, though. It had needed to be done and he'd done it because there was more to do and he wasn't going to help anyone if he was dead. Clint swallowed hard and pushed the thoughts to the back of his mind. He still had an objective to complete.

Clint holstered the Sig and took off running again. He could see the second man farther ahead and poured on the speed, legs aching and breath starting to rasp in his chest. He was too far away for any kind of accuracy with the pistol but if he could get the guy's attention and distract him from the chase maybe-

Clint's spotted a body on the ground and instinctively altered course towards it. It was the young man from the Honda . He was lying chest down in grass with his head turned towards Clint. His face was slack and his wide eyes stared at something no living person could see. Blood soaked the back of his tee-shirt so thoroughly that Clint couldn't tell what color it was underneath the dark stain. He knelt and checked the man's pulse at his neck but he knew it was pointless. From the position of the bullet hole in his back and the amount of blood on the ground, Clint guessed that he'd taken the round straight through his heart or aorta. The kid had probably bled out before Clint had taken down his killer.

Teeth gritted in anger, breath coming in deep, angry surges, Clint turned his attention to the other man and started after him. He didn't run full out this time but jogged until he thought he was close enough to be heard. He drew the Sig again and shouted, "Hey, asshole, hold it right there!"

Clint had his weapon up even as the man turned with his own pistol leading the way. He had known it would happen. The man had to have heard the exchange between Clint and his partner so he'd known what to expect. The pistol kicked in the man's hand as he started firing.

Clint didn't bother going for cover. Instead he dropped into a kneeling stance and started squeezing off rounds. Images of Sarah flying through the air, the hounds, the bloody scene at the Warner home, the kid bleeding into the grass, Arlo in his head; all of these flashed through his mind with each shot and he felt the anger and frustration and confusion that came with them all bleeding into his face.

He didn't even hear the other man's weapon going off. When it was done and the last shot was nothing but a fading echo among the tombstones, Clint was glaring at the other man with rage etched in every line of his face.

Clint watched as the man staggered backwards and then slumped to his knees before falling face down in the grass. He kept his eyes on the man while he reloaded the Sig but there was no movement. Clint rose, his face still tight, and looked around.

Sirens wailed in the distance, the pop of gunfire continued from the street behind him, but none of that concerned him. His eyes swept over the cemetery looking for any sign of-

He spotted her near the far edge of the cemetery. She had already reached the opposite side from where they'd come in and was near one of the exits on that side. She was peeking out from behind a big Magnolia tree at him. There was easily one or two hundred feet between them but even from that far Clint could see the fear and apprehension in her stance. She cradled a package to her chest like she was protecting it.

He holstered the Sig and raised his hands to show her they were empty. "Hey, it's okay," he shouted. "I'm not going to hurt you!"

She ran for the exit.

Clint cursed and took off after her but he was already winded and his legs fatigued. He pushed through it, though, and exited the cemetery by a small back gate the led up a rise to a single lane road with a small, empty playground on the other side. Thick trees and a high rocky face ringed the depression where the playground was situated.

The young woman with the cryptical was nowhere to be seen.

CHAPTER TWENTY-TWO

Jasmine ran.

She had run past Dead Children's Playground and into and through the woods until she'd come out between two houses on a cul de sac. Then, she'd kept running up the street. She ran from the guys with the guns and the cemetery and the sirens and Andy-

Oh, God. Andy. He was dead. That man had killed him. They hadn't even said goodbye. He was just on the ground all of a sudden and he was bleeding so fast and he wouldn't answer her and there was just so much blood. A fresh wave of tears rode in on that memory and she wiped at her eyes with her free hand. Her other held the package tight under her arm.

She still didn't understand why she had grabbed it when Andy had fallen. The whole point of tracking down Professor Warner's address was to hand it off to him like Andy was supposed to but they'd gotten there and found the place surrounded by police tape and a guy having a seizure or something on the porch. Then those other people had shown up and started shooting at the people on the porch. She'd decided pretty quick after that that she couldn't drive away fast enough.

A sudden sensation prickled through her and she stepped off the street and ducked down behind a row of shrubs. The chill October air had deprived the plants of most of their leaves but she suddenly felt safe there, though she had no idea why. She watched the intersection until she saw two white and blue police cruisers speed by with strobes flashing and sirens wailing.

Even after they'd passed she knelt there for a minute trying to figure out why she'd done that. She hadn't known they were coming. She'd heard the sirens, sure, but they seemed to be coming from everywhere right now. Besides that, she hadn't done anything, right? She hadn't broken any laws or anything. Come to think of it, when the guy that had shot the bastards who'd killed Andy had called out to her she'd wanted to just throw the box in his direction and take off but she hadn't. Why hadn't she? She didn't even know what was in the damned thing. Drugs, maybe? Money? Whatever it was it wasn't worth all this. It wasn't worth watching Andy die.

An unfamiliar anger swept through her and she felt a grimace cross her face. She knew damn well why not because that guy had to be a cop. She'd seen all the police tape around Professor Warner's place so he was in a crime scene, right? She'd seen him there, so yeah, and he'd shot those other guys down like a cop would and, if she was keeping it real, she was a black woman getting chased by a white cop and the odds of that turning out good was like playing the slots in Vegas. She seen enough YouTube videos-

Jasmine shook her head. What the hell was that? No, she didn't think like that. She knew better. She'd had police officers living in her neighborhood growing up. They were good and bad like everybody else. She should take the box to one of them. She was pretty sure Mr. Anderson worked at the headquarters over by the county jail. She could try to call him and-

The anger swelled in her again and she gritted her teeth against the sudden flood of images that scattered through her brain. Tears welled in her eyes and she gritted her teeth against an angry scream. No! The police were just fascist, racist bastards who wore smiles to lure you in. She couldn't trust them, any of them, white or black. She'd just end up dead like Andy if she did that,

She shook her head again, desperate to clear it. No, Mr. Anderson was black. Andy was white. How could she think-

Wrong. Andy had *been* white before they'd killed him for getting with a black girl. That was the way the old police were and they were all old, murdering, racist, bastards. Hell, you could look anywhere on the Internet for proof of that.

Jasmine gritted her teeth. No, that wasn't-

She couldn't trust them. They would shoot her down just like Andy. Sweet, nerdy Andy who was nothing but a pile of meat and bone and blood sprawled out in the dirt while the cops stood over him probably talking about what a great shot that was-

She clinched her eyes closed tight against the unfamiliar thoughts and the tears that came with them. No, no, no, she had no real reason to think any of that. She knew Mr. Anderson. He could help her, he would-

She saw him in her mind's eye then. Standing before her with a maniacal grin crossing his normally strong, kind face and madness dancing in his eyes while blood dripped and ran from his features like rain. Andy's blood.

Jasmine bit back a scream and knelt there in the dry limbs battling anger she hadn't known she was capable of. She tried to reason through it all. Reason, logic, evidence; these were the things that she had tried to build her life around. The images and the anger, though, it just kept coming and sweeping away her rational thoughts like sandcastles caught in the surf.

She heard it, then. It was gentle at first, kind of like a soft brush at the back of her mind. A whisper that she could hear but not understand. It grew and grew until it started to make sense though she couldn't pick out any specific words that made it so. It soothed the anger and suddenly she felt like she had a direction.

She couldn't give the box to the police, she realized, but she didn't have to keep it either. She could hide it. She could hide it someplace in the dark and the deep. Someplace in the earth where the sun didn't go and the police wouldn't follow. It belonged there, she realized, it belonged there and it wanted to go there.

Jasmine drew in a deep breath and stood up. Her tired legs trembled slightly as she did so but she scarcely noticed. She walked to the edge of the street and turned left towards downtown. She was certain that she could avoid the police long enough to get downtown if she paid attention and let the whispers guide her. There was a place there, she was sure of it, and once she got the package there everything would be okay.

Jasmine tightened her grip on the package and walked on with the whispers leading the way.

CHAPTER TWENTY-THREE

Southline Consolidated Headquarters
Bank of America Financial Center
600 Peachtree Street NW
Atlanta, Georgia
29 October, 9:32 A.M. EST

Jeffrey's phone vibrated against his desk with a whirring hum. He looked at it, back at the spreadsheets that filled the two monitors on his desk, and then back at the phone. With a frown he snatched it up and checked the caller ID. It read 'Brian Griffin' in flat, white letters.

His frown deepened. That was the name he had assigned the Huntsville team he'd sent to assist the Favored. They shouldn't be calling him. Not unless something was wrong in a big way.

He sighed and tapped the green 'accept' button. He'd hardly finished saying hello before the caller started speaking.

"High Adherent," a deep male voice said, "I'm speaking for the Master of Hounds, Favored of the Mother. My words are his." There was a nervous tremor in the man's words. Jeffrey thought he recognized the voice but couldn't attach a name to it.

"I understand," he said, keeping his tone calm. "How may I serve the Favored?"

"The Favored needs more congregants. We have lost five in an encounter with the Pickmen while pursuing our prize. You will send them immediately and accompany them personally."

"Excuse me?"

There was a nervous breath from the other end of the line and the sound of the caller switching hands. "My words are the Favored's, sir. Those are the orders."

"Why isn't he telling me this?"

"Refuses to use a phone, sir. He's got a thing about technology. He even complained about having to ride in my truck "

Jeffrey clinched his teeth and glanced at his monitors once more. "I can't just-"

"Sir," the caller said, his voice dropping to a whisper, "due respect but trust me when I say you do not want to argue this point. Not with the Favored."

Jeffrey drew in a deep breath and exhaled it slowly, forcing some of the tension in his muscles out with his breath. "What the hell happened, congregant?"

Jeffrey heard the man on the other end shuffle a little. It sounded like he might be looking over his shoulder. "We were watching the house where the Favored fought with the Pickmen," the man said, his voice still low. "The Favored thought that this package he's looking for might show up there so he wanted eyes on the place. We had five people split between two vehicles on the house when a known target showed up."

"Who?"

"Arlo Dandridge. He was there was two other Pickmen."

Jeffrey closed his eyes and bit back a curse. "Dandridge was there? You're sure it was him?"

"Yes, sir. Cell phone photo matched what we have on record. It was him, ten rings and all."

Jeffrey slowly shook his head and said, "Then what?"

"Well, one of the congregant teams decided they could carry out the standing kill order on Dandridge. Another of the Pickmen's team seemed to be having some kind of… fit, or something, and it looked like the target was distracted. So, they made a play. It went sideways and ended up in a pursuit that led to a shootout. We have three dead, one wounded, and one in police custody. The Favored wants replacements for our losses and he wants you to personally bring them. He also says to bring people who aren't- and I'm quoting here - 'damned fools and who know enough about fighting to actually do some good'."

Jeffrey shook his head and mentally repeated the strongest curse word he knew. "And Dandridge?" he asked after a moment.

"The target remains," the congregant said.

"Of course he does," Jeffrey muttered.

"So, you're coming?"

"Of course I'm coming," Jeffrey said, his voice a whip. "A Favored has commanded it. What else am I supposed to do?"

"Sorry, sir. I just… I've never met one of them before. I wasn't sure they were real."

"They are declared by The Mother's Holy Writ, congregant. Do you doubt her?"

"No, no, nothing like that, sir. It's just… I know The Mother's power is true but there are so many stories about the Favored. You can't help but wonder and then to have one giving you orders is kind of… unreal. I didn't doubt The Mother or The Writ but so much of what I've heard is just people telling stories. I wasn't sure what to expect."

Jeffrey sighed. "Honestly, congregant, neither was I until I met him. What did you call him? The Master of Hounds?"

"Yes, sir. He says that people who speak Swahili have a name for him and that's what it translates to. It's like their bogeyman or something. He seems to like that a lot."

"I'm sure he does. Tell him to expect me within the next two to three hours. I'll call this number when I land to find out where to meet you."

"Yes, High Adherent. Thank you, sir."

Jeffrey hung up the phone without responding.

Twenty years. Twenty years he had been a member of the congregation and not once had he opened the church up to Pickman scrutiny. Now, in the space of twenty-four hours, this Favored had brought them toe to toe with one of the highest ranking members of the organization and arguably the most powerful magus in North America. Jeffrey had successfully avoided Dandridge's attention for more than the last decade despite the fact that they lived in the same damned city. Now, though, that was all in jeopardy.

He wasn't concerned about the congregate that was in custody talking. Anyone sent into the field on the church's behalf agreed to certain precautionary bindings that made it impossible for them to betray the Congregation. No, it was more the Favored's insistence that Jeffrey join the field team that concerned him. He wasn't a celebrity or anything like that but he attended enough high profile social events that he'd had his picture in the media more than a few times. Though he had never met Dandridge directly- the young man was a notorious social recluse -he was aware that they knew many of the same people. If Dandridge spotted him in Huntsville, it wouldn't take much effort to put his name to his face. If that happened and Dandridge decided to start digging into his background then things could get complicated quickly.

Jeffry had been very careful over the years to keep his public records as clean as any man in his position could but Dandridge was a powerful magus. With the magics at his disposal all it would take is a hint of a connection to anything eldritch and he'd come looking for Jeffrey. If that happened it was just a matter of the right spell before Jeffrey's secret was out in the open and his life was torn apart by the powers that be.

He gritted his teeth at the thought. Twenty years potentially down the toilet because of one botched operation. A part of him wondered what would happen if he refused to go but he already knew. He'd done his homework on Jubal Mott and it was all scary. He didn't want to think about what could happen to him and his family if he disobeyed.

Still, though, there was something off about this situation and the so-called Master of Hounds. There was something in the Favored's demeanor that nagged at him but he couldn't really put his finger on it. Not that it mattered, really. The Mother had instructed him to give Mott all the aid he required and disobeying her was never an option.

With a resigned sigh, Jeffrey opened his phone's calling app and started making arrangements.

CHAPTER TWENTY-FOUR

Maple Hill Cemetery
202 Maple Hill Street SE
Huntsville, Alabama
October 29, 8:39 A.M. CST

Of all the crazy things that Clint had seen in the last day or so, he found that fact that he wasn't arrested and on his way to jail to be the most amazing.

After he'd lost sight of the young woman in the cemetery, Clint had headed back for the Tahoe to check on the rest of his team. He'd made it about halfway there before a dozen Huntsville PD officers had come at him with weapons drawn, shouting for him to get on the ground. Since he wasn't a complete idiot, he'd done as he was told. By the time Jim had come jogging up to them with his credentials out for everyone to see, Clint had been handcuffed, relieved of his Sig, and was on his way to the back seat of a police cruiser.

That hadn't lasted long, though. Jim had pulled the senior officer aside and talked with him for a couple of minutes before the cop had ordered one of the other officers to uncuff Clint and give him his weapon back. The senior officer had taken a brief statement from Clint and asked him to stick around while they sorted things out. Clint had agreed and then headed for the Tahoe after a gesture from Jim.

He'd been sitting in silence, staring out the passenger side window at the small army of police officers that had responded to the shooting for nearly ten minutes before Rani spoke.

"Are you all right?" she asked.

Clint didn't look at her or respond for a few seconds. She had cranked the Tahoe, which didn't seem all that worse for the wear after the shootout, and the heater hissed a faint, steady chorus to fill the silence.

Finally, he said. "I assume you're not asking me if I'm injured."

She smiled and gave him a shrug. "I watched you as you walked over. I think I'd have noticed if you'd gotten shot."

Clint nodded but still kept watching the cops go about their work. Yellow tape was strung everywhere. It flapped and rippled in the breeze. The clear, bright day didn't seem to fit the scene. Clint thought things like this should happen under a cloudy sky.

"At this point in my life," he said, "I've shot enough people to realize that I don't like doing it. In the service, I was always far enough away that they were just targets. Just shapes. I couldn't see their eyes or their expressions. This was different."

"Do you regret it?"

Clint drew in a breath and met her eyes. "Regret it? No. I have no doubt those two would have killed me without blinking. I defended myself and that woman who was running away. I just hate the fact that I had to. I also hate that I am still not entirely sure why I had to. Doctor, I can't get my head around all of this. It's just coming at me too fast."

She nodded. "Well, first of all, after what we just went through I think it would be all right if you called me 'Rani'."

"Okay, then. Call me Clint."

"I realize this seems like an impossible thing to take in, Clint, but I also want to point out that you are handling it better than anyone I've ever seen. Your level of calm is impressive, to say the least."

Clint thought about that and then shrugged. "I don't know what to tell you. I feel like I should be freaking out six ways to Sunday but I'm not. You guys keep coming at me with things that I'm sure are impossible but then I see them with my own eyes and you'd think I'd flip out or something but I don't and that's weird because even I think I should."

Rani smiled. "Someone once wrote that the eyes see only what the mind is prepared to comprehend. That's a truth. It's one of the reasons that magic stays off the public radar."

"I get that," Clint said. "Arlo filled me in on the whole 'mental circuit breaker' thing but how is anyone ever prepared for all of this? Ever since the other night, it's like my built in reactions are muffled or something."

"Make sure you mention that to Arlo. He's determined to find out how you survived that attack."

"Yeah, about Arlo. I'm getting the distinct impression this job is bullshit. He didn't say anything to me about chasing gun toting bad guys. And now this-" he gestured out the windshield. "Why don't you fill me in on what he's up to."

Rani shook her head thoughtfully. "Arlo can be very single minded. Once he's got his mental hooks into something, there isn't a whole lot he won't do to satisfy his need for understanding. What did he tell you?"

Clint told her about his understanding with Arlo and the things he had told him at the Birmingham hospital. When he was done, she was shaking her head like a weary parent.

"Like most things with him, that's mostly true but partially not. Not in the sense that he lied to you but, rather, committed a lie of omission. The work that our field teams do is very dangerous on multiple levels."

"Yeah, those two guys I just dropped agree with that."

Rani opened her mouth the speak but the two back doors opened and Jim and Arlo got in. She quietly said, "Later", and twisted in the driver's seat to face them.

Before she could say anything, Arlo passed his cell phone to Jim and said, "They didn't have IDs but I got prints off the three here and the first one that Mercer dealt with. Run them by Dante and see what he finds. Mercer, what happened? Why didn't you retrieve the cryptical?"

Clint clenched his jaw for a second to give his sudden irritation a chance to level out. " I think it's pretty obvious, Arlo," he said with as even a tone as he could manage. "I chased the two kids with the box but one of them got shot and the other one had too much of head start so I lost her. Oh, and I killed a couple of guys who were shooting at me. I'm fine, by the way. Thanks for asking."

"Of course you're fine. Where's the cryptical?"

Clint shrugged. "I don't know. Did you miss the part where I said she outran me?"

Arlo glared at Clint, his only movement a slight twitch beneath his left eye. "Lonebear?" he said, switching his gaze to Jim.

Jim was holding Arlo's phone and watching the screen intently. "Loading now, boss," he said. "Just another second or two… there, all four came back. Let's see here… all have Georgia addresses, some criminal stuff,-"

"Tell me what I care about, Lonebear."

"Two known and one suspected congregants, boss. Looks like they know about the book."

"What are congregants?" Clint said.

"The Congregation of the Black Cosmonogy," Rani said. "They're an eldritch cult. Very secretive and very aggressive. We've crossed paths with them before. If they're here for the cryptical then things just got more complicated. We need to secure that thing immediately."

"Obviously," Arlo muttered, though without any particular feeling to it. He seemed to look past Jim as his eyes glazed over into a vacant stare. For just a couple of seconds, Clint thought he was having some kind of neurological event. Before he could say anything, Arlo's eyes refocused and he said, "That will have to wait. Mercer, where did you lose sight of the female?"

Clint looked at Rani. She gave him a reassuring nod.

"Where, Mercer?" Arlo said, the impatience creeping back into his voice.

"Dead Kid's," Clint said.

"Excuse me?"

"Oh, sorry," Clint said. "It's a hangout from my high school days. It's on the other side of the cemetery. It's-"

"Show us," Arlo said. "Rani, drive."

CHAPTER TWENTY-FIVE

"The official name is Drost Park but all us locals call it Dead Children's Playground," Clint said, gesturing to the small array of picnic tables and playground equipment. "We called it Dead Kid's Playground or just Dead Kid's when I was in school."

They were standing at the edge of a small depression in the landscape looking down at a long, steel swing set and a large play set complete with a slide and short, plastic climbing wall. There was a stone bluff surrounding the depression and a cleared play area that was currently filled with winter browned grass. Sparsely leafed trees, oaks and hickory for the most part, ringed the play area and grew right up to the bluff's edge. A covered pavilion with a few well used picnic tables stood to the right with gray, cracked concrete steps leading down to the playground.

"This is cemetery land?" Rani asked.

Clint nodded and gestured to the gate that the woman had run through. It and the garden of headstones beyond were clearly visible through the trees. "I understand they tried to close it a decade or so ago but there were a lot of protests from the public. It's kind of an unofficial public landmark. The story goes that back in the forties there were a bunch of child abductions. They never caught the guy who was responsible but eventually found all his victim's bodies right here. Hence, the name."

"That's a creepy landmark, PJ," Jim said.

Clint shrugged. "Yeah. But it's ours. We've got others, too. Kildare Mansion, the cave under the courthouse, Eggbeater Jesus…"

"And this is where you last saw the woman with the cryptical?" Arlo asked in a terse voice.

"She ran through that gate but I didn't see which way she went after that."

Jim grunted. "Just at a glance I can spot five routes out of here that would be hidden from the cemetery view. Don't beat yourself up, PJ."

"Wasn't planning on it," Clint said with a smile.

"You shouldn't be so flippant, Mercer," Arlo said. "You had a chance to end this and you let it slip away."

"I didn't *let* anything happen, Arlo," Clint said taking an unconscious step towards the man. "She was fast and I was too far away. Period. Besides that, I didn't sign on with you to chase people through graveyards. I'm an RN, not a cop."

Arlo's eye was twitching again. "You should have stopped her. You should have gotten it. You too ignorant to understand what's at stake. You shouldn't have failed." The twitch spread to Arlo's cheek and his voice started rising with each word.

"I did the best I could," Clint said, his own temper making his words hard.

"It wasn't enough. You didn't try hard enough," Arlo said.

"I just killed two people, Arlo!"

"And you should have killed her, too!" Arlo screamed. "You should have shot her and taken the book! You should have-"

"Arlo!" Rani snapped in a voice like a gunshot. "Come with me right now!"

Arlo spun on her. His head was softly jerking to one side as the twitching spread. His eyes were wild. The muscles in his jaw clenched and unclenched as his breath rasped through gritted teeth.

"Now, Arlo," Rani said in a more controlled tone. "Assess yourself."

Arlo stared at Rani as Clint watched. After a moment, the magus nodded and said, "Yes. You're right. I need an injection."

Rani gently took him by his arm and led him to the back of the Tahoe.

Jim stepped over to Clint and said, "Let's take a little walk and give the doc some room to work, PJ."

"What the hell is this, Jim? Is he serious?"

The two men stepped away from the Tahoe and towards the picnic pavilion. "Look," Jim said, "the boss is always a little too blunt but he only gets like this when things are really serious. It's like the stress makes him burn through his meds faster or something. Doc says that's not it, exactly, but that's how it looks from this side. Normally, he wouldn't have gone off on you like that."

"He's sick. I get it," Clint said, "but what I don't get is how he's running around out here armed and doing this kind of work if he's that unstable."

"Because we need him and most of the time he's fine. I know you're still getting used to all of this but here's a solid fact for you; he's the very best there is at what he does. There's maybe ten, twenty other people on the *planet* that can even attempt the things that he can do. He's like the Usain Bolt of magic. I guess living with all that crazy is just the price he pays for it."

Clint looked over at the Tahoe. Rani had opened the rear hatch and was pulling some supplies from the small, red cooler that Clint had seen earlier. Arlo was rolling up one sleeve with short, angry motions. "Is that why he's got a doctor with him all the time?"

"The doc? No. Neither of us are usually here. Deana looked after the boss in the field. Part of her job was to keep him leveled and give him meds when he needed them. The doc trained her how to handle all of it and when to call her if things got weird. We're only here because we lost Deana."

Clint looked back to Jim. "Did he really expect me to shoot that woman to get this book?"

He expected the big marine to say of course not, that was just the mental issues talking, that killing an innocent woman to get what they wanted was not what they did. Instead, he averted his eyes from Clint's and said, "Maybe. I know it's hard to understand, PJ, but some of what we do falls well within the 'by any means necessary' category."

"It's a *book*."

"I told you before; it's never just a book. Hell, for all we know that thing's as dangerous as a nuke with a tricky timer but it's got the boss worried and that's more than enough to get my full attention."

Clint shook his head and looked away. The trees around the park moved with the October breeze, cracking and rustling like they were whispering to one another. Clint listened for a few seconds but if there were any answers in those whispers, he didn't understand them.

"The boss said you saw it," Jim said. "Like, really saw it. The way he can sometimes."

"I'm not sure what I saw, man. I'm not sure about any of this. It feels like I've been hallucinating for the last two days."

Jim shook his head. "That never goes away completely but you're not on any kind of bad trip.

You saw what you saw and I know you must've seen something because I know what I saw."

Clint looked back at him. "What do you mean?"

Jim kept his eyes on the playground. Clint noticed he was scanning the area without actually turning his head like someone who had stood more than his fair share of sentry watches.

"Your eyes," Jim said, finally. "They changed. Back at the house when the boss was doing his spell."

"Changed how?"

"You know those lights they use in nightclubs? The ones that make white stuff glow really bright?"

Clint nodded. "Sure. Blacklights."

"Yeah, like that. Glowing and everything. No offense, PJ, but it was freaky as hell."

Clint thought back. He replayed the series of events in his mind and then said, "Wait a minute; you drew on me. I was a little out of it but now I remember. You pulled your weapon on me when things started getting all fuzzy."

Jim nodded. "Yeah. Your eyes turned all bizarre and… well, let's just say I've learned to approach 'bizarre' with a healthy measure of caution."

Clint started to say something about potentially getting shot but another memory flashed through his mind and stopped him. His brow furrowed and he said, "My eyes. They were that purple color? Like a blacklight?"

Jim nodded.

Clint closed his eyes against the memory of Jubal Mott threatening him in the hospital parking garage.

"What?" Jim said.

"That's what his eyes looked like," Clint said.

"Who's?"

"Mott. That night at the hospital. I remember thinking that exact thing about him, that he had blacklight eyes."

Jim looked at Clint with a concerned frown on his face.

"What the hell did he do to me?" Clint said. His voice sounded smaller than he'd wanted it to.

"It wasn't just him," Arlo said, walking over to join them as he rolled his sleeve down again. Clint caught a quick glimpse of multiple tattoos between his wrist and elbow.

"What do you mean, boss?" Jim asked.

"Exactly what I said. I don't think that the warlock is solely to blame for Mercer's situation."

Clint faced Arlo. He could have asked the question but he was reasonably sure he already knew the answer.

Arlo must have seen that in his expression. He nodded and said, "What's happened to you is as much my fault as Jubal Mott's."

CHAPTER TWENTY-SIX

Clint didn't reply immediately. He studied Arlo's face, assessing it for any twitches or other signs of potential mania. The man looked tired but otherwise in control.

"You look better," Clint said. "Must be one hell of a cocktail the doctor gave you."

"It is fast acting but I'm still feeling the effects of my episode. I should not have lost my composure like that. I'll do my best to make sure it doesn't happen again."

Clint nodded. "I'm going to need an explanation right about now."

Arlo drew in a deep breath, nodding slightly. Clint could tell he was trying to collect his thoughts so he waited in silence for the magus to begin talking.

"From the available evidence," Arlo said, "I think that what you've been experiencing is an exceedingly rare form of supranormal visual acuity.

A more common vernacular for it is 'Truesight'. Do you follow?"

"Not even a little," Clint said.

Arlo nodded and took another breath. "Right. So, you remember when I told you that you should have died the other night?"

"It rings a bell, yeah."

"Of course. Well, I think you actually did die but only for an instant."

Clint blinked a couple of times. "Okay," he said, intentionally keeping his tone flat.

Arlo shook his head. "All right, Mercer. I wish we had the time for me to explain the specific methodologies and differences of Eldritch and Arcane Magic traditions but we don't. So, I'm going to summarize and you just need you to trust me on a few things."

"I'm pretty sure we're already on that ride, Arlo," Clint said.

"Right you are but bear with me, Mercer, because to understand what's happened to you then you're going to need to understand what I'm about to explain."

Clint nodded.

"Magic, the kind of Magic I use, comes from the world around us. Everything in existence creates it from gravity to the changing weather to the neurological energy firing through every living creature's brain and nervous system. All of it flows and weaves and radiates into a kind of field that covers the planet like a massive aura. A rare, few people, like me, can feel this aura and, with proper study and training, learn to manipulate it. That's what we call Arcane Magic. Can you accept that?"

Clint shrugged. "Sure."

"Good because there are other places, countless other worlds or dimensions or planes, the labels don't really matter. What does matter is that those places are not *here* and the things that live there are not *us*. Because of that, magic drawn from those places and those entities are different and more corrupting for human beings than the magic that we draw on from our own world. We call those corrupting magics Eldritch Magic."

"Like Mott," Clint said. "You said warlocks had something inside them from one of these other places that let them do what they do."

Arlo pointed a finger at Clint and grinned. "Just so. Very good, Mercer. Now, bearing all that in mind, I want you to cast your memory back to the parking garage. I was waking up, Mott was about to attack you with a working that I recognized as lethal, and I reached out to protect you with a working of my own. Do you remember?"

Searing pain, darkness, more fear than he'd ever known in his life to that point; yeah, Clint remembered that.

"That's when I think it happened," Arlo said. "I think that the warlock's eldritch attack was a transauric discorporative working from one of the more obscure youggothian traditions intended-" Arlo stopped suddenly holding up his hand with the palm out as though cutting himself off. "That's too much," he muttered, drawing in a deep breath. "There's no reason they would know what that means." He closed his eyes and opened them again a second later as though nothing had happened.

"I think that the spell that he used on you was intended to shred your energy- your soul, if that term suits you -and scatter it across the dimensions from which the warlock draws his power. I interrupted, though, with a working of my own that was drawn wholly from *this* world. That created an anchor that kept you from being discorporated. It saved you, yes, but for one fraction of a second, your energy was dispersed across transdimensional space. You were, quite literally, occupying multiple planes of existence simultaneously. There's no way to tell how many- a few, a million, we can't know - but for whatever number it was, in that brief instant, you could see everything in those realms. When the moment was over, the anchor I had inadvertently created snapped you back to your body in this reality. My working was intended to shield you completely from the attack but I'd only infused enough of it into you to protect your flesh which is why the experience wasn't fatal in the biological sense. Are you following me so far?"

"I think so, yeah."

"All right. Your body was injured but functional for the most part. Your energy, though, your mind, had just been through something extraordinary, a one of a kind event to the best of my knowledge. I think that it came back to your body changed. Even if you can't consciously recall it, your mind witnessed who knows what in the time that it was stretched through the multiverse. I think that's why you can see the things you can, now. From what I saw of your memory, Mercer, you can see everything. Weaves of Magic, auras, the very Aether itself; one mental twist- the flip of a switch, if you will -and you can see things that I have to work very hard to even catch a glimpse of. That's what's happened to you. That's what you can do."

Clint instinctively opened his mouth to call bullshit on the entire story but stopped before he'd made a sound. Jim had been right. It was all real and Clint knew damn well what he'd seen even if he didn't understand any of it. Put that with everything else that had happened and he realized he really didn't have any choice but to accept Arlo's explanation. It seemed to fit the facts and was, quite frankly, all he had to work with. He looked at Arlo and said, "All right. Can you fix it?"

"Fix what?"

"My eyes or mind or energy or whatever. Can you correct whatever happened to me?"

Arlo's brow furrowed in confusion. "Why would I?"

"Why? Because this is screwing up my life, Arlo. I didn't ask for any of this and, frankly, probably wouldn't have wanted to know about any of this had I been given the choice. I liked my life the way it was."

"I don't think you understand what this means, Mercer. You can see the truth of things, the stains on a person's aura, the-"

"And then what, Arlo? I don't understand any of what I saw. All I know is that things looked weird, felt wrong, and, quite frankly, scared the shit out of me. What good is seeing the 'truth of things' if I don't understand any of it? Not to mention the fact that if I tell anyone they'd think I'd lost my mind. Sometimes the truth is overrated, Arlo. Especially when there's nothing you can do to fix it."

"That is a very naive point of view, Mercer."

"Is it? Aren't you the guy who spends his life hiding the truth about magic and monsters from the world because it would be too dangerous for the truth to come out? Isn't that what all of you do? You don't get to do that and then call me out for not wanting to see that side of things. So, stop trying to sell me on what a grand and glorious gift this is and tell me whether or not you can fix it."

They stood like that for what felt like minutes, staring each other down. Clint could feel the angry expression on his face. Arlo was staring at him like he was something between an idiot and a child or maybe some combination of the two. That smug gaze just made Clint angrier.

Finally, Arlo said, "I don't know. Most of what I've told you has been my theory. As I said, it was a one of a kind event."

Clint nodded. "Okay, fine, but you turned it off in my head, right? Flipped the mental circuit breakers and all that?"

Arlo shook his head. "That won't last. It was just a temporary fix so we could deal with the congregants. Besides, we need your sight if we're going to find the cryptical."

"What do you mean?"

"You saw its aura in the car. That much power in one vessel is going to leave an eldritch stain on the world. You should be able to see it and follow it."

"Oh, hell no," Clint said, shaking his head.

"You saw the cryptical, Mercer," Arlo said, his voice near pleading. "You *saw* it. The power in that vessel, the potential for harm, is enormous. We have to get it before Mott or The Congregation can. You've seen what lengths they'll go to. Do you think that girl is safe? Do you think they'll just say please and thank you and be on their way when they get the cryptical? Forget about the book, Mercer. Think about that young woman. Save her."

Clint studied the smaller man for a minute and then let out a deep breath. "Don't think I didn't see what you did there."

"So long as it worked."

"She couldn't have gotten far. Surely the cops will find her."

"They might've if I'd told them about her."

"What?"

"She has the cryptical, Mercer. Trust me when I tell you that the fewer people that interact with it, the better. Remember what you saw. Power like that can get into a person's mind and the last thing we need is for it to influence a bunch of armed police."

Clint considered it. He really had no desire to look at the world through blacklight eyes again but Arlo had a point. The men in the cemetery had killed that kid without any hesitation. There was no reason to think that the young woman would be any safer. If what he was saying about this book was also true… well, that clinched it for him.

"Fine. What do I need to do?"

CHAPTER TWENTY-SEVEN

Arlo had told Clint that he needed a few minutes to make some preparations before they did whatever it was that was needed to trigger Clint's Truesight again. He'd found a relatively clean picnic table in the pavilion and sat down on it, resting his feet on the bench portion while he waited. That few minutes had turned into a lot more than a few, some of which Clint spent watching Arlo argue in whispered tones with Rani while simultaneously tapping at the laptop from the Tahoe. It occurred to Clint that they did that a lot, which made him curious about the specific nature of their relationship. Rani was easily in her late forties while Arlo couldn't be more than thirty at the very outside. He doubted that there was a romantic element to it but he'd seen older doctors and younger nurses in relationships more times than he could count. Still, though, Rani hadn't struck him as the type to sleep with a patient.

He dropped his head and closed his eyes. He knew it was none of his business just like he knew that he was using it as an excuse not to think about what he was about to do. The idea of seeing the world in those washed out tones and blurred edges again made him a little nauseous. He hadn't liked admitting that it had scared him but he figured he needed to be straight about things, male ego be damned.

He raised his head again and looked around the playground. It had changed a lot since he'd been one of the teenagers that invariably ended up hanging around the place after hours but enough of the bones were there that his memories had no problem bubbling to the surface. A group of kids hanging out in the dark, trying to scare each other without laughing about it, and more often than not trying to get next to whatever crush they happened to have that week. Things like that had seemed so important back then. He smiled at the thought of simpler times.

Footsteps crunched through the brown grass behind him. He turned on the table to face them as his three companions came over to join him. Arlo wore his usual stern, focused expression while Rani was more concerned but trying to smile through it, the wrinkles around her brown eyes crinkling up just enough to stand out. Jim glanced at him but only for a second as he kept his eyes moving over the area.

Arlo reached him and held out a pair of dark sunglasses. Clint took them, shrugged, and said, "These aren't mine."

"They are now," Arlo said. "Camouflage. As Lonebear said, your eyes manifest a noticeable energy while your Truesight is active. Those might help to cut down on the glow and save us from some awkward encounters with the public."

"How'd you know he told me that?" Clint said. "You were getting your shot."

"I'm really good at reading lips. Learned to do that when I was twelve."

Clint laughed a little and shook his head. "Of course you did. So, what's the plan?"

"I've been doing some Truesight research," Arlo said. "Most of what I found supports my theory that this is what has actually happened to you but there is very little in the way of firsthand accounts of the phenomena. Still, I found references in both the Zend Avesta and the Third Text of Pahlavi referencing a Zoroastrian monk from the fifth century B.C. who practiced a kind of messianic-"

Clint held up a hand to stop him. "Bottom line it for me, Arlo."

Arlo seemed to think it over for a moment and then said, "I found some stories about a really old monk who had the Truesight and controlled it with a particular kind of meditation and practiced focus. I'm going to try and teach that technique to you."

"Do we have time for that?"

"We do if we do it psychically."

Clint groaned. "This shit again? Believe it or not, Arlo, I don't like people poking around in my head. Every time you do it I feel like you should've bought me dinner first."

Clint heard Jim try and suppress a chuckle.

Arlo ignored the big man and nodded. "I understand that. If it's any consolation, it's an exhaustive process for me, as well, but we are bordering on desperate times here, Mercer. There will be no poking around in your memories this time. Frankly, I don't have the energy. I'm going to undo what I did before and then we'll try some exercises to help you control when the sight comes over you. That way, we won't have to worry about a repeat of the events at the Warner house."

Clint drew in a breath and met Arlo's eyes. He knew what he needed to do but really didn't want to do it.

Arlo rolled his eyes impatiently and said, "Oh, for pity's sake, Mercer. Get through this and I'll buy you dinner. I'll buy us all dinner. I'll buy you all a damned restaurant, if that's what it takes but can you please just close your eyes so we can get on with it?"

"Fine," Clint snapped, shutting his eyes. "Just give me a little-"

Arlo grabbed Clint's head.

White. Silent.

"Arlo?" Clint thought into the void.

"I'm here, Mercer."

"God, this is weird."

"I suppose it must be for you but I've been doing this for most of my life. Now, be quiet. I'm working."

Clint stayed quiet. He wasn't sure how long it really was but it felt like hours before he said, "How's it going?"

"Slowly, I'm sorry to say. There's another influence here that I'm having to work around. I can't tell if it's from the warlock or if it's something else. Maybe a side effect of your spiritual transcorporation. I can't be sure. Now, be quiet. This is tiring and the amphetamine Rani gave me will only last so long."

"The what? Are you telling me you're amped up right now?"

"Oh, that's right. You're a nurse. I keep forgetting. Relax, it's not a regular part of my drug regimen. Rani hates doing it but in cases like this, I sometimes need something mixed into my normal injection to offset the fatigue that comes with working mymMagic. You know, like I'm doing right now? So, be quiet."

"She mixed psychotropics with amphetamines in the same dose? I'm pretty sure that's really dangerous, Arlo."

"Were I an average person, it would be, but I am not average, Mercer. I am magus. My brain chemistry is somewhat different than other people's. Rani knows what she's doing. Now, please, shut up."

Clint didn't want to shut up but he did. Questions bounced around his consciousness like out of control ping-pong balls. He ignored them.

Finally, Arlo said, "Okay, I think we're ready to try this."

"I don't feel any different," Clint said.

"That's because I'm very good at what I do, Mercer. All right, I need you to picture an eye."

"A what?"

"An eye. Realistic, artistic, stylized, simple, complex; I don't care. Whatever is most comfortable for you. I just need you to picture it in your mind and really concentrate on it. Focus is key here. Oh, and it needs to be closed. That's important, too."

"Closed eye. Got it. Just one? They usually come in pairs."

"You must have gotten a perfect grade in your anatomy class. One is all we need, Mercer."

"I guess those injections bring out your inner smartass, too. Just one eye. Got it. So, what? I just imagine it? That seems redundant considering we're already in my imagination."

"Actually, we're not. I avoid that part of other's minds. Some people have… well, let's just say that things can get disturbing in there sometimes. Just picture the eye however you normally would. Trust me and just concentrate."

"Okay. Here goes."

It was harder than Clint thought it would be. Imagining an eye wasn't that hard. He'd seen thousands of them in his life both real and depicted in different visual mediums from textbooks to cartoons. Picking one, though, just focusing on one, that was the hard part. Every element of one seemed to remind him of another which would break his concentration and blur them together into a distended mess.

The void responded to that. It swirled and twisted in smears of broken color as he tried to tighten down his focus.

"Use your feelings, Mercer," Arlo said. "Try to think of a time when you were happy and safe. Find those emotions without losing your concentration on the eye."

"Whatever you say, Obi Wan."

"Who?"

"Seriously? Star Wars?"

"Never mind. Just do as I say, Mercer. We don't have an eternity to get this done."

Clint didn't reply. He'd never thought of emotions as something he could just call up at a whim. They came and he'd either ignore them or react to them. Thinking of things didn't really trigger them like Arlo seemed to think. Clint wasn't sure how he could-

A memory rose up in his mind, then, something that had he been thinking about only minutes or moments before; simpler times.

The mass of smears and breaks swirled into a cohesive whole. The image of a closed eye appeared. Mascara painted the lashes in long, dark lines. The lid was closed but eye shadow the color of a midnight sky highlighted the eye's pointed oval shape. The whole image was framed by a pattern of hardened white that radiated outward in erratic lines that reminded Clint of shattered safety glass.

"Not bad," Arlo said. "Who is she?"

"Wendy," Clint said. "A girl I knew in high school."

"Good enough. Hold on to that image. Burn it into your memory until it's part of you. In the simplest of terms, Mercer, you're constructing the inner eye that will be the mental mechanism by which you will open and close your Truesight. Recalling this mechanism and the feelings of calm that are associated with it will be the…switch, for lack of a better term. When you open this eye, so too will you open your sight. Close it to the opposite effect. Do you understand?"

"I think so."

"Good. When I tell you, I want you to will this inner eye open but there's one more thing before that. Once we return our perceptions to the physical realm your sight will be active. Try not to look at the cemetery unless you absolutely have to."

"Why not?"

"Well, like I've told you before, most everything you've heard of is real, just not how you've been taught to think of it."

Clint considered that for a second. "Arlo, are you telling me that I can see ghosts?"

"Mercer, I've already told you that you can see everything. That includes the lingering energy fields of those who died while in extreme distress. I'm concerned you might not be ready for that."

"So, ghosts, then?"

"More or less, yes."

"Right. Okay. You realize that's kind of like telling someone on a ledge not to look down, right?"

"Heed the warning, Mercer."

"Copy that. Ready when you are."

"Good man. We'll go on three…two…one…open."

The eye snapped open.

Clint's eyes snapped open.

There was no pain this time but a wave of dizziness washed over him as the indistinct shapes and colors flooded into his eyes. Strong hands steadied him and he heard Jim say, "Easy, PJ. I got you, brother." He felt the sunglasses in his hand and squeezed them, just to make sure they were real and solid. They felt just like they should even though they seemed transparent to his eyes.

"Mercer, listen to me," Arlo said. "Take it slowly. Close your eyes until you're steady and then open them again until your mind has time to adjust to the new stimuli."

Clint closed his eyes and nodded, waiting for the dizziness to pass. He went through this twice more before he opened his eyes and told Jim he could let go.

The world was as it had been before but more clear this time. Everything was still in the same silver gray wash that he'd seen before but the colors were brighter, the edges more defined. He looked at

Jim and saw the white glow surrounding him that he had seen before but the gray lines that shot through it were darker now, more slate than cigarette ash.

Jim smiled and a ripple of blue radiated out through the glow. "PJ," he said, "you look freaky as hell right now but in the coolest way possible."

"You're… glowing," Clint said.

"You're seeing his aura," Arlo said. "Lonebear, get back here with us. Mercer, don't look at any of us just yet. Try to keep the stimulus to a minimum. Don't even look at the sky. Remember to keep the cemetery behind you and we'll do the same. Look at the playground and the trees around it. Look for anything that looks like what you saw around the car that was carrying the cryptical."

Clint looked around. The edges of the playground equipment blurred into tracers that reformed as he moved his head. He blinked a few times to clear his vision and the lines grew more solid. He looked towards the far right tree line and spotted what he was looking for. It was an inky stain on the ground that wisped trailers into the air around it. It wasn't large, but it was distinct and led further into the trees.

For an instant, he hesitated. He could lie. He could say he didn't see anything then close this third eye and never open it again. He could say goodbye to all of this and go back to his life and his routine. The whole idea of taking out the warlock-the thing, he realized now -that had killed Sarah was misguided at best. It was a decision made out of grief and anger. Clint knew that he was out of his depth and that was someplace he never liked being. All he had to do was tell one, little lie and then walk away.

He could have done all of that. Instead, Clint slid the glasses onto his face and said, "This way. She went through the trees."

CHAPTER TWENTY-EIGHT

Big Spring International Park
200 Church Street SW
Huntsville, Alabama
October 29, 10:48 A.M. CST

The whispers pushed Jasmine forward. They were louder now, loud enough that she could tell that it was just one whisper repeating over itself and giving the illusion of multiple voices. She couldn't understand the words. They were in a language that sounded deep and thick with too many consonants and a rhythm that brought to mind slow, fat bubbles breaking the surface of steaming tar.

The lack of understanding didn't slow her down, though, as she crossed the street on the west side of the downtown square. A car horn blared but she barely noticed it. Deep below the whispers, there was some tiny voice screaming at her that this wasn't right, wasn't sane, but that voice was just background static. She knew she had to get to the park, the spring, and into the deep and the dark.

Big Spring International Park sat in a natural depression across the street from the Madison County Courthouse which loomed over the downtown square like a boxy monolith that was probably stylish fifty years earlier. The entrance to the park from the courthouse side was a series of four sets of steps leading down to a small public pavilion and then finally to the park itself. The spring for which the park was named was surrounded by walkways of concrete and cobblestone that all led to the spring. A half circle of concrete steps enclosed the pool and led down to the water's edge. A tall stone bluff rose forty or fifty feet into the air on the flat side of the semi-circle.

Jasmine stumbled a little as she stepped from the second set of steps and onto the pavilion. People looked up at her from the Irish themed bar and grill that had set up shop there. She didn't notice. She focused on the next set of steps and headed for them, her mind a cloud of conflicting urges and unnatural voices.

"Miss? Hold up, please. Police."

Jasmine heard the voice, recognized the authoritative female tone, she didn't have time to stop. Besides, they must have been talking to someone else. She had to get to the spring, nothing else mattered. Surely they realized that.

"Miss? Police. Stop right there."

She heard it again and wished that whomever they were talking to would just stop already.

All of a sudden, there was someone in front of her. Jasmine stopped short, looking up and focusing on the dark uniformed police officer that was standing there. The woman was just shy of middle aged, a little heavy set, and had her blonde hair pulled back away from her face. She was holding her left hand up for Jasmine to stop with her right side angled away from her.

"Miss?" she said, studying Jasmine's face. "Did you not hear me? I told you to stop. Are you feeling okay?"

Jasmine stared at her and then shook her head. "No… I mean… I'm fine. I thought you were talking to someone else."

The officer nodded. "Okay. Well, you crossed the street a long way from the crosswalk back there and you didn't look too steady on your feet. You sure you're feeling all right?"

Jasmine nodded. "Yeah, I'm fine. I just need to go. I gotta go."

The officer glanced behind Jasmine and then back to her face. Jasmine wondered what she was looking at.

"I hear you," the officer said, "but just take a minute, okay? You don't look too good."

The whispers rallied in Jasmine's head. Anger burned through her like a fuse flaring to life. Fascist, racist, bastards were just everywhere, just waiting for a chance to bleed her like they had Andy. Why wouldn't they leave her alone?

"Look, I've got to go, okay?" Jasmine said. Her voice sounded small, she thought. "I just need to get to the dark and then everything will be fine. Just leave me alone."

"The dark? What do you mean? There's a comic book shop called The Deep. Is that what you mean?"

"Just leave me alone!" Jasmine didn't think she shouted but from the look on the officer's face she realized she might have.

"You need to settle down. I'm just a little concerned about you, all right?"

"I'm going into the dark now," Jasmine muttered, her eyes fixed on the fountain in the park below.

"What do you mean? What do you have there? What's in the bo-" The officer stopped short and stared hard at the package under Jasmine's arm. Her eyes flicked to Jasmine's other hand and then she took a long step back, one hand dropping onto the Taser on her belt. "We've got blood here," she said in a loud voice. "Miss, you need to calm down and put that package on the ground for me, all right? Nice and slow."

Jasmine was confused. Blood? What blood? What was this racist bitch trying to say about her? She lifted her free hand and looked at it. Dark smears covered her fingers and palm like sticky, black syrup on her rich, brown skin.

Blood.

Andy's Blood.

The whispers became a roar. The fuse that had been her anger exploded through her and she screamed at the officer, rushing towards her as the roaring filled her with strength and speed like she'd never experienced before.

The cop didn't even have time to pull her Taser before Jasmine collided with her. She shoved the woman hard in the center of her chest and sent her sailing through the air and down the steps to the cobblestone sidewalk that ran along the spring. She landed hard, one arm twisting painfully beneath her. Something between a whimper and a scream burst from her lips.

Jasmine didn't care. Hate filled her. Every bitter word she's ever heard, every hate mongering video she'd ever watched, every scene of deep seated racism that she'd ever come across; all of these coalesced into a river of rage that was so deep, so overwhelming, that it felt completely alien to her yet still sent her running towards the injured officer.

The whispers filled her ears like the wind from hurricane. All she could see was a thing that needed destroying, a thing that was in her way, a thing that was keeping her from the dark, a thing that needed to die. She still held the package tight but her free hand was outstretched, the fingers curled like a claw. She screeched like an animal as she descended on the woman.

She had just enough time to register a muffled popping sound before her world became a blank slate of pain that started in the center of her back and radiated out. She almost fell but the unnatural roaring in her ears kept her up, kept her standing despite the vibrations coursing through her muscles.

Jasmine spun and saw another officer with his Taser leveled at her, two thin wires trailing back to his yellow and black weapon. This one was younger, closer to her age, and his eyes were wide with disbelief.

Jasmine took a staggering step towards him slapping at the wires awkwardly.

"Son of a bitch!" the cop said, squeezing harder on the trigger.

Jasmine couldn't see the injured officer as she rolled onto her own back and drew her Taser with her good hand. All Jasmine heard was another muffled pop before the pain that coursed through her doubled and she felt herself falling and saw the cobblestones rushing up to meet her face.

CHAPTER TWENTY-NINE

Steiner Residence
199 Brownsboro Road
Brownsboro, Alabama
October 29, 11:01 A.M. CST

The flight from Atlanta had been smooth despite the heavy clouds that were rolling in from the west. To Jeffrey and his congregants, it looked as though they were flying into a wall of gray smoke but the flight was a short one and they had started their descent long before they'd reached the clouds. They had landed at Huntsville International Airport and immediately transferred to a pair of bland colored sedans that were waiting for them. The drive to the address he'd received had taken nearly as long as the flight from Atlanta.

They arrived at an isolated country home built in the middle of a large lot that was bordered on three sides by thick forest. Jeffrey could see two out buildings of some kind behind the large farmhouse that dominated the lot. Beyond that was a large swath of land that was plowed into neat rows but looked to be lying fallow. A man came down the porch steps to meet them as they pulled into the drive. Jeffrey knew his face but couldn't attach the correct name to it.

He was Jeffrey's age, or close to it, and carried himself with a kind of directness that suggested that he'd spent a lot of time in uniform though whether military of police, Jeffrey couldn't say. His skin was pale and his hair looked as though it had once been dark but was heavily peppered with gray that showed despite the stubble short cut. As he approached him, the man stopped and bowed his head, eyes closed.

"High Adherent," he said, "welcome. The Master of Hounds awaits you at the rear of the house." Jeffrey recognized the voice as the one he'd heard on the phone.

"Lift your eyes, adherent," Jeffrey said. "Forgive me but I've forgotten your name."

The man looked up and half smiled. "No reason you should remember it, sir. I'm Zack Brady. We met a couple of years back."

Jeffrey nodded. He vaguely remembered meeting the man when he'd been part of a security detail. "Of course," he said. "Zack. You were part of the Lake City Crusade. "

"I was, sir. As I understand it, that poor excuse for a mega-church had to be condemned. Praise to The Mother."

"Praise be," Jeffrey said. "So, the Favored prefers… 'Master of Hounds', is it?"

"Yes, sir. He's pretty stuck on the name. Suits him, though."

"How so?"

Brady grew a little pale. He opened his mouth to speak, thought better of it, and then said, "That's something you'll need to see for yourself, sir. I'll get these congregants settled while you go out back and speak with him. Just…" He trailed off, his eyes widening as though looking at a memory that was too dark to really focus on.

"Adherent?" Jeffrey said.

Brady's eyes snapped up and he swallowed. "Just be prepared, sir. His power is… humbling."

Jeffrey studied the man's eyes for a moment. They were distant, almost haunted. He nodded and said, "Thank you, adherent. See to your brethren."

Brady gestured for the others to follow him. Jeffrey watched them go and before long was standing alone in the driveway, considering what Brady had told him. Whatever the Favored had done to frighten the man must have been something impressive. Zack Brady did not strike Jeffrey as the kind of man who scared easily. With this thought in mind, Jeffrey took a deep breath and headed for the back of the farmhouse.

He found the Favored standing in front of a weather worn outbuilding that looked as though it was designed to house farm equipment. The large, roll up style door was partially raised but the interior was far too dark to make out any details. The Favored was standing barefoot next to a large wheelbarrow dressed in a pair of dark slacks and nothing else. Jeffrey spotted dark stains spattered across his torso as he flung something from the wheelbarrow into the partially opened door.

"Master of Hounds, Favored of The Mother, how may I serve you?" Jeffrey said. He had stopped a respectable distance from the Favored and had no desire to get any closer when he realized what the stains on his body were.

The Favored did not respond for a moment, staring hard at the darkened building's interior. "They don't like the light," he said finally. "They can work in it, don't think they can't, but it's under the moon that they really shine."

Jeffrey glanced at the building, not sure how to respond. "As you say, Favored. I have brought more congregants to your service. They're anxious to serve you and The Mother through you."

The Favored nodded but said nothing, his eyes locked on the building.

Jeffrey had stood in silence long enough that he thought he might have been dismissed when the Favored said, "The Chthon live in the dark, too. Did you know that? Just like my hounds."

Jeffrey nodded slowly. "Yes, sir. They are deep dwellers in their native realm so that stands to reason."

"Do you know why I went to Africa?"

"No, Favored. I would not presume to question you."

"For decades I was the reason that folks in these parts were scared of the dark. Me and my hounds, the other critters we hunted with. When the sun went down we ran the woods and the fields while the prey locked their doors, stoked their fires, and cradled their rifles thinking that'd keep them safe. Those were good days for us," he said, keeping his eyes on the garage.

Jeffrey opened his mouth to reply, realized he had no idea what to say, and shut it again.

The Favored's hand dropped into the wheelbarrow. It rested there while he said, "Then some damned fool went and invented electric lights, automobiles, better guns, and all the other things that make all these modern folk so soft. It got to the point where it was damned near impossible to hunt anybody without spotlights and helicopters lighting us up like a summer day. It just wasn't worth the effort anymore."

He pulled something from the wheelbarrow and gestured with it as he spoke. The bloody limb looked to have been a woman's arm, torn away at the shoulder. The wrist and elbow flopped about sickly and Jeffrey swallowed hard against a sudden wave of nausea.

"Africa, though," the Favored went on, waving the limb in the air like some kind of grotesque conductor's baton, "that's a big place. Lots and lots of open space where modernization has barely touched the world, lots of alpha predators to challenge, and lots of darkies to hunt. Surprising as this might sound, I liked it there."

He tossed the arm into the dirt a few feet outside the partially opened door. It landed in a limply crooked position that made Jeffrey's stomach roil, though he did his best to keep his revulsion off his face. He watched as a huge paw, easily the size of one of his wife's fancy dinner platters, stretched out into the light and covered the severed arm. The thing was ink black and covered in something that looked more like fleshy tendrils than anything resembling fur. With casual ease, the paw slid back into the shadows taking the limb with it. Thick claws left behind inch deep furrows in the dirt. There was a faint crunch from within the garage.

When Jeffrey looked away, the Master of Hounds was staring at him, his eyes a cold mixture of ink black and swirling crimson. He glanced at the wheel barrow and said, "The previous occupants. They were in the way and I like to give my best hounds a treat before a big hunt. Seemed like a win-win."

Jeffrey nodded and swallowed bitter bile. "You have a hunt in mind, Favored?" he said over his nausea.

The Favored nodded. "Now, why do you think Mother would call me back from Africa for this? To track down one of Hsan's Seven Crypticals? The Fourth, to be exact. The one that allows man to summon dark dwellers and bend them to our will. Why *me* for that when she has so many loyal followers here already?"

"I would not presume to know The Mother's mind, Favored."

He grunted, almost laughing. "Well, I've been in her army a might longer than you, boy, and I can tell you that sometimes she expects you to figure things out on your own. Trick's knowing when. She is a female, after all."

Jeffrey stood silent again, forcing himself to meet the warlock's eyes without flinching.

After what seemed like an eternity, The Favored turned back to the garage and said, "We go as soon as the sun's full down. Me and mine can track the cryptical and you and yours back us up with your toys. Go let the rest know." He reached into the wheelbarrow again.

Jeffrey turned away before he could see what came out.

CHAPTER THIRTY

Randolph Avenue Southeast
Huntsville, Alabama
October 29, 11:10 A.M. CST

"This is giving me a hell of a headache," Clint said. He reached under the dark sunglasses and rubbed at his closed eyes. They'd been walking for the better part of an hour and he'd been looking at the world through his blacklight eyes the entire time.

"Not surprising," Arlo said from behind him. "I imagine that you're using whole new neural pathways in your brain to process all these unfamiliar inputs. Are we still on the trail?"

Clint repositioned the glasses on his nose and took a look at the street. The black stain that marked the otherwise silver-gray world was dead ahead. "Yeah," he said. "She stopped ducking off the road and taking detours as much once we crossed California Avenue."

"We're getting further from the cemetery," Arlo said. "All the police were heading that way. She was avoiding them."

"Well, another mile or so and we'll be downtown. That's not the best place to avoid law enforcement. Jim and Rani still with us?"

"They're still following. Focus on the trail."

"I am focused, Arlo. Hence the damned headache."

Clint thought he heard the magus chuckle. "Point taken, I suppose."

They continued in silence for a minute or so before Clint decided to bring up something that had been nagging at him. "You know," he said, "you don't seem very… wizardly."

"Excuse me?"

"You know, magical or whatever. Wizardly. You don't sound all-knowing and mysterious. You're more like an irritable professor."

"What exactly did you expect, Mercer? Round spectacles and a scar on my forehead? Maybe a long, pointy hat and a fondness for little people?"

"Well, no. I just didn't expect to hear you use terms like 'neural pathways'. Sounds more scientific than magical."

Arlo grunted. "What did I tell you about letting popular and established culture color your assessments of evidence?"

"To not too," Clint said in his best hillbilly accent. "Seriously, though, even that statement sounds like a something a researcher would say even though I know for a fact that you can do magical things that would make the average neuroscientist's brain melt."

"Why are you so certain that magic and science are mutually exclusive?"

"Aren't they?"

Arlo sighed. "Yes and no. Among the arcane community there are diverging thoughts on the nature and use of magic. Many are traditionalists who would probably fit your idea of what a wizard should be. Others, like myself, are more progressive. The traditionalists are content to practice the craft without challenging the historically established norms. I seek to understand it on a deeper level, though. Magic and science coexist in this world and there is an intersection to that existence that I think holds a greater potential for understanding both. I've devoted my life to that understanding. At least, I have when I'm not out in the field doing things like this."

Clint nodded. "You're in the field a lot, I guess."

"More often than not. I haven't gone home in nearly three weeks."

"Where's that?"

Arlo didn't answer.

After a moment, Clint shook his head and said, "Come on, man. You've literally been inside my head and you're still playing this secret agent shtick with me?"

Arlo sighed and said, "Atlanta. Just outside the city, actually. I've got other properties around the country but that's one of the better ones for my work."

"Why's that?"

"Ley lines. Look, Mercer, I understand that you're just making conversation but the need for secrecy in our work isn't just a 'shtick'. Aside from the fact that magic is dangerous in the hands of untrained talents, we keep secrets to protect ourselves. No one gets through a life in this line of work without making enemies. Even if they don't know our names, they despise us just the same. I'm sure you can see the logic in keeping personal details secret under those circumstances."

"Operational security," Clint said. "I get that but I think that I've proved I'm not a threat to your operation, right?"

"You have. And, I'll admit, now that we know there are congregants in town the need for secrecy isn't what it was. All that matters now is who gets the cryptical first."

"Right. So, tell me something. What's this group you work with called? What exactly is it you do? I'm sure most of your enemies know that much, at least."

"Oh, yes," Arlo said with a bitter laugh. "I've got a number of groups that would like to see my head on their mantle." He was quiet for moment as they walked until he finally said, "Fine. It's called The

Pickman Institute. Think of us as a kind of private military and investigative contractor specializing in all things paranormal. Most of the time we act as a buffer between the government and any fallout from eldritch threats that get out of hand. Did you ever watch that old television show *Mission Impossible*?"

"I've seen all the Tom Cruise movies."

"There were movies? I wasn't aware. Anyway, it's a lot like that but with supernatural threats."

"That's how you guys scored the DHS covers."

"It is. Believe me, though, if this operation goes bad and gets too far into the public eye, we will get disavowed and have the full weight of federal law enforcement come down on us like Thor's hammer. They'll need scapegoats and we've agreed to fill the bill if it comes due. That's the risk we take for the ease of access those covers provide."

Clint took that in as he rubbed at his eyes again. "So how'd you end up here? In Huntsville, I mean."

"A CIA tip, actually. There are a number of spots globally that have or are suspected to have significant eldritch activity. Most of them are remote and difficult to get to but world governments do what they can to keep them monitored and isolated. Apparently, one such site in Nepal became the subject of a group of archaeologists interest. They found a reliquary-"

"A what-a-what?"

"Reliquary. For most people, it's a container that holds holy objects; bones of saints, that kind of thing. For us, though, it's kind of a magical lock box. The container is infused with substantial arcane power that binds and restrains the eldritch artifact within or vice versa. Anyway, one of the good doctors knew enough about our side of reality to not try and open the thing. They decided to ship it back to the states for analysis along with some other things they'd found. Part of that trip involved a layover in Egypt. That's where someone stole the shipment."

"Let me guess," Clint said. "Black market antiquities types? I heard a lot about those guys when I was overseas."

"It's an enormous business with an even deeper level when you factor in artifacts of a magical nature. Regardless, the shipment was lost until pieces of it resurfaced in Morocco. By then, the archaeologist that had originally found the reliquary had gotten word of the theft and raised an alarm with people that knew enough to be worried about such things. Some of our agents along with some clued in CIA people tracked down the location where the shipment was being sold with the intent of raiding it and securing the reliquary. Instead, they found a massacre. Some damned fool opened the reliquary and exposed the cryptical. I can only assume that it forced its influence into the minds of everyone in that room. A dozen men murdered each other for it."

"Damn," Clint whispered.

"Regardless, they managed to track the individual that had survived the fight and fled with the cryptical. As it turned out, though, he was badly wounded and near death when they finally caught up with him. He'd gotten rid of the cryptical at some point along the way. The agents investigated and the only thing they managed to come up with was the name 'Edward Warner' and the fact that he was in the states."

"Sounds like a needle in a haystack situation."

"It was but we finally managed to find the correct needle. That was what led us to your fair city. You know the rest."

"Mostly. Who was this Warner guy?"

"Professor of Mathematical Physics with a respectable expertise in theoretical physics and quantum theory. Amateur geologist and spelunking enthusiast, husband, father, grandfather, and a devout worshiper of the Dark Old Ones."

"Of the what?"

"Just think of them as ancient entities of enormous power that some people consider divine."

"People like these congregation guys?"

"Correct."

"How do you know he was like them?"

"Our people found a collection of books. Reprints, mostly, no real power to them but all the rituals and rites were there. As near as I can tell, he worshiped in secret for most of his life. Likely his wife, as well."

Clint was quiet as they crossed over Lincoln Street. The dark stain they were following was a steady line through the hazy gray world. It seemed to be leading through the old brick buildings that made up most of the downtown square and straight towards the tall courthouse at the center.

"You have a weird job, Arlo," Clint said.

"So do you, at the moment."

"Just at the moment. I get plenty of normal crazy coming through my E.R. on a regular basis. You guys deal with some next level crazy that I can barely get my head around. Once we make sure this girl is safe, you can fix my eyes and I'll gladly go back to my normal crazy, thanks."

They walked another block before Arlo said, "There might not be anything to fix, Mercer."

Clint took a deep breath and measured his response. "Not what I want to hear, Arlo. I wasn't like this before I carried you into that garage."

"I know. What happened to you, though, it wasn't like something that was already there got broken. It's more like you were disassembled and remade into something new. I suspect that this is your normal now and you're just going to have to embrace that."

"Fine. I'll just shut it all down and never use it again."

"You could but I'm not sure that will work. The things you've seen won't just go away. For the rest of your life you're going to see what most people call ordinary and wonder what's beneath the surface, what truth might lie hidden there. You'll know you have the means to uncover that at your disposal. How long do you think you could go without using those means? You're going to need help understanding these things. You've seen into the abyss, Mercer, and it has seen into you. There's no coming back from that."

Clint didn't respond. He focused on the trail before him and let Arlo's words settle into him. He wanted to argue, wanted to curse, but how could he? He was no closer to truly understanding what had happened to him than he had been when he'd woken up in Birmingham. Plus, Arlo had a point. If this was his new normal, he'd never understand it if all he did was try to ignore it.

"The trail turns left up here," Clint said, pointing. "It looks like she crossed the street on the other side of the courthouse."

"Anything of note over there?"

Clint shrugged. "Big Spring Park, the art museum, the civic center a little further back. Nothing that screams 'destination' to me."

"Keep going," Arlo said. "I'll update Rani in case they need to circle around the park."

Clint kept walking while Arlo made the call. He followed the trail past the west side of the downtown square and then down a set of steps to Big Spring Park. The trail grew erratic there, zigging this way and that down the steps into the park proper. There were smears of brilliant crimson in the black lines and it slowly dissolved into nothing the closer it got to the water. Clint stopped at the edge of the spring and looked around for some hint of a direction.

"Mercer!" Arlo snapped in a low voice. "Cover your eyes. There are civilians here."

Clint lowered his head and raised a hand to his brow as though he were nursing his very real headache. There weren't a lot of people in the park but he had passed more than a few on the street. He wondered if anyone had noticed the lights behind his sunglasses.

"What is it?" Arlo said. "Why did you stop?"

"It's gone," Clint said. "The trail stops here."

"What do you mean? What are you seeing?"

Clint described it to him.

Arlo cursed and said, "There's no other sign of it anywhere?"

"Nowhere that I can see."

"Stay here. Close your inner eye. I'll be right back."

Clint nodded and closed his eyes, focusing on the mental image he had created back at Dead Kid's. It took him minute but when he opened his eyes again, it was to sunlight filtering through drifting clouds and all the colors in their proper places. He looked around for Arlo and saw him walking back from an Irish grill that he had frequented a few times.

"It's what I thought," Arlo said. "Acts of violence leave an auric signature. That was the red staining that you saw. The worse the act, the longer they last. Our quarry had an encounter with the police here and was injured. The bartender over there says an ambulance took her and one of the officers away. He says that the girl threw the cop like she- and I quote - 'had superpowers or something'."

"The cryptical?"

Arlo nodded. "Obviously. It's influence is stronger than I thought if it gave the girl enhanced physicality."

"Why did it bring her here?"

"Did it? This could just have been on the route when the police got involved. We don't need to speculate, though. We know the girl was transported to the hospital and the cryptical most likely taken into evidence. All we need to do is find out where so that I can ward and secure it before we lose it again."

"Won't it just get in someone else's head? Someone with a badge and gun?"

"Probably, but if it's in an evidence bag in the trunk of a cruiser, though, we might have some time before it takes effect. Let's go back to the square and meet the others. Luck might finally be with us."

Clint glanced at the fountain once more and followed Arlo back up the steps towards the square. For some reason, he wasn't feeling lucky.

CHAPTER THIRTY-ONE

En Route to Crestwood Hospital
Madison Street SE
Huntsville, AL
October 29 11:45 AM CST

It took a couple of phone calls but they finally managed to find out that the girl had been taken to a hospital across town despite the fact that the one Clint worked at was closer. Jim had flicked a switch that activated some strobes in the Tahoe's grill and drove the big SUV like he was daring anyone to get in his way. Their route took them past Clint's ER and he watched it as they passed. Police barricades and tape surrounded the ambulance bay. The glass doors were shattered and bent off the slides in some places. There didn't seem to be any sign that any repairs were underway yet. He shook his head at the sight. At least he didn't have to worry about not showing up for work.

They reached Crestwood in record time and piled out of the Tahoe, heading for reception. Arlo stabbed a finger at his phone screen, ending a call he obviously hadn't enjoyed. He snapped at Jim to get someone who could tell them where they'd taken the cryptical on the line. Jim pulled out his own phone and started dialing. Clint took the lead as they headed through the doors, Rani at his side. She veered towards the information desk but Clint waved her off. He knew the way to the ER and reasoned that's where the two patients would have been taken.

They got to ER reception and, after flashing their fake IDs, found out that the officer had been released only minutes before they arrived. The girl, though, had been transferred to one of the neurological units. She hadn't regained consciousness despite the fact that her head injury wasn't that severe and the doctors were concerned that she had as yet undiscovered brain trauma. She was already settled into her room by the time they made it to the correct floor. A uniformed police officer was standing post by the door but waved them in when Arlo flashed his ID.

Rani went to the nurse's station to get some information on the young woman's condition while Jim kept speaking into his phone. The big man was looking more and more flustered.

Arlo guided Clint to the woman's side and said, "Take a look. Quickly, before anyone joins us."

Clint looked down and checked patient wristband the woman was wearing. Her name was Jasmine Ives; early 20s, African American, what looked like a bandaged wound above her right eye, swelling around that eye, steady breathing-

"No, Mercer. I didn't say *assess* her" Arlo said. "I said *look.*"

"Oh," Clint said. "Right." He closed his eyes, focused, and opened them again. The world shifted back to the silver-gray shades of his new sight. The hospital room was all hard lines and defined features. It was much clearer than it had been while they'd been outside.

He turned his attention to the patient. Black threads of eldritch energy were wrapped around her head like some kind of inky cocoon. The threads spread out and unraveled down her body, passing through her limbs and torso like tiny needles. As he studied them, Clint realized that there were gaps in the threads, gaps that were slowly getting larger, as though the residue was breaking apart or dissolving somehow. He relayed the information to Arlo.

"Good," the magus said. "It sounds like time and distance from the cryptical's influence will be enough for the eldritch weaves to degrade and dissipate, allowing her natural auric energy to replenish itself. From what you're saying, if she'd held onto it much longer the effects would have gotten concentrated enough to attain permanency."

"So, she's going to get better?" Clint said.

"Didn't I just say that?"

"I'm really not sure, Arlo. You said words but-"

"Close your sight," Arlo said. "Rani's coming with the nurse."

By the time Clint was opening his eyes to the world in all its normal colors, Rani and a heavy set, middle aged woman with pale skin and hair the color of coffee with too much cream were standing at the foot of the bed. Clint half listened as they discussed the girl's medical status. He was distracted by Jim, who had stepped to one side and was speaking into his phone in terse, aggressive whispers.

He caught Arlo's attention and nodded towards Jim. Arlo shrugged but Clint could see the muscles in his jaw flexing in frustration.

Clint put one hand to his head and massaged his temples with his thumb and fingers. The headache had subsided somewhat on the ride over but was back in full force since he'd used his sight again. He stood there with his pounding head and listened to the combined chatter of Rani, Jim, and the nurse all talking over each other. His frustration swelled and he said to Arlo, "I'm going to go find a men's room. I'll be right back."

Arlo gestured towards the room's lavatory. "There's one right there."

"I just need a minute away from all this, Arlo. I'll be right back." He turned and headed into the hall without waiting for a reply. For a half a second, he thought Arlo might follow him but when he looked back the magus had moved closer to Jim and seemed to be listening in on his conversation.

Clint didn't know a lot about Crestwood's layout beyond the Emergency Department but he managed to find the public restroom without much effort. He was relieved to find it empty and went straight to the sink and splashed cold water on his face. He stood at the sink with his eyes closed and spent a few minutes just taking deep, controlled breaths in hopes that it might ease the pain behind his eyes. He was wondering if he could sweet talk a couple of Tylenol or something out of one of the nurses when he heard the door open. He heard someone come in but kept his eyes closed until he heard a voice say, "Just the man I'm looking for."

Clint looked up and found himself in the company of three police officers. One of them, the one that had spoken, was dressed in a polo shirt with the Huntsville Police Department logo over the left breast. He was a dark skinned man with a stocky build that suggested he was more sturdy than soft despite his girth. His face was round and had the look of someone who didn't laugh much. There was a pistol clipped to one side of his belt and a badge to the other. The two men behind him were larger than he was by a couple of inches, younger, and wearing their dark uniforms like they were very comfortable in them. None of them were smiling.

"Remember me?" polo shirt said.

It took Clint a second but then it came to him and he nodded. "Yeah, you were the senior officer or whatever back at the cemetery."

"That's right. I'm Sargent Vance Bellmon."

Clint nodded. "Well, Agent Lonebear's over in room-"

"I know where he is," Bellmon said. "Don't want to talk to him, though. I'm looking for you."

Clint stood up straighter and faced the trio of men. "Probably best if you just talk to Lonebear. I'm just a-"

"Special consultant. Yeah, I know. Thing is, after you dropped those two guys at Maple Hill, I got a good look at you. Now, in my job, you see a lot of faces, you hear a lot of names, and they can get all jumbled up together but sometimes they really stick out. That's what yours did; stuck in my head. I knew I'd seen you before but I could not remember where to save my life."

"I'm pretty sure we haven't met before today, Sargent."

"We haven't. You couldn't be more right. That doesn't mean I haven't seen your face, though. Then, all of a sudden, it came to me while I was back at the station making a fresh pot of coffee. You're that nurse. The one that survived that emergency room mess the other night."

Bellmon paused, as though waiting for Clint to confirm it. He didn't.

"Yeah, it's you. Looked at your picture on my phone before I walked in here just to be sure. Showed it to these guys, too. They agree with me. See, the problem is, the thing that's confusing, is that you were supposed to be severely injured. They had to rush you off to some specialists or something down in Birmingham. Yet, here you stand; Clinton Mercer, RN. Looking strong and fit enough to shoot down a couple of gunslingers this very morning."

Clint swallowed and tried to keep his apprehension off his face. "Sargent, my instructions are pretty clear. Agent Lonebear-"

"Oh, 'Agent Lonebear'," Bellmon made air quotes around the words, "is about to have problems all his own. See, my bosses don't like the fact that there have been more violent deaths in the last forty-eight hours than we had in all of last year. That all started when your friends came to town. So, we've got people checking out their bona fides. What I'm curious about, though, is how a guy who was an emergency room nurse suddenly ends up as a 'special consultant' for some DHS folks who, quite frankly, look shady as hell. I'm curious enough about it, in fact, that you and me and these two fellas are going to take a ride to my office to talk it over. Get what I'm saying, Mr. Mercer? You can consider yourself under arrest."

"For what?"

"Suspicion of felony conspiracy, suspicion of acts of domestic terrorism, whatever else we can come up with. Trust me, enough bodies have dropped around you in the last couple of days that I had a list of judges that were more than happy to sign a warrant."

Clint gritted his teeth and let his eyes sweep over the trio.

"Now, don't go getting foolish," Bellmon said, holding his hands up in a calming gesture. "I read enough about your service to know that you could give us a fight if you wanted too. I also read enough to know that you should be able to recognize bad odds when you see them. So come on, now, Clint. Do the smart thing and surrender that weapon so we can do this nice and peaceful like."

Clint studied the man's face, his mind racing for a way out or around that didn't end with somebody getting shot.

Finally, he handed over his Sig and let them cuff him.

CHAPTER THIRTY-TWO

Huntsville Police Department
Evidence Security Station
815 Wheeler Ave NW
Huntsville, AL
October 29 2:42 PM CST

Jimmy Harrison leaned his considerable girth back into his chair and studied the array of digital playing cards floating on his monitor. He dragged a stack of three cards starting with the three of spades and descending to the ace of spades onto the longer stack next to it. He gave himself a little smile as the complete suite scrolled down to the bottom of the screen. After almost twenty-five years in uniform, he could think of worse ways to spend the golden years of his career.

He leaned back, stretched, and filled the quiet evidence room with a loud yawn. It wasn't a particularly large room, not like those warehouses he always saw on the cop shows on TV but it was big enough that he took a little pride in making sure everything was tagged, accounted for, and easy to find when needed. Huntsville wasn't that big, really, but with asset forfeiture laws being what they were he could easily find himself responsible for a million or more dollars worth of evidence if the guys on the street took down something big.

Jimmy took a pull from his fourth cup of coffee. He knew his wife would give him a good shot of the stink-eye if she knew he was drinking that much caffeine in a day. That's why he'd gotten that fancy Keurig machine for the office and not his house. He knew her heart was in the right place but after two decades together that woman had taken nagging to the level of high art. Besides, it was just coffee. It's not like he spent his days drinking on duty or anything.

A buzzer sounded and Jimmy hauled himself out of his chair. He walked the few steps to the thick Plexiglas that separated the evidence room from the rest of the world and saw a familiar face. Jimmy shot the young man a smile and said, "Officer Stapler. How's my favorite rookie?"

"Tired," the young, sandy haired officer said. "Crazy afternoon."

"Yeah? What happened?"

Stapler shook his head. "Anne spotted somebody acting hinky over by the square. We stopped her to check it out and things went sideways. Anne got hurt."

"Damn. She all right?"

Stapler nodded. "Yeah, she's okay. Cracked her wrist pretty good so she'll be on office duty for a while. Not sure who they're going to have me riding with."

"Did the suspect break her wrist?"

Stapler shook his head. "That's the crazy part, Jimmy. We stopped her over at Big Spring Park, right? A little younger than me, talking crazy, and holding this package like her life depended on it. Then, Anne spots some blood on the suspect and calls it out to me. Next thing I know, the little psycho is throwing Anne off the steps coming down from the square like she didn't weigh a pound. She landed on her wrist."

"Holy crap," Jimmy said, grinning. "What'd you do, rook?"

"What do you think? I tased the bitch."

Jimmy nodded. "Good move, kid."

"You'd think so, right? But, no, she turns and looks at me like she was more pissed off than subdued. I'm telling you, Jimmy, I hit her square in the back with both darts and she was trying to walk it off. Anne had to light her up with her Taser before she dropped. Craziest thing I've ever seen."

"Oh, come on," Jimmy said. "They don't call getting popped with those things 'riding the bull' for nothing. You must've had a glitchy weapon or something."

"I guess. I'll tell you, though, man, the way that girl looked at me, I was tempted to draw down on her."

"Hey, you be careful with that shit, rook. If she wasn't armed then you did what you needed to."

"I know," Stapler said. "Still, the whole thing freaked me out a little."

Jimmy laughed. "Well, here's hoping you get a few months of being bored before you have that much fun again. That's the job, kid."

"Yeah, whatever you say, old timer," Stapler said with a grin. "I'd better get going."

Jimmy wrinkled his brow and glanced at Stapler's hand. He'd been holding a large, paper evidence bag the entire time they'd been talking. "Forgetting something?" Jimmy said, nodding towards the bag.

Stapler looked confused for a moment and then glanced down at his hand. He stared at the bag as though he'd forgotten it was there.

"Oh," he whispered. "Right. This is the package that the suspect was holding. I need to log it in."

Jimmy nodded. "Okay. Do you know what's in it?"

"No. DA says we can't just rip it open. Turns out it's addressed to one of the victims from the Maple Hill shooting this morning. They want to do 'due diligence' or something before they find out what's in it."

"No shit?" Jimmy said, raising the Plexiglas window to take the package. "Your suspect involved in that?"

Stapler shrugged. "Maybe. I mean, the package has one of the victim's names on it so there's got to be some kind of link."

Jimmy nodded. "She talking?"

"Banged her head pretty hard when she finally went down. She's in the hospital. Unconscious, last I heard."

Jimmy nodded and looked at Stapler, waiting. Stapler just stood there looking back at him with a small, vacant smile on his face.

"So, are you going to give me that thing or what, kid?"

Stapler started at his voice and said, "Yeah, yeah. Sorry. Zoned out for a minute."

"You okay?"

Stapler nodded and placed the bag on the small shelf on his side of the window. "Yeah, I'm good, Jimmy. Like I said, crazy day."

Jimmy nodded and scribbled his ID number on the evidence bag label. He scanned the bar code on that same label with a light gun and made sure it was registered into the system.

"All set," he said, looking up. Stapler was staring at the bag with an expression on his face that Jimmy found a little obsessive. He closed the Plexiglas window with a sharp snap.

Stapler blinked and looked up at him.

"Are you sure you're good? You seem a little off."

Stapler nodded but didn't say anything.

Jimmy picked up the bag and said, "All right, then, rook. Go grab some lunch or something. Coffee, whatever. Shake off the day."

Stapler met his eyes and seemed to think that over. "Yeah, you're right. I missed lunch. Thanks, Jimmy. I'll see ya later."

Jimmy nodded his farewell and watched as the young cop turned, hesitated, then shook his head and walked away. So far as Jimmy knew, today was the kid's first taste of a violent suspect. It seemed to have shaken him up more than he wanted to admit. Jimmy wasn't too worried about it, though. He'd been on the job long enough to spot one of the good ones and Stapler had the look. The kid would shake it off, he thought. He had 'good police' written all over him.

Jimmy turned towards the shelves and started forward. Suddenly, he remembered the solitaire game and cooling mug of coffee that he'd left at his desk. There was very little he hated more in life than a cold cup of coffee. He hesitated, a little confused, and then headed for his desk. Cold coffee just would not do and he really didn't want to waste the k-cup he used to make it. He was paying for the damn things out of his own pocket, after all.

Jimmy settled back into his chair and placed the evidence bag on the floor next to him. He took a sip from the mug, still hot, and smiled as he turned his attention back to the computer screen.

He barely noticed the whispers creeping into his thoughts.

CHAPTER THIRTY-THREE

Huntsville Police Department
Interview Room
815 Wheeler Ave NW
Huntsville, AL
October 29 4:22 PM CST

Clint shifted in his metal chair and sighed, letting his frustration flow out with the breath. He looked down at the handcuffs securing his wrists to the steel table and shook his head, wondering where he'd be right then if he'd called in sick two nights ago. The hospital would probably still be trashed and all this insanity still going on but he'd be somewhere other than in cuffs. Maybe, just maybe, things might have played out differently for Sarah, too.

Clint took a look around the tiny room for the hundredth time. He gotten some training in counter interrogation techniques when he'd been in the service but it wasn't something he'd ever had to put to use. He remembered enough to recognize the scenario, though. They'd left him in a small space that would feel cramped once the two cops- and he was certain there would be two -came in to start questioning him. There were no light switches or thermostat controls and it was just warm enough to be uncomfortable. He'd been alone in the room for hours while the cops were out doing… what? Investigating? Watching him through the two way mirror that dominated one wall and snacking on Krispy Kremes? He didn't know. That was the whole point, really. Get him to feeling like he had no control or comfort and then start throwing him little concessions while brow beating him into some kind of confession or something. The cuffs seemed like overkill, though. He suspected Bellmon was trying to make some kind of point.

He wanted to put his head down on the table, maybe catch a quick nap, but with the position of the table and the way his wrists were cuffed in front of him that was actually a less comfortable position than sitting up straight or letting his head hang onto his chest. With the way his head was aching, he might just consider confessing to something in exchange for a handful of Excedrin.

He had closed his eyes and leaned back into the stiff chair as best he could to try and ease it. He wasn't sure how much longer he had been like that when the door clicked and he looked up.

Bellmon came in with another cop behind him. She looked a little older than Clint with dark hair and skin that looked like it got a lot of sun in the summer but had paled through the winter months. She was dressed in slacks and a no nonsense blouse. Her badge and gun were clipped to her belt and when she looked at Clint with her slate gray eyes, he got the distinct impression that she didn't really care whether he lived or died.

"Sorry to keep you waiting," Bellmon said. "You want some water or something?"

Clint shook his head. He was thirsty but he knew he'd rather not have a full bladder while tied to a steel table. He glanced at the female officer as she took up a position just over his left shoulder while Bellmon sat down across from him. It was another trick he recognized. No matter which way he turned his head he wouldn't be able to keep them both in his sight. It was like they'd gotten the tactic from an *Intimidation For Dummies* book or something. So, he turned his back on the female officer and decided to ignore her. He met Bellmon's eyes and waited.

"You sure you don't want anything? It's no problem."

Clint shook his head again.

"All right, then. Suit yourself." Bellmon made a show of opening a manila folder and a small notebook. He spent a moment scanning the pages of the notebook and then looked at Clint as though he'd just remembered something that was nagging at him.

"So," Bellmon said, "once I recognized you it wasn't that hard to get some information on you. The hospital was helpful with your employee records, most of your military stuff that isn't classified was useful, we even found your Jeep in that parking garage. My question, though, is what happened to your ID? You didn't have it or a phone on you when we picked you up and they weren't in your vehicle. Hell, I even checked your locker at the hospital and walked that crime scene looking for a wallet or something that the crime scene guys might have missed. Checked the evidence room for all the things they didn't miss. Nothing. Where's all your stuff, Mr. Mercer?"

Clint shrugged. "I lost it."

Bellmon nodded. "So, that's it? You lost it? That's all you got?"

Clint nodded. "That's it. I had it, now I don't. Lost it."

Bellmon studied him for a moment. "So it's gonna be like that?"

"Looking that way."

Bellmon nodded. "Well, as I was saying, I managed to dig up a lot on you. Huntsville born and raised, varsity track and basketball in high school, above average student, military, college… you're just a straight up all American boy. Hell, by now you should be all set with a picket fence and a family. You're not, though, are you? Why is that?"

Clint shrugged. "Guess I just haven't met the right woman yet. Know anybody?

Bellmon snorted a laugh. "Hell, I'm too busy trying to get my own kid to settle down. I'm not about to take on your personal issues."

Clint allowed himself a little smile.

"Which brings me to the topic at hand. How is it a straight up all American boy like yourself ends up running with a bunch of shady types claiming to be Homeland Security?"

"Claiming?"

Bellmon shrugged. "Can't prove it but my bosses are digging pretty deep to remedy that. See, it just seems a little off that you get caught up in a domestic terrorist attack, supposedly get injured real bad, and then suddenly turn back up with those folks without a scratch on you. There's a lot of blanks in your story that need filling in."

Clint watched the man's eyes. They were steady, firm, and patient. This wasn't the kind of man that just accepted the company line. Clint gave it to him, anyway. "Talk to Lonebear. I'm under orders."

"Orders? Man, you've been out of uniform for years now. Don't give me this orders crap. Look, you and that bunch of fake feds have been running around shooting up my- no, *our* -hometown and I want to know why. What do those folks at the cemetery have to do with the SCL?"

"The what?"

"The SCL. The Sons of Confederate Liberty? Are you trying to tell me you've never heard of them?"

Clint thought back, trying hard to remember anything that might link back to the name. It took a second but he remembered seeing it on the television back in Birmingham. He nodded, "Right. Sorry, the abbreviation threw me off."

"Uh-huh. What aren't you telling me?"

Clint met the man's eyes again. He realized he was actually starting to feel a little bad for the guy. Bellmon seemed to be nothing more than a good cop trying to do his job to the best of his ability but he was working on problems that didn't actually exist. All he knew was what he was being told by his superiors and whatever evidence Arlo's people had given up or manipulated. In that moment, sitting across from the man, Clint felt a wave of guilt, though he wasn't entirely sure for what.

"You know how it goes when the government gets involved, Bellmon," Clint said. "Does anyone ever truly know what's going on?"

"So you're standing by the DHS story?"

Clint shrugged. "They've got the badges. Talk to them."

"Hell, I've got a badge. Damn near everybody in this building has a badge. That don't make any of them honest by default. No, you know something you're not saying. Something important. And you know what? I think you want to tell me. I think you're a decent, standup guy who got pulled into something bigger than him when all that crap went down at Huntsville Hospital. Come on, Clint. Just tell me the truth. How are you mixed up in all of this? What's your connection to the SCL? Who were those shooters in the cemetery?"

For just a second, Clint considered telling him. He could just spill his guts about magic and monsters and the whole screwed up enchilada. He even thought he might give him a look at his fancy new eyes just to prove it. The moment passed, though, and he said, "I don't have any ties to the SCL. The people I was working with are on the more secret side of the fence than most DHS. That's probably why they seem so shady to you. Look, this… SCL, the people causing all the problems for the city; they're monsters, Bellmon. It's like there's something in them that tore up the human parts. That's what that DHS team does. They hunt the monsters so the rest of us don't have to."

"Yeah, well, they're doing a piss poor job at the moment and if there are people like that in this town, me and mine need to know about it."

Clint shrugged again. "It's a tough gig. Look, the point is that you're better off getting out of their way and letting them work. The people behind all of this are next level bad. They're bad like you've never seen."

"So what are you saying? They've got overseas connections? Middle East? Russia? What?"

Clint closed his eyes and shook his head. "Talk to Lonebear," he said. "I respect that you're just trying to do your job but I've said all I'm going to on the matter. Talk to Lonebear."

Bellmon slapped his notebook closed. He stared hard at Clint for nearly a minute before he stood up and gestured the other officer out of the room. He looked back as he was leaving and said, "I'll be back in a little while to see if you still feel that way. Think about this while I'm gone; how much can you really depend on people like that? People that lie about who they are and work in secret doing God knows what? How do you know they aren't going to let you take the fall for all this? You already look like an inside man for the hospital mess. Are you sure they aren't just going to throw you to the wolves to take the heat off of them?"

The door clicked shut behind him as he left. Clint stared after him for a few moments and then let his head fall back. "Hounds," he whispered. "He calls them hounds."

CHAPTER THIRTY-FOUR

Steiner Residence
199 Brownsboro Road
Brownsboro, Alabama
October 29, 5:44 P.M. CST

"The sun's getting low, sir," Brady whispered to Jeffrey. "The troops are wondering if you have any idea what his plan is for sunset."

Jeffrey looked over at the man. Everyone but the Favored was gathered in the house's large dining room. If Jeffrey had to guess, this had probably been the place that all the extended family gathered for holidays and family events because the dining table was long and looked well used. Family photos covered the walls displaying an array of smiling faces and traditional milestones. The congregants had raided the pantry and the leftover boxes, bags, and sandwich fixings were scattered about. The hushed collection of conversations died as Brady asked his question.

"The Favored will inform us of our purpose in his time, congregant. If I had to speculate, though, I'd say his hounds have some way to track the cryptical. He's just been waiting for dark before he begins his hunt."

"But how-"

"Zack, we have to be patient. I know as much as you do right now. Let the Favored do as he will and have faith that his will serves The Mother and through her our interests."

"Of course, sir," Brady said. Then, in a louder voice, "All praise to The Mother."

"Praise be," came the broken chorus of responses.

"Praise be, indeed," Jeffrey said. "Have patience and hold to your faith, congregants. Soon, the Favored will define our purpose and our hands will become The Mother's instruments. Until then, contemplate the cold glory that awaits the faithful."

The room returned to its rustle of low conversations. Jeffrey looked at Brady and said, "You handle them well."

"Thank you, sir," Brady said. "I was a squad leader in the Army back in the day. It was that experience that brought me to The Mother."

"Tell me."

Brady shrugged. "Not really a special story or anything, sir. Like a lot of soldiers, I had a couple of really bad days that got stuck in my head and my heart. Things I just couldn't let go of, not even when I was sleeping."

"PTSD?"

Brady nodded. "That's what the docs at the VA called it. Four little letters to sum up something that shreds your life. Anyway, I was on the meds but they only helped so much. I wasn't sleeping, I wasn't eating right, drinking too much… all the usual suspects, you know? That's when I met an adherent who told me about The Mother's Holy Writ. At first, I figured it was just another fly by night, wanna be religion looking for a sucker with a credit card. But… well, she just touched me and I felt better. It was just for a second, you know? But it was enough. A week later, I was an initiate and the adherent had worked a ritual that called on The Mother's power to heal me. I felt it, sir. Cold and overwhelming and filling me up. It was… I'd never felt anything like it before. When it was over, I was better. I mean, I still remember those bad days and everything, you know? Remember them clearly. They just don't matter anymore. The pain and confusion and concern are all just gone. The people that died… well, they just died, you know? I see a bigger picture now with The Mother at the center. The Mother is all."

Jeffrey nodded and gave the man his best deal closing smile. "It is glorious how she frees you from the confusion and shame of the unbeliever's existence."

Brady nodded. "It's awesome. I never feel bad about anything anymore."

"All the better to serve," Jeffrey said.

"Praise be."

Jeffrey was about to reply in kind when the Favored's voice boomed through the house. "Join me. It's time."

Brady was the first on his feet and led the way for the others. Jeffrey stood, holding back as he offered nods of assurance and The Mother's blessings as everyone filed out. He never let the confident smile drop from his face but he was happy to have the others between him and the Favored. There was something about the Master of Hounds that set off a warning chime in his mind but that was not something he was about to say out loud.

They found him in about the same spot where Jeffrey had spoken to him hours earlier. The sun was a strong glow over the low foothills in the west with iron gray clouds pushing the color out of the sunset. There was still just enough light to see by. The wheelbarrow sat where it had before, empty save for a sheen of dark blood. The Favored faced them and spread his arms wide as he spoke.

"The time is upon us brothers. The sun is low enough in the sky that my best hound and I can take to the trails and the shadows. We'll track the scent of our prize like a predator tracking its prey and you, in your machines, will follow. When we find what is ours, we will lay waste to them and theirs as a lesson to others that The Mother does not tolerate the defiance of non-believers. We will write her name in their blood across the night sky as a testament to her power."

Jeffrey stood at the rear, close enough to be part of the group but far enough that at least a few of the congregants were between him and the Favored. He smiled at the words as a few excited murmurs rose up.

"Favored," Brady said from the front. "I apologize for my ignorance, sir, but how are we going to follow you if you're with your hound and we're in our vehicles?"

The Favored grinned. "That is an excellent question… Zachary, was it?"

Brady nodded nervously. "Yes, sir."

"Come here, Zachary, and I'll show you."

Everyone seemed to draw back even as Brady took a few hesitant steps forward. All eyes were on the Favored.

Suddenly, so fast that Jeffrey could have missed it if he'd blinked, the Favored surged forward and grabbed Brady's head, a hand on either side. He tilted the man's face slightly and leaned in as though he were about to kiss him on the mouth but stopped with a couple a inches between their faces. Deep, violet light flared in the Favored's eyes as a stream of black, oily things that resembled earthworms shot from his mouth and onto Brady's face. They stuck there for an instant before squirming and winding their way into his mouth and nostrils.

Brady bucked and choked in the Favored's grasp but the warlock did not let him fall. After a couple of seconds that seemed like an hour, the Favored released Brady. He fell to the ground and rolled around violently there making a sound like something between a choke and a scream.

The Favored stepped back to give the man room to convulse. He looked over at the rest of them as he wiped gray slime from the corners of his mouth with the back of his hand.

"Just wait for it," he said.

Jeffrey stood and watched, listening to the congregants around him. Some of the men sounded alarmed, others amused, but none of them spoke while Brady twisted in the dirt. Minutes passed before he stopped moving.

"Here we go," the Favored said with a grin. "This here's the good part."

As though on cue, Brady's body jerked, his limbs snapping straight for an instant before the man rolled to all fours and sprang to his feet with far more speed and agility than he had displayed before. He squatted there with his head faced down. Jeffrey thought he heard him sniffing, as though smelling the air. He turned his eyes towards the congregants. Each of them stared wide eyed at their former brother. There was more than one excited smile.

Brady raised his head and looked over at them. His face was changed. Black veins showed through his skin. His nose had flattened and twitched as he sniffed at the air. His breath scraped over lips that were pushed out of shape by a mouth that seemed to have sprouted another set of teeth. Dark, jaundiced eyes shot through with crimson blood vessels fell on the Favored and Brady whimpered at the sight of him.

"Ah, come here, boy," the Master of Hounds said. "Let's have none of that. You're more suited to service now than you've ever been. Get up and let's have a look at you."

Brady rose. He seemed hesitant, as if he weren't sure whether or not his legs would lift him up.

The Favored grabbed him by the shoulders and said, "You feel us now, don't you? My hound and me? Yes, I can see it in you. You're with us now, one of the pack. You'll know where we go and you'll lead these men to us. You understand, hound? You point the way for them."

Brady nodded and grunted his response. Jeffrey stared at the man's deformed features and wondered if he could even speak anymore.

The Favored stepped away from Brady and walked towards the out building he'd been throwing his hound's 'snacks' into earlier. A sound came from within, a deep growl that sounded like it belonged on the African Savannah more than an Alabama farm. The Favored turned back to face them and said, "You boys try and keep up."

The thing burst from the building behind him. It was an inky black shape the size of a small horse but wider at the shoulder than any horse Jeffrey had ever seen. The thing's head was raised to the night sky and it howled at the clouds with a snarling sound that made Jeffrey's guts quiver. A think mane of writhing tendrils ran from the top of its stunted head all the way down the length of its body and gathered into a heavy tail that whipped in the shadows. Crimson eyes came to rest on all of them as the howl ended. It growled and showed them two rows of long, gray teeth that dripped something dark from its lipless mouth. The look only lasted a moment before the thing charged towards the Favored.

The thing was coming so fast that Jeffrey thought it was going to run the warlock down. Instead, he watched in awe as the Favored leaped into the air in a perfectly timed jump that brought him down on top of the hound as it passed under him. Rather than just landing on the thing and riding it, though, the Master of Hounds sank into the beast amid a halo of dark light until he had completely merged with it.

They all ducked instinctively as the thing continued its charge without slowing and jumped over all their heads into the shadows at the side of the house. Jeffrey stared after it, his heart pounding in his chest and his breath coming in sharp gasps as another howl tore through the freshly fallen night.

He looked back to see Brady already moving towards the cars. "This way," he said, every word coming on the back of a growl. "The master hunts tonight."

CHAPTER THIRTY-FIVE

Huntsville Police Department
Interrogation Room
815 Wheeler Ave NW
Huntsville, AL
October 29 6:31 PM CST

Clint's neck hurt. He'd been sitting with his head hanging for so long that he'd developed a tight line of pain at the base of his skull. He rolled his head on his shoulders trying to loosen the ache but it was hardly worth the effort. After sitting for as long as he had with his range of motion limited by the cuffs the only thing that was going to help was to get up and move around. That and a massage the first chance he got.

He leaned forward again and closed his eyes. He was getting pretty fed up with the whole situation. He knew that Arlo and Lonebear were getting the run around from the powers that be at the police department so he figured that it would take them some time to get him freed. Still, he'd expected them hours ago and there wasn't any sign that they even knew where he was. There were at least three police stations that he knew of in the city so it was kind of a crap shoot for them trying to find him with no cooperation. Whatever was happening out there, Clint was starting to feel like he wasn't much of a priority.

Bellmon's warning about them leaving him in the wind came to mind but he dismissed it just as quickly. He knew that there was no way Arlo was going to leave him sitting in jail cell while he still possessed his ability to use the Truesight. It was obvious that made him an asset that the magus wasn't about to abandon.

A laugh bubbled up in his throat and he let the sound of it bounce off the stark walls. He was sitting there thinking about his new superpower and how valuable it was to his wizard friend. When exactly had his life gotten that absurd? Not for the first time, he wondered if this whole thing wasn't some kind of pre-death hallucination. Was he still in that parking garage getting electrocuted by that psychopath with the dogs? He'd heard stories about that kind of thing but always questioned them because if they were pre-death experiences then who was around to talk about them? The people that he'd help resuscitate over the years had only ever talked about there being nothing but black, like a dreamless sleep.

He shook his head and let the laugh play itself out. Regardless of whether or not he was hallucinating, he had to see this through to the end. If it was just his consciousness in its death throes, then the end was predetermined. If it wasn't, though, if this was his new normal like Arlo had said, then he damn sure wasn't going to just sit back and watch it happen around him.

He glanced up at the camera in the corner of the interrogation room. He'd thought about using his Truesight to see if there was some way out of the cuffs but the camera had stopped him. He didn't want out of them so that he could escape. Clint had counted at least nine cops in the rooms outside counting Bellmon and the two bruisers he'd had with him when they'd arrested him. That and the two security doors that separated him from the rest of the world was more than enough to convince him that even if he did get out of the room he was in, the only place he'd be going was right back in. No, he wanted out of the cuffs because it was plainly obvious that they weren't needed. That and the fact that he'd just love to see Bellmon's face when he walked in and found Clint leaning back in his chair with his feet up on the table. The camera, though, ruined that idea. He could only imagine what would happen if they caught him with his eyes lit up on digital HD.

He spent a few more minutes scooting his chair around the floor trying to find a more comfortable position before he heard the door click and then open. Clint looked up, expecting to see Bellmon and the female detective coming in for another talk. He felt a grin crack his face when Arlo slipped into the room with a quick step and close the door behind him.

"Well, it is abou-"

Arlo faced him and held a finger to his lips for Clint to be silent. His face was pale and sweat beaded across his forehead.

"Arlo, what-"

"Shut up," Arlo whispered in a sharp hiss. Clint noticed that there were misty streamers of light flowing from each of Arlo's rings and into his arms. "This is difficult. Do not distract me with needless talk."

Clint had no idea what was going on but nodded like he understood.

"No one can see me unless I allow it," he said. "Once you're free, get behind me and put a one hand on my shoulder. Keep it there no matter what until we clear the building. Understand?"

Clint nodded again.

Arlo moved in and leaned over Clint to place one of his palms over his right wrist. Feverish heat rolled off him in a sweat scented cloud. There was a sharp click and Clint felt the pressure release from his wrists. He slid his hands from the cuffs and stood up, moving behind Arlo and latching onto his left shoulder with his left hand.

A sudden feeling of lightness coursed through him, like he was somehow as insubstantial as the air he breathed. He tightened his grip as Arlo said, "Don't let go. Don't speak. Don't touch anyone but me."

Clint squeezed the other man's shoulder to let him know he understood. Arlo moved carefully to the door. Clint could feel the heat coming off the man and he was breathing in tight, controlled breaths as though he were trying to keep from panting. Arlo drew a deeper breath and opened the door.

An image of a dozen cops with weapons drawn flashed through Clint's mind as they moved into the hallway. Instead, they stepped into an empty corridor that was separated from a room filled with low cubicles by a half-wall topped with reinforced glass and steel frames. A few of the officers that Clint had counted earlier were still at their desks talking on phones or tapping at their computers. No one looked their way.

Arlo moved without hesitation, heading towards the exit with smooth, quick steps. He hesitated and then pushed Clint back against the wall. Instead of switching hands, Clint turned and faced the wall, looking back over his shoulder at whoever was coming down the hallway.

Clint's heart jumped in his chest as Bellmon came around the corner, talking on his phone. Clint heard him say his name but couldn't understand anything else the man said. He walked towards them, intent on his call, and then right past them without hesitating. Clint was sure the man's eyes had swept right over them but he acted as though there was nothing there.

For a second, he thought Bellmon was headed back to the now empty interrogation room but the detective turned and went through a heavy door and into the cubicle room. Arlo started forward again and Clint whispered into his ear, "That was my interrogator. We need to double-time it."

Arlo didn't give him any kind of acknowledgment except to pick up his pace.

They made it past the first security door by whatever trick it was that Arlo had used to unlock Clint's cuffs. They had to actually open the door, though, and Clint was worried someone might notice that but they made it through with no one the wiser.

They had to press themselves against the walls twice more before they reached the last security door. They managed to slip past this one as it closed behind a couple of uniformed officers carrying trays of takeout food. The smell of beef and refried beans hit Clint's nose and his stomach grumbled like the neglected organ it had become.

They went through the glass doors at the front of the building and Arlo made a sharp right into the parking lot and out of sight for anyone entering or leaving the building. He let out a sudden breath and leaned heavily against the wall. The light faded from his rings. The sun had set and full dark was over the city but there was enough light from the parking lot for Clint to see how pale Arlo was.

Clint didn't bother asking Arlo how he was. "Do we have a ride?" he said.

Arlo held up his phone and panted, "Lonebear… favorited contacts. He's waiting close by."

"Is Rani with him?"

Arlo shook his head. "She stayed with the girl. Wanted to be there when she woke up."

The phone was powered down so Clint activated it and started tapping icons once they appeared. "I think you might've kicked a hornet's nest here, Arlo. It won't be long before they know I'm gone."

"They're suspicious already," he said, his breath stronger. "Our government contacts will support us but that takes time with officials as stubborn as these are being. I need you now. Relax, this is not my first jailbreak."

Clint grunted a laugh as he found Lonebear's listing in the phone. His finger landed on it just as the screen skewed into pixels and went blank. Clint stared at it in confusion for a moment, tapped at the screen a couple of times, and then said, "It died."

When Arlo didn't respond, Clint looked up and found him staring at the parking lot lights. They were all flickering on and off. Loud clicks stuttered through the night with every flicker. The lights on the building started following suit when Clint said, "Arlo?"

Arlo didn't answer. He headed for the front of the building again, muttering something under his breath as he went.

Clint started to call after him but thought better of it. He was not all that anxious to follow him to the front doors of the place he'd just escaped from. When the lights closest to the street popped and went dark, though, he muttered a curse and hurried to catch up with him. He found him near the edge of the parking lot staring down the main entrance lane between a loose assembly of parked cars. When Clint followed Arlo's gaze, he felt a sudden cold spread through him.

Jubal Mott, naked save for a pair of filthy slacks, was walking up the parking lane with his hands relaxed and hanging at his side. His eyes were pinpoints of dark violet in the stuttering light. One of his hounds walked beside him like a nightmarish, stalking wolf the size of a small car. Mott turned his gaze on them a laughed softly.

"Perfect," he said. "Oh, so perfect. Everything I want all in one place. And you, boy; I remember you from the hospital. I don't know how you're alive but I promise to rid you of that condition forthwith. You and this sad excuse for a magus."

Mott threw his hands up and his head back. *"Nog forth hounds ot n'ghftyar,"* he shouted. *"Nog forth hounds ot n'ghftyar! Nog forth hounds ot n'ghftyar!"*

For an instant, nothing happened. Then a line of violet light split down the center of Mott's chest. The warlock screamed… or laughed… Clint couldn't be sure. It was some twisted mixture of the two that only got louder as the line started to separate his chest cavity into two parts, like a set of swinging doors on hinges of flesh and breaking bone.

There should have been blood and viscera and all the other things that one would expect to see in a suddenly vivisected human body. There wasn't. Instead, a swell of blackness shot through with purple sparks grew out of the warlock's chest and hung in the air like some sort of enormous growth.

Hounds suddenly started leaping from it. They were smaller than the one that had come in with Mott but they were all still larger than any dog that Clint had ever seen or even heard of. They hit the ground all snarling teeth, crimson eyes, and tentacled manes that whipped an excited frenzy in the cold air.

Clint was frozen. He watched in fascinated horror as dozens of the things erupted from Jubal Mott's chest while the warlock laughed and screamed with every arrival. They arranged themselves around him, standing on and between the cars, snarling at the humans that stood in their way.

Sometime during the spectacle a misty drizzle had started to fall, the gray clouds finally making good on the day's promise. The warlock was on his knees and the largest of the hounds was standing over him like a guardian demon while his chest cracked and snapped back into place. Clint could see Mott struggling to catch his breath.

Cars pulled into the parking lot behind Mott and the hounds. When Clint saw the rifle wielding men getting out, he realized that they weren't with the police.

Still on his knees, Mott looked at Arlo and Clint with dark violet virtually burning in his eyes. His face twisted with hatred and he screamed, "Attack! Kill them all!"

CHAPTER THIRTY-SIX

Clint had been so distracted by the hideous display that he didn't know about the cops that had come out of the building behind him until they were shoving him out of the way and pointing their weapons at the pack of hounds. Shouts of 'freeze' and 'drop your weapons' filled the air but they were suddenly lost under the cacophony of gunfire and snarling howls that filled the night.

Clint grabbed Arlo and pulled him down behind a parked car. Someone screamed as more police came rushing out of the building, an assortment of weapons in their hands. The hounds came at them all, leaping over their fellow officers like the weapons just didn't matter.

"It's here," Arlo shouted over the din. "It must be here in the evidence room! Why else would Mott be here?"

"I think we've got bigger concerns," Clint shouted back. "Will bullets work on those things?"

"Only if there's a lot of them for every barghest. They need to coordinate their attacks."

Clint snapped a glance over the car and saw the police fighting for their lives against hounds and gunmen alike. The cops didn't have a line so much as a collection of officers scrambling from cover to cover while shooting and trying to avoid the hounds that were charging them. In the distance, he could see the flash of multicolored strobe lights as patrol units raced to respond to the chaos. Clint had to duck down again as a body came sailing through the air and slammed, broken and bleeding, into the brick wall behind them. The body slumped over and the woman's dead eyes stared up at Clint. With a start, he recognized Bellmon's unsmiling partner from the interrogation room.

"We've got to help these guys," Clint said.

"We have to get the cryptical," Arlo snapped back.

"Arlo, these people are going to get slaughtered! Can't you… I don't know! Throw a fireball or something? Use your magic to at least give them a chance?"

"We have to get the cryptical, Mercer! It's a much greater danger than these beasts."

"And it's secured in an evidence locker. We can save lives here and still get the book. Come on, Arlo! I can't believe that you're okay with letting these cops die when you can help save at least some of them."

"You don't realize what you're asking."

The largest of the hounds howled as the growing wail of sirens mixed with the cacophony. "Maybe I don't but I can't just watch people die, Arlo. Not again. You go, I'll stay and help."

The magus looked up at him. There was something in his eyes that Clint hadn't seen before. Something between curiosity and admiration, he thought, but he wasn't sure. Arlo nodded slightly and said, "That's just what Deana would have said."

"What?"

Arlo shook his head. "Nothing!" he said. "You'll just get yourself killed out here. I'll draw their attention, you go for the cryptical. Listen to me, though, Mercer. I need you to have a singular purpose in mind once you get it and that's to get the package to me. It may well try to influence you so no matter what else you might think or feel, I need you to get that thing to me above all else. That is your mission, Mercer, and the mission comes first. Do you understand? It is very important that you understand."

Clint nodded.

Arlo returned the gesture and reached into his jacket pocket and withdrew a small syringe. Before Clint realized what he was doing Arlo had stabbed it into his own neck and injected the contents.

"Hey!" Clint said. "What the hell, man? What was that?"

"Something to help me light up the night," Arlo said with a smile. "Oh, this is really going to piss off some people at the home office. Once I've got the hound's attention, you go for the evidence room."

Clint nodded and looked back at the dead detective. He crawled over to her as bullets thudded into the wall well above his head. He snatched the bloodied badge from her belt and looked back to Arlo. "Ready when you are," he shouted.

Arlo didn't respond. He had his head bowed and his eyes closed. Words with thick, hard sounds fell in harsh whispers from his lips. Each of his ten rings started to glow, getting brighter and brighter until arcs of energy shot in jagged lines from the rings to his skin. His hands crackled with energy that sent a white glow up his arms and through his body.

The words kept coming, louder and faster, but still in a language that meant nothing to Clint. Arlo's eyes opened and the white energy popped from them like bolts of micro-lightning. The magus rose to this feet, his body alight with his magic. It charged the air around him and Clint was sure he could actually feel the power brushing against his skin.

Some of the nearby cops actually stopped firing as Arlo stepped out from cover and walked towards the nearest of the hounds. Even they hesitated at the sight, the glow from his body seeming to drive them back. Clint heard Jubal Mott scream something at Arlo but he couldn't understand the words. Arlo didn't bother answering except to increase the cadence of his chant until it seemed the words were just one long constant sound that no human throat should have been able to create.

Bullets flew at Arlo but none found their mark.

The light grew brighter, so much so that Clint had to squint against the brilliance.

Arlo raised his hands and his eyes to the night and then suddenly slammed them down onto the ground in front of him.

The parking lot exploded in a wave a light and heat that felt like a sudden summer day. Cars rocked on their suspension, windows shattered and the three hounds nearest to Arlo burst into pieces that thumped onto the ground like huge chunks of fleshy, smoldering charcoal. When the glow faded, there was a momentary pause in the shooting. The magus didn't waste it. He was back on his feet, energy still dancing up his arms and into his eyes as he shouted, "Combine and concentrate your fire on the nearest hound! Leave the warlock to me!"

Mott screamed something incoherent and lightning arced towards Arlo. He raised his left hand and caught the bolt on a shield of what looked like solid white light while he swept his right hand in an arc towards Mott. Clint didn't see any effect from the move except that the front quarter panel of a nearby car suddenly tore itself from the rest of the vehicle as though it had gotten hit by an invisible truck.

Gunfire filled the night again as someone shouted, "Open fire!"

Clint looked towards the shout and saw Bellmon near the front of line, shotgun at his shoulder and firing into the oncoming hounds with measured precision. The detective dropped down to reload and their eyes met. The detective's normally calm, rational expression was a cracking mask over his panic and disbelief. His expression twisted into something that begged for answers.

All Clint could do was give him a reassuring nod and sprint for the doors that led into the station.

CHAPTER THIRTY-SEVEN

Someone started screaming as soon as Clint burst through the doors. He held up his stolen badge and yelled, "It's okay, I'm a cop!"

A woman's head peeked up over the wall that separated the lobby area from the security desk and cubicle farm. Her dark face was nearly gray with fright and it was obvious she'd been crying. "Who are you?" she said, her voicing shaking with barely restrained sobs. "What in the name of Jesus is happening out there?"

Clint kept the badge up high and said, "It's bad, ma'am, you're best off just staying put unless you know a back way out of here but I need to get through the security gates first. Can you open it up for me?"

"I don't know you."

"No, you don't," Clint said, his mind racing for what little he knew about the local police department. "I normally work out of the South Parkway station. I'm a detective. Detective Castle.

Rick Castle." He winced even as he said the name. All he could do was hope that people who worked in real police stations were about as fond of cop shows as people who worked in hospitals were of medical shows. Which is to say, not very much.

"We're always supposed to check folks out before we let them in but the security are all…" she pointed towards the door and barked out a startled scream as something outside exploded.

"I get that," Clint said, "but I think you'd agree that these aren't ordinary circumstances. I really need to get back there."

"How come you aren't out there helping?"

Clint had already thought about that one. "I lost my weapon. I need to re-arm so I can get back out there. I can't get to the guns if you don't open up for me, though."

She stared at him, her eyes flicking back and forth between him and the door. "All right," she said finally. "Let me get around to the- Oh, Jesus!"

The woman's voice was panicked as she spotted something behind Clint and dropped behind the wall again.

Muscle memory honed by long hours of combat drills took over Clint's body. He didn't bother spinning to look at whatever had frightened the woman but instead dropped low and did a tuck and roll that brought him back to his feet at a point on a forty-five degree angle from where he'd been standing. He expected to see a gunman or a hound. It was neither but somehow both.

The man- or what Clint suspected had once been a man -in front of him was crouched low, glaring at him with bloodshot, jaundiced eyes. His teeth were bared in a snarl and Clint was sure there were a lot more of them than there should have been. He flexed clawed fingers as he looked at Clint. Gray drool dripped from his black lipped mouth and his face was a web of black veins.

"What the actual f-" Clint started to say but had to dodge back as the thing lunged for him, slashing at his belly with thick claws.

"The Master's prize is here," the thing said in a deep, growling voice, "but I know you. You were with the Master's enemy. You stink of him. I will please the Master with both his prize and your heart!"

Clint gritted his teeth and said, "Yeah? Well, sorry, Snoopy. I'm not quite done with it yet."

The man-beast howled like a demonic wolf and charged at Clint.

He came in fast and low with his teeth bared and claws leading, ready to shred Clint's legs to ribbons. Clint shifted his legs back and caught the thing with a hand on each shoulder, pushing down to force his already overbalanced body to the floor. With a shout, Clint delivered two fast, brutal knee strikes to the side of the thing's head. Even though it had been years since Clint had regularly trained, there was still enough power in his legs to make that a fight ending move. If, that is, he had been fighting a human being.

Clint backed off fast, thinking he'd brought the beast down but it just shook off the attack and came at him again. It snarled and drooled like a rabid animal as it charged him with its hands flashing through the air. Clint did his best to stay out of reach but the lobby wasn't that big and only provided him with so much room to dodge.

The claws flashed too close and Clint instinctively raised his left arm to block. The claws tore through his jacket and shirt as though they weren't there. Lines of burning pain flared through his forearm.

Clint screamed a curse and felt his anger surge up over his fear. He braced his feet, dodged another swipe of the claws, and then waited for the thing to follow up with the other arm. When it did, Clint slapped at the attacking limb as it passed, adding to its momentum and throwing the monster off balance. Clint stepped fast behind it and slipped his arms under its shoulders. He clasped his hands at the back of its neck and cranked down hard on the top of its spine.

The idea was to get behind it and stay out of the reach. What Clint didn't count on, though, was just how strong the damn thing was. It just flexed and brought its arms down straight, breaking Clint's grip. It spun towards Clint with both arms extended far enough to catch him on the side of his ribcage send him flying across the lobby.

Clint hit the opposite wall hard enough to crack the beige drywall and fell onto a pair of waiting room chairs before tumbling into the floor breathless, aching, and with fresh pain burning in his side where the claws had raked his ribs. He looked up and saw the thing taking measured steps towards him. He would've sworn the thing was smiling around all those dark teeth.

A loud, sudden click off to his left drew his attention. Clint looked towards the sound just in time to see the security door open just wide enough for a slender, dark skinned hand to toss a shiny metal object in his direction. The nickel plated, snub nosed revolver hit the carpet and bounced once just out of his reach as the security door slammed shut again.

Clint didn't hesitate. He rolled towards the weapon and snatched it up, continuing his roll onto his back and bringing it to bear.

The beast must have seen the woman throw Clint the gun, too, because he was practically on top of him before Clint could line up a shot. Clint got a foot up just in time to deliver a kick to the thing's chest that didn't knock it off of him but stopped its advance cold. It raised one hand to slash at the inside of Clint's raised thigh.

The weapon boomed much louder than Clint expected in the small space before the claws could fall. The beast's shoulder jerked back with the bullet's impact and staggered the thing. Clint dropped his leg and raised up just enough to empty the remaining six rounds into the beast's chest.

Every shot forced the beast back another step. Dark blood sprayed onto the walls behind the thing with every impact. As the last report echoed through the room and Clint clicked on a dry chamber, the thing's knees finally buckled and it fell face first onto the floor.

Clint sat there for a minute, ears ringing and wounds burning, until he finally took a look at the weapon the receptionist had thrown him. It was a seven round Taurus snub nose chambered for .357 magnum rounds. He shouted for the woman and wasn't surprised that his own voice seemed dull in his ears.

Her head popped up over the wall again. "Did you get him?"

Clint nodded and held up the weapon. "Thanks. Where'd you get this thing?"

She shrugged and said, "That's my purse gun."

Clint shook his head and started climbing to his feet. He'd love to see what she considered a house gun.

"They're after something in the evidence lock up," he said. "Which way?"

The woman, whose name turned out to be Edmonia, got Clint through the security gates and then promptly retrieved her gun which she reloaded from a small, floral print change purse filled with bullets before dropping both back into her large bag. Clint had hoped she might offer him the weapon but instead all she provided was directions to the evidence room and her promise that she'd be locked up in one of the supply closets with the door barricaded if anyone needed her.

Clint found the evidence lock up at the end of the hall and down a flight of stairs. There was a Plexiglas window that was obviously where things were passed to and from the officer manning the evidence room. Clint looked through the window and saw that the room was empty. He glanced at the heavy steel door next to it and noticed that it was ajar.

A sinking feeling crept into his gut as he pushed the door open and entered. Shelves of boxes and closed cabinets filled the room but there was no one there. Clint glanced back to make sure Edmonia had not changed her mind about following him. When he was sure she wasn't lurking back there with her purse cannon at the ready, he open his inner eye and looked around.

None of the boxes or cabinets showed any sign of the inky blackness that marked the cryptical's presence. There was, however, a familiar smoky trail leading out the door and deeper into the building's lower level. The cryptical was gone.

Clint shook his head and said, "Son of a *bitch*!"

CHAPTER THIRTY-EIGHT

Washington Street and Oakwood Avenue
Huntsville, AL
October 29 6:52 PM CST

Jimmy Harrison sat at the intersection while the light changed to green, then yellow, and then back to red. The car behind him honked furiously but he barely heard it. If some piss-ant wanted to get out and hassle a police cruiser going about its business then he had everything he needed to put them right in their place, no problem. He needed a second, just a moment, really, to decide what to do. He absently let his hand drop on the evidence bag in the seat next to him.

There was a part of him that was nagging that he shouldn't have left the station when the shooting started, shouldn't have abandoned his fellow officers, but, dammit, his job was to protect the evidence. He had to keep it safe, keep it secure, keep it out of the hands of the all piss-ant scumbags that would try to take it. He might not have the knees for riding patrol and chasing down perps anymore but he could do this. He could secure the evidence. He could keep it safe. Stapler had brought him this. The kid was counting on him. Hell, the whole department was counting on him to-

The horns blared again.

Harrison's anger flared and he dropped one hand to his door release and the other to the Glock that was holstered at his hip. If that piss-ant, son of a-

Wait.

He shook his head to clear the sudden rage. He could feel sweat cooling on his skin, his heart thudding in his chest. There was a something in his head, a buzz behind his thoughts. Was it a heart attack? He'd taken his pills that morning like every morning so-

More horns sounded. A car squealed tires as it shot out from behind him. He half expected to see a single finger salute but apparently the driver wasn't mad enough to flip off a police car.

Horns again.

He was blocking traffic. Shit, what was he thinking? What had been going on back at the station?

Another car pulled past him but with less tire squealing.

Harrison put the cruiser into gear and crossed the intersection, whipping into a Jiffy Mart parking lot. The cruiser's radio was a chorus of distress calls;

multiple officers down, shots exchanged, EMS en route. Every moment of training and experience he had told him that he should be back at the station, standing with his own, helping-

He gasped as the buzz in his head doubled. A dull pain bloomed and settled into an ache in his chest.

He shook his head. No, no, no; let the young bucks handle the gun fights. He was too slow, his reflexes too run down to be any good in a shootout. His role was to protect the evidence. It was his function, his purpose, his reason. So long as he had that he was still a part of the force, still contributing, still relevant. He would do it, by God, he would die to fill his role if it came to it.

He felt something tear under his fingers. He looked down and realized that he was gripping the evidence bag that Stapler had given him so tight that his thick knuckles were white from the pressure. He released it and stared at the thing.

This was important. It was the last thing to be logged into evidence before all hell broke loose back at the station. Is this what the scumbags that had started shooting up the place were after? Could that be? If so, how could he have known that? Why had he taken this one piece of evidence when he'd left?

The pain in his chest deepened. The buzz in his head sharpened.

It didn't matter. He'd been a cop a long time and his instincts told him that this was the right move, the straight play, the thing to do. He had to secure it, hide it, keep it safe.

But where?

He needed someplace secure. It had to be hard to find and easy to defend like the evidence lockup had been. An underground bunker or a basement would be ideal. It needed to be hard to get to, hard to access, hard to reach.

Someplace deep. Someplace dark.

An image formed in his mind, full of stone and shadows and the scent of undisturbed soil. There was water there, too, cold and clear and deep and dark.

That was the place. No one would look there.

That was where it belonged.

Harrison hit the switch to activate the cruiser's strobes and sped away from the parking lot.

CHAPTER THIRTY-NINE

Huntsville Police Department
815 Wheeler Ave NW
Huntsville, AL
October 29 7:06 PM CST

Clint came out through the station's main entrance to a sight that reminded him of something from a disaster movie. Strobes from the ambulances and police cars painted the scene in chaotic flashes of red and blue. There was an overturned car burning near the center of the parking lot, injured people were staggering towards paramedics and leaning against cars, and there were bodies scattered about on the asphalt. Some of them, he realized, weren't entirely whole.

Jubal Mott and his congregants were nowhere to be seen, as were the hounds, but Clint could hear them howling in the distance. A uniformed officer groaned and struggled to sit up a few feet from him and Clint hurried to his side, helping him get to an upright position and assessing his condition as he did so.

One of the man's arms was a mess of torn flesh. He was holding one hand over the injured arm's bicep but Clint could see bright blood leaking from between his fingers. Clint told him to keep his hand where it was and stripped the belt from his pants. He looped it around the arm just below the armpit and pulled it as tight as he could. Once he'd looped the excess belt over the arm a second time, he held it in place and started shouting for a medic. It wasn't exactly a textbook perfect technique but he figured it would do the trick until someone with a proper emergency kit could get him treated.

The young woman that came running over a minute later wasn't anyone he knew but she looked focused and calm. She knelt next to the patient and said, "What do we have here?" Her voice was controlled and even.

"Pretty sure it's a Brachial Artery tear," Clint said. "I applied the tourniquet about a minute ago."

"That's pretty specific. Are you a medic?"

"Nurse. Huntsville ER."

"Thanks," she said. "I've got this but look around. We can use all the help we can get."

Clint gave her a nod and stood up just in time to see Bellmon coming towards him like a man bent on violence. His face was flushed and the closer he got, the more dark stains Clint could make out on his police polo shirt. The shorter man came in fast and got in Clint's face. Clint let him but didn't back up even a step.

"Did you know?" the detective said, his voice tight and angry.

"What?"

"Did you know? Did you know this was going to happen?"

"Of course I didn't know! How could I?"

"What the hell is this, Mercer? Who was that? What were those things? Do you know how many cops-"

"I told you," Clint said, leaning towards him and returning the man's glare. "I told you this was outside your experience. I told you that Dandridge and Lonebear knew how to handle these things. I told you to leave the monsters to them."

"This is what happened at the hospital, isn't it?"

Clint nodded. "Now you get it, right? Even if I explained it all, even after this, you still wouldn't believe me because it's just so damned unbelievable. Just take care of your officers, Bellmon. Get them the care they-"

"My officers? Are you deaf? Can't you hear the howling?"

Clint could but it hadn't really registered what it meant. He felt his eyes get wide and he said, "What happened?"

Bellmon shook his head. "He just stopped. The… what did Dandridge call him? Warlock? He just stopped and told his people to pull out. Then he told those… things… of his to scatter. He told them to go into the city and hunt, Mercer. He told them to *hunt*." The man's face had tightened into an expression of barely controlled terror.

"What are we doing about it?"

"Pulling every cop in a hundred mile radius that's willing to come, calling the mayor and the governor, using the cellular weather alert system to try and get people off the streets, what cruisers we have are out looking for those things; we're doing whatever we can. I've never trained for hellhound attack, Mercer. We're all pretty much making this up as we go."

Clint closed his eyes and took a deep breath. "Where's Dandridge? Have you seen him?"

Bellmon nodded. "Yeah, he's with Lonebear. This way. Maybe they have some genius insights because you're no damn help at all."

Clint glanced up at the young paramedic leading the officer with the injured arm to an ambulance. He started to say something to Bellmon but the detective had already turned away. Clint gritted his teeth in frustration and followed.

They found Arlo and Lonebear near the street standing near the Tahoe's opened rear hatch. Arlo had his jacket off and Lonebear was taping off a swath of bandages that encompassed all of Arlo's left forearm. The magus saw them coming and gestured for Lonebear to intercept them. The big marine headed their way.

"Detective Bellmon," Lonebear said, coming in with his hand extended to shake. "I've made some calls. We've got agents and emergency relief aboard helicopters and inbound from Birmingham and Nashville. Estimate for the nearest one is fifteen minutes out."

Bellmon approached Lonebear in much the same way he had Clint though instead of getting in his face, it was more like he was challenging the man's sternum. He ignored the outstretched hand. Lonebear took his eyes off the frustrated detective long enough to nod a greeting to Clint and cut his eyes towards Arlo.

Clint took the hint and headed for the Tahoe. Arlo looked up as he approached and said, "You didn't get it."

The magus looked exhausted with sunken cheeks and an even paler complexion than normal. His clothes were filthy, scorched, and there was a large bruise coming up on one side of his face. As Clint drew closer, he caught the distinct scent of burned hair.

"It wasn't there. How'd you know?"

"The warlock called for a retreat. He'd only do that if he'd gotten the cryptical or sensed that it was no longer here. Tell me what you saw."

Clint told him what he'd found in the evidence room. "I tried to follow. I thought maybe some of Mott's guys had snuck in the back while we were out here. I only got as far as a security door that led out to a back parking lot with some patrol vehicles sitting there. The trail ended at one of the parking spaces. Looked to me like they took one of the cruisers."

Arlo nodded. "It's gotten its hooks into another mind. I assume there was no sign of an officer on duty in the evidence room?"

Clint shook his head.

"He or she, then, most likely."

"Do you think Bellmon could track it for us or something? The trail looks like it got dispersed once the car was moving."

"Under normal circumstances, I'm sure that would not be a problem. Circumstances like this, though, it would take more time than we have. I think I know where it's going, though, so it's a moot point."

"Where? How do you know?"

"Mott let something slip that gave me the final hint I needed. He said that once he had the cryptical that his pack would grow large enough to shake the very earth itself."

Clint waited for him to finish as Arlo slipped back into his jacket. When he didn't, Clint said, "Arlo, let's pretend for a minute that I don't know what that means."

Arlo shot him an irritated glance that quickly softened. Clint thought he saw a spasm twitch the skin under his left eye.

"The cryptical we've been chasing," Arlo said, "is just one in a set called The Seven Cryptical Books of Hsan the Greater. Each book in the set is special and powerfully focused in its own right. Until now I didn't know which of the volumes it was which made it harder to predict what the crytpical was driving its thralls to do. I've worked that part out now."

"Okay. Feel like sharing?"

Arlo called out for Lonebear and then said, "The fourth cryptical contains the rites and means to open a portal to the realm of beings known as Chthonians. Think of them as giant, intelligent arthropods who view humans as cattle. Supposedly, alongside the fourth cryptical's diagrams for transplanar workings there are also instructions for mentally enslaving any chthon that pass into our world. Mott intends to do exactly that; expand his pack out to the potentially billions of chthon that exist on the other side of the portal that cryptical opens."

"Holy crap," Clint said. "How can you be sure?"

Arlo shrugged. "It fits. Professor Warner was an amateur geologist with strong faith in the Old Ones so a potential means of contacting a deep dwelling race like the Chthon would appeal to him. Then there's the police report from the young woman in the park. I didn't think much of it before but she was quoted as saying that she needed to get to 'the dark'. That could easily mean underground. When

Mott let it slip about expanding his pack and shaking the earth, it all kind of clicked since stories about the Chthon usually include earthquakes of some kind."

"Earthquakes?" Clint said. "That's… that's just awesome. How do you know where it's going?"

"You told me," Arlo said. "Remember? At the cemetery? You were listing off local landmarks and mentioned a cave beneath the downtown courthouse. Thirty seconds on Google told me the rest."

Clint did remember and with that came another recollection. "And there's an entrance to those caves in the same park where they picked up Jasmine Ives."

"Who?"

"The woman in the park. The one I chased through the cemetery?"

"Ah, yes. Just so. Was that her name? I never looked."

Clint started to comment on Arlo's overwhelming sense of empathy but thought better of it. Instead, he said, "Why the cave?"

"The nature of the fourth cryptical is such that it wants to be used. It pushes those it influences to do so. The rituals contained within it, though, have to be performed while surrounded on all sides by natural, unprocessed stone and soil. Hence, underground, which is also the Chthonian's natural environs."

Clint was about to comment when Lonebear joined them and said, "All right, boss, I think I've got him distracted enough to hold over until C&C can get here to help sort out this mess."

"C&C?" Clint said.

"Clean and conceal," Lonebear replied. Then, to Arlo, "Where to, Boss? What's the play?"

Arlo reached up and closed the Tahoe's door. "Big Spring International Park. One way or another, this will end there."

CHAPTER FORTY

Krispy Kreme
1218 North Memorial Parkway
Huntsville, Alabama
October 29, 7:08 P.M. CST

Jeffrey sat in silence as he watched a pair of police cars streak by with sirens wailing and lights flashing. The two glazed donuts and large black coffee that he'd ordered sat untouched on the small table in front of him as he tried to follow the police progress without seeming more interested than the average citizen. The stereotypical irony of hiding from the police in a donut shop was not lost on him but he was in no mood to enjoy it.

This whole thing, from the moment he'd found Jubal Mott sitting in his kitchen had felt and gone wrong, just utterly wrong. Favored or not, the Master of Hounds had led them into one of the most public and possibly exposing operations in Jeffrey's lifetime. What had he been thinking? An open attack on a police station? By the Mother's touch, it was madness. They lived in the shadows, they thrived behind the scenes, and they served The Mother with their silence.

Was it possible for a Favored to lose their way? Jeffrey didn't know but he was starting to suspect it was. The very thought seemed blasphemous, though.

Another cruiser sped by, breaking his revere with its rolling sound and light show. An ambulance followed not far behind.

The Favored hadn't even bothered to give them instructions. They'd lost half their congregants and all he could manage was a frustrated scream for them to fall back before he merged with that hound of his again and took off into the dark with the rest of the pack. Jeffrey had ordered everyone into a car and they'd taken off, dropping congregants at random spots with orders to scatter and wait for instructions. Hopefully, they all had sense enough to blend in. He didn't know the man that was supposed to get rid of the car but he'd seemed calm and competent. Jeffry could only hope he knew what he was doing.

Damn it all. He'd kept things quiet in his region for years and now this? A pitched battle with the police, the Pickmen, and Arlo frigging Dandridge? His mind rattled with the possible implications. If they managed to trace one of the congregants they'd lost back to him… it would all be over.

His hands shook a little as he picked up the coffee and took careful sip. It was hot enough to sting a little but he didn't mind. The sensation gave him something to focus on, something to calm him down. He'd been careful. He'd kept out of sight at the police station and he was confident that he hadn't left any obvious trace of his presence in the car or back at the farmhouse. There were no fingerprints or dropped items that might give him away. There was another possibility, though.

Had all the congregants that had gone down in the fight been dead? He hadn't checked. Hell, there hadn't been a way to check without getting shot or mistaken for an enemy by one of those black hounds. He'd gotten a good look at what one of them had done when it had pinned a cop. It wasn't something he was interested in ever seeing again. If one of those fallen faithful had survived and had recognized him… if they betrayed the faith… game over.

He put his hands on his temples and gritted his teeth against a furious scream. The scent of vanilla, sugar, and hot dough wafted up from the donuts and just seemed to highlight his frustration. He didn't even like donuts.

He got up and made his way to the restroom. There was only one thing he could do now, one place he could go for guidance, and he needed privacy to do get there. He went into the men's room, entered one of the stalls, and closed the door.

He took out his silver pen knife and sat down on the toilet without dropping his jeans.

The ritual dish that he kept in his office made contacting The Mother much easier but it wasn't necessary. The magic wasn't in the dish, it was in him and the tiny sliver of The Mother that he carried within him. It was in his faith and his connection to her divine self. It was in his love for her.

He stuck the knife into his thumb until the blood flowed. He used it to trace a sigil on the stall wall and then placed his hand over it, focusing his will, and letting the incantation fall from his lips. The he felt the numbing cold of her presence and smiled. Let the mewling masses bruise their knees begging to all their indifferent deities. When he prayed, his goddess answered.

"Why do you come to me, child?" Her voice was a cold whisper in his mind.

"Praise unto you for your attention, My Mother. I am in need of wisdom and direction in how best to serve you."

"What of my Master of Hounds? Why do you come to me and not seek counsel from my Favored?"

Jeffrey hesitated. This might be a problem. He hadn't considered that she might blame him. If she thought this was his fault for not properly serving Mott, then he'd be better off getting arrested. For a while, anyway.

"Speak!"

The word exploded through Jeffrey's mind like a thunderclap. *"I do not know where he is, Holy Mother. He fled the battle and I-"*

"Battle?" Jeffrey thought he heard a note of surprise in the goddess's voice. *"What battle?"*

Jeffrey spent an instant considering it and then rolled the dice. He told her everything from the moment he'd first met Jubal Mott right up to the current situation. He was especially thorough when he described his conversation with the Favored outside the farmhouse.

"My will was clear. Yet he claimed to know my mind? To assume the prize is his?"

"Yes, My Mother. As he is Favored I did not dare to question or challenge him."

There was silence then. Cold and long and filled with something that made Jeffrey think of waiting for death.

"You have served me well, child," The Mother said finally. *"Gather your flock and return to your homes. Three days hence, call to me again so that I might grace you with further service."*

"Your will is my hand, Mother. I just… No, forgive me. It is not my place."

There was no laugh. Goddesses did not laugh but Jeffrey thought there might be the smallest hint of amusement in her voice.

"You wish to know what is to become of Jubal Mott and the prize he covets? Release such concerns, Jeffrey

Lemaster, for I have taken them on. Go to your rest and come to me again at the appointed time."

Just like that, she was gone. Jeffrey opened his eyes and flattened his palm against the sigil, smearing the sticky blood into just another random stain.

Whatever The Mother had planned, he seemed to be off the hook. More than that, she'd used his name. His *name*. Something told him that held a significance that he could only imagine. Whatever the case, he needed to signal his people to get out of town.

As he pulled out his phone to send the coded text, he was suddenly grateful that he was far away from Jubal Mott.

CHAPTER FORTY-ONE

Big Spring International Park
200 Church Street SW
Huntsville, Alabama
October 29, 7:11 P.M. CST

Jimmy Harrison staggered towards the small spring at the base of the bluff leading up to the downtown square. Sirens and howls filled the night, punctuated by the occasional scream or distant gunshot. He didn't have time for any of it. One thought drove him forward, his breath visible on the night air as he huffed and puffed his way forward; secure the evidence. Get it to a safe place. Get it to a place in the deep and the dark.

He reached the edge of the pool and gripped his chest. He felt like someone had dropped a bowling ball on it. That didn't matter, though. He had a job to do and, by God, he was going to do it. If it was the last thing he did then so be it. At least he would die being useful. Jimmy grimaced and stepped into the frigid water. It rushed up his legs and over his waist sending a violent shiver through his belly and aching chest. His jaw trembled from the cold but he pressed on, gripping the evidence bag tight with one hand and trying hard to keep his balance on the slick, rocky bottom with the other. He fell once but managed to get his footing again and make it to the rough stone wall.

The cave under the courthouse was something he'd known about since he was a kid. The city had closed it off years ago but it was fairly common knowledge that the narrow cave ran from the park all the way across the square to another exit somewhere on Green Street. He'd heard that the Green Street entrance had been accessible by a manhole cover years ago but that had long since been covered with asphalt.

The Big Spring entrance, though, was still easy to get to if you didn't mind getting really wet and even more dirty. The actual opening into the cave was behind a tall, vertical shelf of stone that hid the opening from view unless you were standing at just the right angle. When the city had refurbished the park they had intentionally made it difficult to spot or get to the shelf since no matter how illegal they made accessing the cave, there were always those who would.

Jimmy knew right where to go, though, and squeezed in between the shelf and the bluff with more than a little grunting and cursing. The narrow opening was not meant for a man of his girth and when he finally pushed through, his uniform and undershirt were both torn open around his belly. He hardly noticed that, though, as he fumbled to pull the heavy duty flashlight from his belt and click it on in the small chamber.

The waterproof light filled the space with white, LED brilliance. Jimmy was still standing in waist deep water and he could see that it ran further into the bluff through a heavy steel grate that was bolted into the native stone. He waded over to it and examined the two inch wide steel bands that formed the thick grid.

No, no, no; this wasn't going to work. He wasn't nearly far enough into the dark, not nearly deep enough, to keep the evidence safe. There had to be a way to get past this thing, to get further in, to go deeper. Maybe if he had a pry bar or something he could work the bolts loose. There might be one in the cruiser. Some guys kept small ones handy for car wrecks and the like. He could-

"Well, well, well," a thickly southern voice said from behind him, "if this just ain't a predicament for you, my friend."

Jimmy spun as best he could, sloshing water around as he brought the light to bear.

The man in front of him was thin and leanly muscled. He wore no shirt and his pale blonde hair was wet and slicked back from his face. His smile reminded Jimmy of a growling dog and crossed a face that was angular and defined. Oddly colored eyes caught the light and locked onto the evidence bag in Jimmy's hand.

"Hold it… right there," Jimmy said, doing his best to use his cop voice through his chattering teeth, "police."

The man ignored him, instead staring at the bag. "I can hear it, too," he said. "It's voice is… sublime. Like the music of a great master, no? Do you find it sublime, friend?"

Jimmy's belly quivered as the cold worked on him. "It's… look, this is important evidence. You need to go so I can secure it."

The eyes flicked up to meet Jimmy's. A shudder that had nothing to do with the cold rippled through him.

"Oh, you're right about that, friend. That is important. A whole lot of blood has been spilled over what's in that bag. Lakes of it over the centuries. You, though, have succeeded where so many others have failed and you don't even know it."

"What are you…talking about?" The whispers in Jimmy's mind were like a strong wind through his thoughts. His chested ached and spasmed as the cold just kept seeping into him. If the stranger felt the cold, he showed no sign of it.

"Why, you brought it here. You heeded its call and brought it to the place it needed to go. Now, you're going to finish your part and give to me."

Jimmy tightened his grip on the bag. "No. It's my responsibility. Now, I'm armed so stay back."

One of the man's eyebrows rose a little in what looked to Jimmy like amusement. "Armed, you say? Now, do you really think you can draw that pistol from under the water before I can get to you? Even if you could, you've got to drop either your light or the bag to do it. No matter what, it all ends with me ripping your throat out. Give me the bag, might be that we can avoid that dire outcome."

Jimmy gasped as the whispering got louder in his mind, like waves crashing onto rocks. The pain in his chest tightened into a knot that felt like he was caught in some kind of giant vice. He staggered and slipped in the water as the pain started to overcome him.

"Of course, might not even come to that. You don't look like you're doing too good, friend. I think maybe you don't have the heart for this kind of thing." The man laughed at his own joke while Jimmy's feet slipped from under him and he fell to his back. He managed to keep from sliding under the water by leaning against the chamber wall.

"I'm sorry, I'm sorry," the stranger said, still laughing softly between the words. "My mama didn't raise me to find levity in another white man's misfortune but damn if I don't love me a humorous turn of words."

The man crossed the short space between them. He didn't so much walk, Jimmy noticed, as he glided. Jimmy tried to keep the light up but it suddenly seemed so heavy. Everything seemed heavy and he couldn't catch his breath. If he could just catch his breath-

"I'll take that," the man said, reaching under the water and taking the bag from Jimmy's numb fingers. He lifted it up and looked at the dripping package. The smile on his face only got wider. "Normally this is where I'd make good on that whole ripping your throat out thing but I'm not gonna do that. You're dancing on the edge of your grave already, friend. I figure since you were kind enough to deliver this to me, I'll let you find your fate on your own. So, you just sit right there and keep breathing for as long as you can. I got some work I need to get to."

"What..." Jimmy gasped, every word a spike of pain, "what are you...?"

"What am I going to do? Oh, son, I'm gonna unleash a pack of hounds that will tear the earth from beneath mankind's feet. I'm going to bring it all down and send all you tiny little mortals back to the days of living in caves and warming yourselves by the light of a fire. And, then? Why, then, I'm going to spend the rest of time hunting you all down and gorging on the meat. So you know what, son? You might want to go ahead and die, because that's all any of you are good for, anyway."

Jimmy wanted to respond. He wanted to tell him that he was insane, that there was nothing that could do that, that he was under arrest. Instead, he shuddered even harder as darkness rushed up and swept him away.

CHAPTER FORTY-TWO

Big Spring International Park
200 Church Street SW
Huntsville, Alabama
October 29, 7:37 P.M. CST

Lonebear had parked the Tahoe on the far side of the park from the downtown square according to Arlo's instructions. They'd sat in the truck for a few minutes while misty rain had collected on the windows and Lonebear had scanned the area through a pair of nightvision binoculars, looking for any sign of the warlock or the cryptical. The park was empty as far as he could tell, though he had spotted an abandoned police cruiser on the park's northern side. Arlo had silently nodded at this and told Clint to confirm it with his Sight.

Clint only took a second or two to activate his ability. When he did, he saw multiple trails of ink black energy tangling through the park but all leading to the stone bluff on the far side of the natural spring. It occurred to him that the world looked the same to him as it had earlier in the day even though night had taken a firm grip on their side of the world.

"Truesight doesn't depend on something as mundane as light waves," Arlo said from the back seat when Clint mentioned it. "It's much deeper than that. Shut it down for now, though."

Clint did as he said even as Lonebear asked, "Call it, boss."

"We gear up and go," Arlo said. "They've obviously beaten us here and gotten into the cave."

"Want me to divert some of our incoming agents this way?"

"Obviously," Arlo snapped. "But we have to go now. Mott has the cryptical and is already underground with it. We could be too late already."

"The city sealed that thing off from what I know," Clint said. "No one's supposed to be able to get in there. It's dangerous."

Arlo's expression was something short of disgusted when he looked at Clint. His eye twitched visibly in the dim light. "Really, Mercer? You saw what this warlock is capable of back at the police station. How long do you think a fence or a locked door is going to slow him down?"

Clint shrugged. "Point taken. How're you feeling, Arlo?"

The expression shifted from near disgust to irritation. "Excuse me? Are you my doctor now?"

Clint drew in a breath. "No, but I'm as close as you've got at the moment. You threw down pretty hard back there and it looks like that's about to happen again. You're getting irritable, you've got a visible eye spasm-"

"I am fine, Mercer," Arlo growled. "I don't need your second rate nursing assessment."

"Bullshit," Clint said, twisting in his seat so he could lock eyes with the other man. "You're supposed to be so damned smart, so unmoved by your emotions. Prove it. Assess yourself, magus."

An actual spark flashed in both of Arlo's eyes, lighting up his face for an instant and casting shadows over his angry scowl. As fast as they came, though, they faded. Clint made sure he never broke eye contact.

Arlo looked away first. "You may have a point, Mercer. You two get ready and I'll see to my pharmaceutical needs."

"I can help you," Clint said.

Arlo actually let out a single, ironic chuckle at that. "In time, perhaps you could but not now. I've got this. You get prepared. Lonebear, bring me my kit, please."

Lonebear got out of the Tahoe without a word and opened the rear gate. Clint joined him as the shutters opened on the weapon cache. Lonebear reached in, grabbed the small cooler and took it to Arlo. Clint was studying the collection of weapons when he returned.

"Pick your poison, PJ," the big marine said as he reached in and retrieved one of the big Mossbergs. It was the same model that he'd trained with when he was in uniform except that Lonebear's was fitted with a pistol grip and collapsible stock. He set the weapon aside, grabbed an armored vest, handed it to Clint, and then grabbed one for himself.

"It's like that?" Clint said, looking at the armor.

"This is as real as it gets," Lonebear said, sliding into the vest. "If we had time, we'd be going in with a fully armed and armored assault team but we ain't got time. That's why I keep these around."

Lonebear pulled down a long panel on the left side below the rear window and revealed a line of six spherical objects that Clint instantly recognized.

"Half a dozen M67 grenades," Lonebear said. "Three for you and three for me. If you can shove them down the bastard's throat, then do that."

Clint slid into his own vest and clipped it tight. He adjusted the sizing buckles and ran his hand down the front, feeling the rows of stitched straps that lined the front of the vest. "Got any Molle pouches for those baseballs?" he asked.

Lonebear was way ahead of him and answered by handing him three black pouches with clips that attached to the straps on the vest. Clint secured them and then put a grenade in each one. Lastly, he lifted one of the M4 carbines and looked it over. It was so pristine he wondered if it had ever been fired. He pulled the thirty round magazine, checked it, and pushed it back into place with a solid, satisfying snap.

"Extra mags over there," Lonebear said, gesturing to Clint's right. "Better to have and not need. Know what I mean?"

"Yeah," Clint said. "I heard that a lot back in the day."

"About that," Lonebear said, "seeing as we're going into mortal danger and all, I've got a question I've been holding on to. Figure I better ask it while I can."

"Go for it."

"I read your jacket. You were good at what you did while you served. Really good. The kind of good that doesn't separate from the military all of sudden like you did. Guys like you either retire or get retired. What happened? Why'd you get out?"

Clint secured the last of three spare magazines to his vest as he considered the question. "Tell you what," he said, "make sure neither one of us gets retired before the night's out and I'll tell you over a glass or three of Jack Daniels."

Lonebear grinned. "So long as you're buying, it's a deal."

Arlo joined them a moment later. He placed the cooler into its holding slot and faced them. He had opened his mouth to say something when a howl split the night air. It was loud and deep and made the hairs on Clint's arms bristle.

Lonebear lifted the Mossberg into a ready position and said, "That was close by."

"It was," Arlo said. "Let's hurry. If Mott's ritual is drawing the hounds to him then we could well be overrun soon."

They jogged across Church street towards the park, weapons ready. They were spread out with Clint and Lonebear flanking Arlo by ten feet or so on either side. The mage's glowing rings left short, dim light tracers as they moved through the air. Clint kept his head moving side to side, watching the shadows and the spaces between the trees looking for anything that didn't fit, shadows that were out of place. That's what saved his life.

The barghest came charging out from behind a small stand of decoratively placed dogwood trees that were deep in the shadows of a nearby building. Clint shouted, "Contact right!" and brought his rifle up, sighting through the ACOG scope and putting the blood red cross hairs towards the center of the thing's bobbing head. It wasn't that hard. Cling recognized the hound as the one that had been with Mott before he'd summoned the others at the police station. It was the size of a small horse and was easily the biggest of the pack.

Clint squeezed the trigger and the M4 triple kicked against his shoulder as three rounds rocketed from the barrel towards the target. The thing flinched away from the impacts but kept coming.

Clint squeezed off another burst and then instinctively darted to one side as the beast leaped into the air with its snarling, black maw opened wide and ready to rip him to pieces.

He was fast enough to avoid that but had to duck so low that he stumbled, staggered and then managed to come back to his feet off balance and facing the wrong direction. He turned fast and brought the M4 up but the hound was already coming at him like something from the pit of hell, its eyes burning crimson in the cold, rainy night.

A blazing white sphere of fire the size of a softball exploded against the thing's side, knocking it off course enough for Clint to see Arlo rushing forward, his hands aflame and flinging pure white fire at the monster. Lonebear wasn't far behind with the Mossberg up, angling around Arlo for a shot.

Though the sudden attack knocked the hound's off its straight line charge, it was still coming towards Clint and large enough to do some damage if it ran over him. With no time to line up a shot, Clint darted to the side again but wasn't fast enough to avoid getting sideswiped.

It felt what he imagined getting hit by a pro linebacker would feel like. The blow was a glancing one, though, and knocked him off his feet rather than crushing his ribs. The M4 went flying as he slipped and skidded on the wet grass. He landed hard on the paved walking path that cut through the center of the park, his forehead smacking into the rain soaked concrete.

Everything went white.

CHAPTER FORTY-THREE

He dreamed the dream.

The chopper bounced in the air, the flood waters rushed by below, the rain pelted him in the face, the survivors wept and groaned behind him, and the people he couldn't save drowned and died while he watched.

Except…

He turned. She was there again, standing solid and still among the survivors, oblivious to the rocking and shaking aircraft. She was there but different somehow; Sarah but not Sarah. Her features were too defined and severe, her expression too serious, her stance to precise. She was dressed in some kind of Asian looking business attire, he thought, with a tab collared jacket that was secured up the front all the way to the top with pearl white buttons. The suit was pewter gray with slacks and shoes that matched it exactly.

"Hello, Clint," she said. Her voice was sharp and precise, with only a hint of any emotional inflection.

Clint looked around. There was something wrong, something off. "I shouldn't be here," he said. "Arlo and Jim-"

"There's time," Not-Sarah said. "We need to talk a moment."

"No," he said, staring around the crowded cargo bay. "I don't have time for this. There's a man and-"

"A man?" she said, one eyebrow raising in curiosity. "Is it a 'man', Clint?"

"What? What do you mean?"

Not-Sarah gestured around her. "Who are these people, Clint?"

Clint looked around him. "They're flood victims. The one's we could rescue. We couldn't get them all."

Her expression softened a bit and she walked the couple of steps between them and knelt down next to him. "I've had time to adjust to your reality," she said. "I understand things better now than I did the last time we talked. Do you remember that?"

Clint nodded.

"Good. Then you should remember asking me who and what I am. I will answer that now. From time to time throughout the history of your race, there have been a few of your kind - Abram, Jeanne d'Arc, Michel de Nostradame, Lovecraft, some others -who have transcended the boundaries of your reality through various and remarkable circumstances. The problem with that is that your kind are… well, in the grander scale of the evolved multiverse you are but infants and not prepared for such transcendence. So, whenever this has

happened, one of my kind attaches themselves to the transcended as a guide, of sorts. A counselor. My kind are much older than yours and have no wish for harm to come to your world or your race because of something you did not cause or intend."

"You're talking about the Truesight."

"Yes, Clint. You are of the transcended. Even among that number of your kind, though, that is a very rare gift. I am here to aid you in understanding it so that you may realize your potential."

"You sound like Arlo."

"Yes. The magus is well intentioned but when all is said and done, he's still very much a human."

"And you're something else."

She nodded and then gestured at the assembled passengers. "Who are they, Clint?"

"I told you. Look, I need to wake up. My team is in trouble and I need to help them."

"You've done this before, Clint. You know there's time."

Clint took beat to consider that. He remembered the car chase when his sight had first manifested and said, "Speed of thought."

"Exactly. Now, who are they?"

"Survivors. We saved them."

She studied Clint so intently that it felt as though her eyes were slicing into him. "This thing that you call Truesight, Clint, will show you all that there is to see. It will show you truth in as much as a human mind is capable of framing that construct. It will not care for your feelings or your opinions. It will simply show you what is and leave you to adjust to that knowledge. Some truths can be maddening for your kind if you cannot accept them objectively. You must train yourself to have the kind of mind that can see the truth and process it without it breaking you down. You must have the kind of mind that refuses to deal in falsehoods no matter what the source may be. Especially when that source is yourself. Anything else, any other path, is folly. Now, I ask you again, Clinton Mercer; who are they?"

Clint looked at the passengers. They were the same grieving, bedraggled faces that he had always seen. He knew the faces. They belonged in the memory but not in the way he saw them. Not in the way, he realized, that he had put them there. The faces were right but in the waking world they had never looked at him from inside the chopper. They had all looked up at him from rising waters and crumbling homes.

"Who are they?"

He shook his head. He didn't want to say it.

"Truth, Clint. Face what is; always and only."

"They're…" he choked on lump in his throat before he could finish. "They're the ones we let die."

Not-Sarah nodded and said, "Show me the truth, Clint."

He watched as the passengers burst into a wave of brackish water that vanished even as it splashed to the deck. When it was gone, the bay was empty except for Clint, another uniformed man with a name tag that read 'Robards', and four civilians. The civilian contingent consisted of a borderline obese, middle-aged man with pale skin and thinning hair, an attractive blonde woman at least a decade younger than him, and two frightened boys who had yet to reach their teens. The woman was holding the boys close with one arm and had the other firmly attached to a large rolling suitcase. The man was on a satellite phone having an angry conversation that Clint couldn't hear.

"I found out later that he was on oil executive," Clint whispered. "He'd insisted on staying in his company's private compound when the storm warnings came out. By the time they realized that they'd made a mistake, the area was already too flooded for land travel. So, he called some politician or another, they called somebody else, and then they called somebody that could authorize an off the books extraction."

"Go on," she said, nodding.

"I was on the standby rotation that day, so I got tapped for it. They put me with a pilot and another airman that I didn't know. The op was straightforward; chopper in, extract the exec and his family, then return to base and forget it ever happened. It really couldn't have been more textbook."

"So what went wrong?"

Clint pulled the helmet from his head and said, "During the op? Nothing. It was paint by numbers easy. On the way out, though, I made the mistake of looking out the window. There was this village, tiny place, and the water was high and fast. The buildings that were still standing had people on them. They saw us, we were hard to miss, and they thought we were there to help them."

"You didn't, though."

"I tried," Clint said, his voice wavering. "I told the pilot. I practically begged him. We had the gear, we had the room to get at least most of them, we could've saved at least some of them but they shot me down, both of them. Him and this Robards guy. 'Not the mission' they said. 'We've secured our package," they said. Then the exec told us to shut up because he was on a very important call and had no intention of sharing the flight with a bunch of 'filthy natives'. He talked to us like we were his corporate flunkies or something."

"And then?"

Clint shrugged. "I took his phone away from him, opened the bay door, and tossed it out. When he got in my face about it, I broke his nose."

As he'd been talking, the dream had slowly frozen around Clint, locking into place like he'd pressed the pause button on a video. Not-Sarah nodded and then stood up. "Why did you create this fiction for yourself, Clint? What purpose did deceiving yourself serve?"

Clint rose and faced her. "I loved being a rescueman," Clint said. "I did it to save people who needed saving, not watch people- hell, whole families -die just because some rich asshat had a politician in his pocket. That's what I did, though. That's what I was ordered to do. Why? Because the people who were giving me orders were bought and paid for by guys like him." He stabbed a finger at the executive.

Clint shook his head, teeth clamped together in a barely controlled snarl. "That's not why I signed up. That's not who I want telling me who can and can't be saved. No way, no how. I guess I just wanted to remember it a better way."

"You seek comfort by deceiving yourself."

Clint shrugged. "I guess. But I can't do that anymore, can I?"

"No. Going forward such comforts could prove your undoing."

The dream shimmered, breaking apart into smears and washes of dark color that swirled and coalesced into a small, grassy clearing with low tree covered mountains surrounding the lake that the clearing bordered. The sun shined overhead and a warm breeze washed over him. Clint recognized the spot immediately as one of the Lake Guntersville camping spots that his family had spent summers at. "Did you do that?" he said, looking around and smiling.

"Yes," Not-Sarah said. "This is a shared realm. We both have some power to shape it."

Clint nodded. "How do I know you aren't just some trauma induced hallucination? Lonebear was just asking me why I got out of the military. This could all be from that."

"You don't, I suppose. Time will tell. In the meantime, remember; your gift will show you the truths you seek. You must be focused, though, and open to accepting them without alteration."

"I get it. You know, you're sounding more like Arlo all the time."

"There are overlaps. Speaking of, you're about to recover from your fall. Stand with your friends. Use what you have. Do not falter."

"Don't suppose you could lend a hand? There's this really big hound and all."

"No. That is not my role. I will return when I am needed, whether you realize your need or not."

"One more thing," Clint said. "What's your name? I'm not calling you Sarah no matter how much you look like her."

She seemed to consider the question and then said, "I knew one of your race a long time ago by human reckoning. He called me Dina. That should suffice."

Clint nodded. "What was that guy's na-"

He opened his eyes to dark, cold, and the sound of Arlo screaming.

CHAPTER FORTY-FOUR

It wasn't a scream of pain or fear but rather one that tumbled out in a patterned incantation that was punctuated with focused determination. Thunder filled the night as Lonebear opened up with the shotgun.

Clint shook off the fog from his impact with the concrete and looked towards the fight. Arlo was down on one knee, his hands stretched out in front of him, rings blazing with a silver blue light that formed a dome of energy around him. The barghest was attacking the dome with ravenous fury, clawing and biting at it in a frenzied attempt to get at Arlo. Lonebear was on the beast's far side, pumping and firing the Mossberg with merciless efficiency.

Clint scrambled across the muddy ground and retrieved the M4 from where he'd dropped it. He took a half second to clear the ACOG lens, raised the weapon to his shoulder, and lined up a shot at the hound. He squeezed off three quick bursts and stitched a line of impacts down the thing's flank just as the Mossberg ran dry and Lonebear had to reload. The big marine was so practiced that there was barely any time between the echoes of Clint's shots and the sound of Lonebear's renewed fire.

The hound twitched and jerked with every impact, sliding off of Arlo's shield and swinging its head between Clint and Lonebear. It looked as though it was trying to decide which of them was the bigger threat.

Clint shook his head in disbelief at the amount of damage that the monster was able to absorb and thought that maybe they were more nuisance than threat. Whichever, the hound decided that Lonebear was the more irritating and turned towards him. The agent sprinted for a trio of large oak trees to try and get something between him and the hound.

Clint ran to Arlo as the shield dissolved. The magus was breathing heavy and struggled to rise. Clint helped him to his feet and said, "You okay?"

Arlo answered with a nod.

Across the park, the shot gun roared and the oak trees shook as Lonebear and the enormous barghest circled them, each looking for a chance to get at the other.

"Lonebear won't last long like that," Arlo said, gasping in a breath between the words.

"I know. I've got an idea but I'll need your help. Got any juice left?"

"Just tell me," Arlo said.

Clint quickly laid it out for him. When he'd finished he said, "What do you think?"

"I think it's an idea, which makes it one more than I have. Give me the grenades and get going."

Clint handed over the explosives and then turned toward the hound. It had stripped one side of the oak trees down to the raw, pale wood in its efforts to claw through them to get at Lonebear. For his part, the marine was moving around the trees, mirroring the hounds movements, but he was doing so with a pronounced limp. He had dropped the Mossberg and had a big pistol in his hands, trying his best to line up shots between the three trees.

Once Clint had run far enough from Arlo and had the right angle for a shot, he raised the M4 and started putting three round bursts into the thing's side. The barghest howled and snapped its head towards him.

"Yeah, that's right, Marmaduke," her shouted, ejecting an empty magazine and snapping another into place. "Come get some!"

Clint didn't know if the thing could understand him but it snarled and started charging him like it could. Clint raised the M4 and started firing. There was maybe five hundred feet between them and the barghest was closing the gap fast. Clint kept firing but held his ground as he glanced at Arlo.

The magus had just used three of the fingers on his right hand to simultaneously pull the safety pins on all three grenades. Instead of throwing them at the hound, though, he tossed them straight up into the air and spread his fingers wide as his rings flared to life again. The grenades stopped in midair, hovering in place for just an instant before Arlo shoved both hands forward. The grenades rocketed away from him with the motion, flying through the air and curving towards the charging barghest.

Clint clicked dry on another magazine as the grenades thudded into the beast's side so close that Clint could hear them strike home. He dove away from the charging monster but knew it was too late to make a difference. He'd underestimated how fast the thing could cross the distance between them. There was no way he was going to be outside the blast radius. He had hit the ground and tucked into a fetal position with his arms covering his head when the grenades went off.

The sound was like a thunderclap in his skull. He expected pain. He expected to die. Instead, a second or two later, he lifted his head, ears ringing from the blast and looked towards what he had thought would kill him.

A sphere of silver blue light hung in the air where the barghest had made its final leap for him. Within the sphere, the hound's body lay motionless, one side a mess of black meat that seemed to be smoldering. The burning crimson eyes were cold and dark.

Clint looked at Arlo and saw him standing with his hands uplifted, muttering something unintelligible. The same silver blue light as the sphere pulsed from his rings. He had used the same spell that had protected him earlier to shield Clint from the explosions. He had contained the explosive force with his magic.

The two men's eyes met and Arlo dropped his hands. The spell faded and the hound's body fell to the ground with a wet thud. As Clint watched, the magus likewise fell to his knees and then face first into the wet grass. Clint shouted his name and ran for him.

He slid down next to him in the grass, calling his name. He moved the magus onto his back and put two finger to his neck, checking for the carotid pulse. He found it, weak but steady. Arlo was pale in the dim park lighting. Blood trickled from both nostrils, whether from the fall onto his face or exertion Clint didn't know. His eyes opened in slow, heavy blinks. They were rimmed in red and his pupils were tightly constricted despite the low light.

"Not dead," he mumbled. "Good. Help me up. The cryptical. We have to get the cryptical."

"You can take a second to catch your breath, Arlo. Jesus, man, what you just did-"

"We don't have a second to spare, Clint. He could be a second away from killing this whole city right now," Arlo said through gritted teeth. Blood seeped from his gums and highlighted each tooth.

"It's 'Clint', now, is it? What happened to 'Mercer'?"

Arlo met his eyes and even as battered as he was, only partly managed to hide a smile. "I'm severely injured," he said. "It's affecting my judgment."

Clint just shook his head and helped the magus to his feet.

CHAPTER FORTY-FIVE

They found Lonebear propped against one of the trees that he had been using for cover. He had stripped off his shirt and jacket and had them tightly bound around his right thigh.

"Damn thing got a lucky swing in between the trees," he said. "Stepped right into it. Got me deep but I don't think it hit anything important."

"Let me look at that, Jim," Clint said.

"No," he said, waving him off. "I've already called for backup. There are people inbound. You get in there and slow Mott down. Take my grenades. They worked on his pooch so maybe they'll work on him. Soon as I see some heavy hitters, I'll send them in after you."

"Other hounds may come," Arlo said.

Lonebear grinned and held up his pistol. "Let'em. I got a whole bunch of forty-five caliber hellos and I'm feeling friendly."

Clint couldn't help but smile at that.

"Boss," Lonebear said, "my phone was acting hinky when I made that call. Whatever he's doing, I think it's building to something big."

Arlo nodded and said, "Let's go, Mercer."

Clint took a few seconds to collect and secure Lonebear's grenades then he and Arlo headed for the spring. When they reached it, Clint pointed and said, "Right there. All the tracers headed into that bluff. The cave entry is hidden by a stone shelf there on the left."

"On the other side of the ice cold water," Arlo said, frowning. "Of course it is. Lead on."

They waded into the pool and both did their best no to slip on the uneven bottom. Once they'd negotiated their way past the jagged, moss covered stones they squeezed into the crevice. The water seemed to glow the further they got into the crevice and Clint saw why as soon as he crossed into a larger chamber. A police officer in a torn, filthy uniform was propped against the far wall. He was older, heavyset, and pale. His dead eyes were open and staring. His name tag read 'Harrison'. Apparently, he had dropped his flashlight into the shallowest part of the pool and it was waterproofed enough to still be working.

Clint didn't need to check the cop's pulse to see that he was gone but he did it anyway. As Arlo squeezed into the small chamber behind him, Clint just looked up at him and shook his head.

"The evidence room officer, no doubt," Arlo said.

Clint nodded. "You know, Arlo, I am really, really over people dying for this damned thing."

"Then you've almost caught up with me. Let's go put an end to this." He gestured behind Clint.

Clint looked over his shoulder and saw a gaping hole in the wall that led farther into the bluff. A large, steel grate had been torn from its mounting bolts and leaned discarded to one side. Clint didn't need to ask who'd done the tearing.

"So, he's magical and super-strong. Awesome. How do we play this, Arlo?"

"We follow. I can't tell you more beyond that until we find him and see what he's up to."

Clint nodded. "Hey," he said as something occurred to him, "what was that stuff about Jim's cell phone?"

"Active magic tends to wreak havoc on sensitive electronics like cell phones. If whatever's happening underground was affecting his phone in the park, then it's likely powerful magic. Now, if you're finished stalling?" He gestured towards the opening.

Clint frowned and waded up to the passage. "I wasn't stalling. Just curious." The M4 had a small tactical light attached to the barrel so Clint switched it on and shined it into the passage. Arlo retrieved the fallen officer's light from under the water and raised it up, adding to the illumination.

The cave was really more of a crevice that ran at a slight upward angle from the pool they were standing it. The floor of the cave was still covered in water but it was a little more than ankle deep as opposed to the waist deep water they were currently enjoying. Clint took his time getting up the incline, picking his steps and working his way around the ruined grate. Once he was in the passage, he reached back and gave Arlo his hand so he could negotiate the slick stones. The magus looked even more exhausted than he had earlier.

"Are you sure you're up for this?" Clint said.

"Does it matter? He has to be stopped and we're the ones who are here."

"Yeah, but-"

"No, Mercer, there are no 'buts'. You should understand that by now. We do the job. Me, you, Lonebear, all of us are expendable when weighed against that because if we don't, if we indulge in the time it takes to lick our wounds, then this city *will* die. And it will only be the first. Surely you can see that by now."

Clint fell quiet as they advanced down the corridor, squeezing through where the walls closed in, ducking under low hanging sections, and watching their steps from holes or stones that might trip them up. All the while, he kept replaying the dream in his mind and the things that Dina had told him.

"Yeah," he said, finally. "I see it. Mission first, so long as it's the right mission."

Arlo shined his light up the passage and said, "What's that?"

Clint adjusted his own light up the passage. A collection of stones had fallen across the small stream they were wading through. They were different from the other stones that they'd been working around, though. The light hit them and bounced back in tiny glints of silver and blue, like distant stars on a moonless night.

They made their way closer and saw that the rock wall had been shattered on one side of the passage. The small reflections they were seeing was from the broken pieces that had never gotten covered in the mud and lichen that seemed to coat everything else.

Clint shined his light into the space beyond the break. "Another chamber," he said. "Looks a little wider than this but it leads down. The entrance is a little higher so there's no water to contend with." He swept his light across the chamber floor. Footprints from a barefoot person was the only disturbance in the ancient soil.

Arlo looked in and said, "At least it's dry. Press on."

Clint took stepped up into the new passage and then helped Arlo up. The passage wasn't as cramped as the original one but it led down at a steep angle. The further they went, though, the more Clint realized that some of the stones weren't natural. He shined his light over the walls in front of him and saw strange symbols and crude pictures etched into the rock. He was about to comment on it when his tactical light started flickering. Arlo's flashlight started doing the same a second later.

"Kill the lights," the magus said in a low voice. "We must be getting close."

Clint clicked off the tactical light. Darkness like you can only get when deeply isolated from the open sky closed around them immediately.

"It's really dark," Clint whispered.

"Really? Whatever could you possibly do about that?" Arlo said. The sarcasm in his tone was like a verbal eye roll.

Clint took his meaning and said, "You know, Dandridge, you're kind of an asshole."

"That's not exactly a state secret. Activate your Sight and I'll keep a hand on your shoulder."

Clint opened his inner eye and the cavern was suddenly visible in the familiar shades of silver-gray. This time though, there was a filmy black haze over everything. It was like a mist that was made from oil instead of water vapor.

"Eldritch residue," Arlo said after Clint had described it to him. "Mott will likely have to saturate the cavern in it to power the working. We need to hurry."

"You should get that printed on a tee shirt."

"I'll consider it. Now move."

Clint felt Arlo's hand grip his shoulder. He started forward again, whispering warnings back to Arlo when there was a tripping hazard or a sudden change in the passage gradient. The going was slow but they hadn't gone very far before Arlo whispered, "Hold on. There's a light ahead. Stay concealed as we get closer. I'll tell you when to shut down your Sight."

Clint moved closer to the wall and told Arlo to put a hand out so he'd know where it was. They crept forward with slow deliberate steps. Clint could see the end of the tunnel gradually opening into what looked like a much larger space. The oily mist was a lot thicker there.

"I can see on my own now," Arlo whispered. "Go ahead and switch to your physical eyes."

Clint paused for a beat at the words but then shook his head. He could ask Arlo what he meant by 'physical eyes' later. Assuming, that is, that they got to have a later.

He opened his eyes to a tunnel washed in dark, violet light. The color seemed to cast darker shadows than normal and made everything look like something might be hiding there. Clint gritted his teeth against his rising paranoia and kept sneaking forward. When they reached the point where the tunnel fully opened into the cavern, he held up a hand for Arlo to stop. By slow degrees, he leaned forward until he could see into the chamber.

There was an altar of some kind in the center of a cavern that was roughly half the size of his high school gymnasium. It was a circular thing with a terraced edge leading up to a platform that was carved from the bedrock. A stone ring, easily twice as high as Clint was tall, stood on its edge in the center of the platform, glowing with veins of dark light. Jubal Mott stood before it, one hand extended before him and the other dribbling dark blood from his closed fist. An unfurled scroll hovered above his extended hand, glowing and pulsing with the same dark light as the huge ring.

"It's him," Clint said. "He's doing whatever it is he's doing in front of a big Stargate looking rock thing."

"R'lyehien Portal Ring," Arlo said. "That makes perfect sense but they're almost exclusively a west coast phenomenon on this continent. Remarkable to find one in this part of the country."

"Yeah, that's downright amazing. Let's blow it up."

"If we can get the cryptical from Mott we won't need to. Barring that, sure. We can blow it to Hell and gone."

"I'm thinking we rush him while he's distracted, right? Hit him hard, grab the scroll, get the hell out of here. Easy-peasey."

Clint could see that Arlo was considering the plan. "I think I can manage a working or two," he said, "but you have to promise me you'll get that cryptical to the surface, no matter what. I mean it, Mercer. You grab it and you run. No looking back."

Clint met his eyes. He could see that Arlo was resigned to whatever fate awaited him, that stopping the warlock was the one and singular thing that mattered. Clint was also pretty sure that Arlo could see how much the idea of leaving him behind bothered Clint. It was a moment of unspoken understanding that ended with Clint's reluctant nod. "I get it, Arlo. I can do the math. I'll get it done."

"All right, then. We need to disrupt his working. I'll hit him with something that will knock him off his feet. You reinforce that with your rifle. At the very least, it might give us the second we need to grab the cryptical before he finishes."

"Grenade?"

Arlo shook his head. "They likely won't kill him outright and you might need those to collapse the tunnel behind you if he ends up chasing you out."

They didn't say another word. Clint rolled his shoulders and neck to loosen them while Arlo held up his fists and closed his eyes in concentration. A kind of luminous rippling started forming in the air around the magus's hands as his rings started to glow with white light. Arlo's eyes opened and the same light glittered in his pupils.

Without a word, Arlo stepped into the open, his closed fists pulled back to his chest. Clint came out a couple of steps behind Arlo and an arm's length to his left.

Arlo shouted something and shoved his fists toward the warlock. A wave of rippling, white light shot from his hands and streaked through the cavern straight for Jubal Mott.

Clint had the M4 up and was drawing a bead on the warlock when the rippling wave suddenly rebounded and washed back towards them. It was so fast that neither man had a chance to do anything before they were lifted from their feet and flung backwards through the air.

Clint hit the ground and skidded to stop against the far wall. Arlo wasn't as he lucky since he had been standing closer to the corner that they had been hiding behind. He slammed into the stone wall in mid-flight and fell in heap onto the rock and sand strewn ground.

Clint took a second to catch his breath before he scrambled to his feet and brought the M4 up again. He spotted Arlo on the ground then shifted his attention to the stone dais.

Jubal Mott was looking right at him. The warlock grinned and said, "I was wondering when you boys were going to show up."

CHAPTER FORTY-SIX

Clint opened fire.

Three round burst after three round burst stuttered out from the rifle in a deadly rhythm. He kept the ACOG's cross-hairs on center mass, adjusted for recoil, even dropped into a kneeling stance for better stability but the warlock just kept looking at him, an amused smile on his face. It was like the bullets just disappeared before they reached him. Clint had emptied an entire magazine, his last, before he stopped firing and got back to his feet.

Mott grinned. "You about done? That thing's a might loud and I am trying to work here."

"Guess we weren't as sneaky as we thought we were," Clint said. He did his best to keep his voice light despite the icy fear churning in his guts as he hurried to check on Arlo. The magus was out cold but his pulse was present, if not strong. Clint dropped the M4 onto the ground next to him. Without ammo, it was just a club.

"Hell, son, I knew you two were here the second you came through that door I made in the wall up yonder. Your friend, there, he's a mighty powerful one. It's hard to miss that kind of aura. You, though, you're different from last time. How come you ain't dead?"

Clint stood up and shrugged. "Just lucky, I guess."

Mott chuckled. "Well, looks like you might've used all that luck right up. Another couple a minutes or so and that ain't gonna be a good place to be standing."

Clint took a cautious step towards the dais. Mott didn't respond except to look back at the cryptical.

"Come on over if it suits you. Ain't nothing you can do to stop me," the warlock said.

Clint moved with slow, cautious steps. He moved behind the warlock and said, "You seem pretty chatty. I thought all this magic stuff required a lot of concentration."

"Well, I reckon you got that from your friend over there. I been at this a whole lot longer than him. You might say I've mastered the art of multi-tasking."

Clint noticed that the warlock spoke without trying to turn and look at him. Despite what he said, a large part of his attention was devoted to the cryptical. The ring of stone pulsed with interwoven threads of light and a shimmer of identical light was starting to glow at its center. Clint glanced at Mott one more time to make sure his back was still to him then opened his inner eye with a single, slow blink.

The cavern clarified into shades of silver and gray. The black mist that he had seen earlier was more like a heavy fog now, obscuring his vision beyond a few feet. It flowed out of the cryptical like smoke from an oil fire, through the man shaped blot of inky dark that was Jubal Mott, and out into the cavern. The ring seemed to be pulling it in like a low powered fan venting smoke from a room despite the fact that there was an intricate web of eldritch power erected all around the dais. Clint suspected it was this web that had protected Mott from their attacks.

All of this came into focus for Clint but it was not what captured his attention. His eyes were affixed to what he saw within the ring itself. The image was slightly blurred, like looking through a dirty plate glass window, but clear enough that he could make out the shapes on the other side.

There were creatures there, huge things, the smallest of them easily ten feet long from what Clint could see. Their bodies were that of thick, bumpy worms with pale, veined flesh and a coating of slime that fell from their skin in thin, clinging threads. They slithered around the portal like fat snakes with heads that were nothing more than a mass of dark, writhing tentacles lined with suckers that puckered and flexed in response to some unseen stimulus. There were thousands- no, tens of thousands -of the things sliding and slithering beyond the portal. Beyond them, structures likes uneven, lumpy buildings rose as high as skyscrapers into a strangely solid sky. These stretched farther than Clint could see.

The fear that had chilled his guts before surged like frozen bile in his throat and Clint turned away before he lost control of himself. "My God," he whispered, every word a testament to his sudden terror. "What are you doing? What are you doing?"

Mott laughed, a cold hard sound in Clint's ears. "Your God?" he said. "Your God is a mute, absentee father with no love for His creation or the children he spawned. Your God abandoned you long ago and you bunch of pathetic, mewling mistakes of creation just keep begging and pleading and crying to a Father that isn't there and doesn't care to be. You're just cattle with delusions of importance. You're just meat that doesn't know its place.

"I'm correcting that. My Goddess, my Mother, she has given me what I need to make that happen. She guided me to this place and this tome of knowledge to expand my pack a thousand fold so that I could tear it all down, start over, put all the prey and the lesser races back in their place, put things right again. Make the world-"

"Stop!"

Clint flinched against the word as it echoed through the cavern like a crack of thunder that vibrated in his brain. He staggered back from the dais, instinct and training telling him that he was under attack and needed cover. No attack came, though, and as Clint watched the dark mist started swirling away from the ring to a spot a few feet to Mott's left.

It coalesced into a woman's nude, pregnant form. The shape was clear, but undefined. Clint realized that though he could feel a new presence in the cavern, there was no one else physically there. Whatever he was seeing must have been some kind of projection or manifestation formed from the eldritch mist because it trailed wisps of the stuff like smoke curling off burned wood. Without his Truesight, Clint figured he wouldn't even see the figure. Something about that sent up warning bells in his mind.

"Mother," Mott said, his voice suddenly filled with excitement. "You honor me with your presence at the moment of our victory."

The thing he called Mother walked with careful steps until it stood on the opposite side of the hovering cryptical from the warlock. *"Our victory?"* it said, its voice a whispering hiss but no less powerful for it. *"What victory do you speak of, Houndsman? You were to bring me the prize. Not release its power."*

Clint couldn't see Mott's face but his voice betrayed his surprise. "I know but I understand what you truly wanted, why you choose *me* for this. I can grow the pack to the size of an army. We can tear this world down, raise you up as the goddess of all, as you should be, we could-"

"You dare claim to know my mind? You forget yourself."

Mott was silent for a moment. Clint couldn't tell if that was from fear or something else. A moment later, he got his answer.

"Forget myself? Forget myself? I have served at your whim for nearly two centuries! You and that so-called Sovereign Union. There's nothing unified about you! I've watched you all this time, watched you waste opportunities, watched you sniping each other! I can correct all that now! Give you a world where you can sort it all out and have nothing but the strong fighting for you!"

"You," the voice was more growl than whisper, *"forget yourself, Houndsman. Cease this ritual immediately and come to me for correction. I will not say it again."*

Clint could hear Mott breathing. His shoulders rose and fell with each breath. "No," he said. "No more. You're not even actually here. I will build my pack and then I will come to you. No, bitch, I will come *for* you."

There was only a moment's hesitation before the manifestation replied, *"So be it, my Houndsman."*

Jubal Mott screamed and fell to his knees. Something that looked like crude oil spilled out of him from every orifice, streaming out from his face and ears and trickling down over his shoulders and chest. It exploded from his mouth and nose in a violent spray as he screamed again and bent over double, clutching at his abdomen.

"What… what…?" he stammered.

"You served me well for a time," the Mother said, *"but this failure, this hubris, cannot be overlooked. What was given is now taken, Jubal Mott."*

There was a sudden clatter of wood against stone as the cryptical fell to the dais. Clint looked at the portal just in time to see the last of the light fading from the ring. He released a breath he hadn't realized he'd been holding.

The Mother's wispy form was swirling in the air around Mott. Clint was trying to figure the best way take a run at the cryptical when the first of the hounds came trotting past him.

Clint nearly screamed at the sight and brought his hands up to fight but the thing made no move to attack. In fact, it didn't seem to notice or care that he was right there. Clint looked back towards the entrance and saw more of them coming down the access passage. They walked right past Arlo's limp form, even stepping over him as they headed straight for the dais.

"What did you do? Why can't… why can't I feel them?" Mott stammered.

"What was given is now taken," the Mother repeated. *"And what was summoned must now return."*

Mott looked up, his face twisted in horrified realization. He staggered to his feet, backing away from the advancing pack. "Stop there," he shouted. "Obey me! I am your master! Obey!"

He looked at Clint with a pleading, desperate expression for an instant before the first of the hounds leaped for him.

Clint expected the beast to savage him with tooth and claw as it had so many others. Instead, mid-way through its leap, it shifted into a inky black smear of eldritch energy that shot into Mott's body, striking him low on his right side.

Mott staggered as though shot, his eyes growing wide and his mouth opened in a silent scream. Clint looked at the spot where the bolt had struck him. There was a hole there the size of a baseball. Another hound leaped forward and shot into Mott, this time striking him in his left thigh. Another bloody hole appeared completely through his leg and the former warlock dropped to one knee. He found the air to scream then and the rest of the pack surged forward.

Clint looked away and didn't look back until the only thing he could hear was his own breath hissing hard and fast from his lungs. When he finally turned back, the dais was empty and still save for the cryptical and a mass of mangled, bloody flesh. Clint focused on the former and did his best to ignore the latter.

The dark mist still floated around him but it was considerably thinner than before. Clint hesitated at the edge of the dais to make sure there was no barrier in his way. Satisfied, he stepped onto the platform and snatched up the cryptical. He'd been expecting a book, some sinister looking thing bound in human skin or something. Instead, it was just a long, simple scroll whose ends were secured into two pieces of smooth bamboo. Clint just shook his head and rolled it up tight, shoving it between his vest and shirt.

He turned to head for Arlo and found himself face to face with the shimmering, wispy face of the Mother.

"How is it you see me, mortal?" she hissed.

Clint stifled a yelp of surprise. He took a quick step back and felt his boot slip in something. He didn't bother looking down to see what.

"Well," he said after a nervous swallow, "long story short, your boy here gave me the grand-daddy of all LASIK operations. I see pretty much everything now."

"You would do well not to be so glib with your betters. Who are you?"

Clint thought about that for a moment. "I'm the new guy," he said. "My name's not really important."

The apparition swirled in a circle around him. Clint turned, following it. He could see the form breaking apart as the eldritch mist dissipated.

"You ally yourself with those who stood against my Houndsman? Against me?"

That gave him pause. He thought about the last couple of days, the things he'd seen, the things that had happened. His jaw tightened and he said, "You know what? Yeah, I think I do. I think I'll see you brought down for what you and yours have done here."

The mist spun into an oily tornado with him at the center, hissing and screeching like some kind of trapped animal. Clint charged through it without any difficulty and spun to face it as the sound died and the remaining mist twisted into the Mother's face again, hovering next to Clint's ear like a lover.

"I see you, too, Pickman," It whispered. *"And I will know you before you die."*

Then, it was gone.

Clint didn't know how long he stood there, trembling, with the thing's words echoing in his ear before he heard the sounds of booted feet coming down the access passage.

CHAPTER FORTY-SEVEN

Private Care Facility
799 Arrington Blvd South
Birmingham, Alabama
October 30, 10:21 A.M. CST

"And you know the rest from there," Clint said, looking between the two people sitting with him in Arlo's private room. Sun streamed through the windows and Arlo lay in the bed, his rings glittering as they worked to repair his damaged body. A bag a blood dripped steadily into the IV attached to his arm. The familiar, antiseptic smell of a hospital filled the air around them. A cup of black coffee sat untouched on the table in front of Clint.

"I have to say, Clint," Rani said, "that's quite a story. Even by our standards." She sipped her tea and glanced at the other man sitting with them.

Rani had introduced him as Mr. Noble when they'd come in. He was an older man, late fifties Clint guessed, and built like he'd been a bodybuilder once upon a time. His skin was dark with a prominent jawline despite his full face and intelligent eyes that looked like they could cut through you if he decided they should. His hair was gray, thinning, and tightly trimmed. He was dressed in a dark three piece suit with a tie the color of cinnamon candy. He had listened to Clint's story without uttering a word and was looking at him like he was someone that needed to be dealt with.

"Sovereign Union," he said, finally. "Mott used that exact phrase?"

Clint nodded.

"And neither of them mentioned it again?"

"Who are you again?" Clint said, looking the man in the face.

"Mr. Noble," he said. His voice was a rolling baritone that was commanding without being loud.

Clint nodded, waiting for more. When it didn't come he said, "And your role in the greater scheme of things is what, exactly?"

The man settled back in his chair a little and took a long sip from him own coffee mug before answering. "I'm the man that decides which boots kick which asses."

Clint studied him for a moment before he deadpanned, "Wow."

"Mr. Noble is Arlo's immediate supervisor within the institute," Rani said.

Clint was genuinely surprised. "Arlo has a supervisor?"

"Yes," Noble said. "Your level of surprise at that fact should give you some idea just how challenging my position can be."

"I'll bet."

"Arlo is a unique case," Rani said, eying Noble critically. "As you've seen for yourself, Clint, he requires specialized supervision."

"Yeah, I noticed that about him," Clint said. "Hey, how's Jim?"

"Agent Lonebear will make a full recovery," Noble replied. "His injury was serious but not life threatening."

"And Jasmine Ives?"

"She woke up while Jim and Arlo were trying to track down where you'd been taken after your arrest," Rani said. "She'll likely require some counseling but I predict that she'll recover with time. She wasn't exposed to the cryptical for that long, thank goodness. That made a lot of difference."

"And what happened to that damned thing?"

"It's locked away and warded," Noble said. "We have a place for such things."

"Let me guess," Clint said, " 'top men' are studying it."

"No," Noble said, no hint of amusement on his face. "High functioning sociopathic men with assault rifles are guarding it, though."

Clint held the man's gaze for a few seconds and then said, "Okay, tough room. Why are you here?

My experience with debriefings is that they don't usually involve upper command staff."

Noble's lip twitched a little, like the seed of a smirk, before he said, "You're a smart man, Mr. Mercer. You know why I'm here."

Clint nodded. "So, what? This is my job interview?"

"Hardly," Noble said. "Your record and your actions over the last few days have told us everything we need to know about you. I'm just here to look you in the eye before I make you the offer."

"Just my record and my actions, huh? My eyes don't have anything to do with it?"

"Of course they do. Truesight will make you a unique asset in your own right. Partnered with Agent Dandridge, I can see the two of you being formidable. Your ability to observe, his extensive knowledge; that's a winning combination.

Dina's words came back to Clint; *You will see but he will know.*

"Clint," Rani said, "you need to understand that this is demanding life. You have to keep a lot of secrets, you have to travel on short notice, and you've seen for yourself how dangerous it can be."

"And you have to lie," Noble said. "All the time. To everyone. You'll learn truths that can't be revealed. If the general populace discovers that they have the potential to perform real magic we'll be flooded with low rent warlocks in no time flat. It would only take one of them and the wrong eldritch formula to-"

"He gets the point, Leland," Rani said.

"Leland?" Clint said.

"Mr. Noble," the older man said, fixing him with a stern glare. "Or Director Noble. Your choice."

Clint smiled. There was something about the man's directness that he liked. Clint looked back at Arlo. His vitals glowed strong and steady on the monitor. The rings on his fingers shimmered with magic.

Clint turned back to Noble and said, "Where do we start, Director?"

EPILOGUE

The Arcadian Building
Five Points Plaza
725 5th Avenue
New York, New York
November 5, 1:22 A.M. EST

Jeffrey Lemaster stood naked and bloodied before the wall length, plate glass windows that looked out over Central Park and the Upper East Side. A full, golden moon hung in the sky and sixty-nine stories below the rest of humanity slept, rutted, or wandered the night like the lost souls they all were. Lost in the dark, lost in their ignorance, lost without The Mother.

Tears cut the dark stains on his cheeks but he wiped them away, shaking his head and blinking his eyes to clear his vision. It was to be expected. They had begged, his wife and daughter, confused and terrified as they'd been. He'd wanted to explain, explain to them that The Mother had commanded it all, that the ritual required the fuel of their fear and their anger but he hadn't been able to. The incantations had been long and did not tolerate interruption.

It didn't matter. Soon, all pain would be washed away, all confusion lifted from his thoughts, all concern wiped away in the great glory of service.

He was to be uplifted. He was to be powerful. He was to be Favored.

The door opened and The Mother's servant entered. The hairless, pale skinned man had not given a name and Jeffrey had not asked. He had supervised the preparations for the sacrifice and now he walked between the twin altars to join Jeffrey by the windows. Though the man did not smile, Jeffrey got the sense that he was pleased by what he saw.

"You have done well," he said with a voice as smooth as a stalking cat. "The Mother awaits you."

Jeffrey glanced back at the ruins of what had once been his family. "What about-"

"Do not concern yourself," the bald man said. "A narrative will be constructed and you will adhere to it as The Mother commands. The passing of your family will be explained and you will grieve sufficiently enough to satisfy heretics and the non-believers. All will be well, for She is with us."

Jeffrey gave him a shaky nod and whispered, "She is with us."

"Follow," the servant said. "Follow and be granted The Mother's Favor." He turned sharply on his heel and headed for the door.

The Servant's footsteps echoed softly through the large, unadorned room while Jeffrey's bare feet made a slightly sticky sound as he traversed the remains of his night's efforts. He hesitated, only for an instant, glancing between the two altars and memorizing the faces that stared into infinity there.

Then, he followed the bald man into the hall and did not look back.

THE END

AUTHOR'S NOTE

This book was born of bourbon and cigars.

Really.

There's a cigar bar here in town called *SiP* that my best friend and I are fond of. It's near the downtown square and one night, as we were walking from our parking spots to the bar, my friend and I were discussing a field trip my daughter had recently taken to a local cave. We live in what's called the foothills of the Appalachian Mountains so this area is rife with caves of all sorts. "There's even one under the courthouse," he told me.

Now, there are these moments in a writer's life- at least, in this writer's life -where you hear a snippet of conversation or see something that catches your eye or stumble across some obscure fact and just *know* that there is story attached to that thing and you're going to be the one to write it. So it was with the cave under the courthouse. While my friend, the more socially adept of the two us, mingled and small talked at the bar, I smoked a Monte Cristo, enjoyed a nice Woodford Reserve, and googled everything I could about the cave that bisected the downtown square. I'd always wanted to write a book set in my hometown, anyway, and this was the spark that lit that fire.

Master of Hounds was born.

I worked in the same hospital as Clint for many years. I've been to all of the places in this book that he has with the exceptions of the cave itself and one other. I'll leave you to guess that one for yourself. To the best of my knowledge the things that Clint and Arlo found in the cave are not really there and are but products of my imagination. As I said, though, I've never investigated that for myself.

There are two more books planned for Clint and Arlo titled *Child of Magic* and *Mother of Warlocks* respectively. I hope, if you enjoyed this one, that you will return for those. I've already written a short story called *The Invisible Web* that takes place between this novel and *Child of Magic,* so I think that I've got a lot of stories to tell in Clint and Arlo's world.

Thanks for taking the time to join me on this adventure. I hope it gave you all the thrills and chills that I was hoping it would. If you're ever in Huntsville for real, go by Big Spring Park or Maple Hill Cemetery and take a selfie that you can share with me on social media.

If you go to Drost Park, though, do it during the day.

You never know what might be hiding in the dark.

CSM
May 2018